HEADSTRONG

HEADSTRONG

EDEN FINLEY

HeartEyes
Press

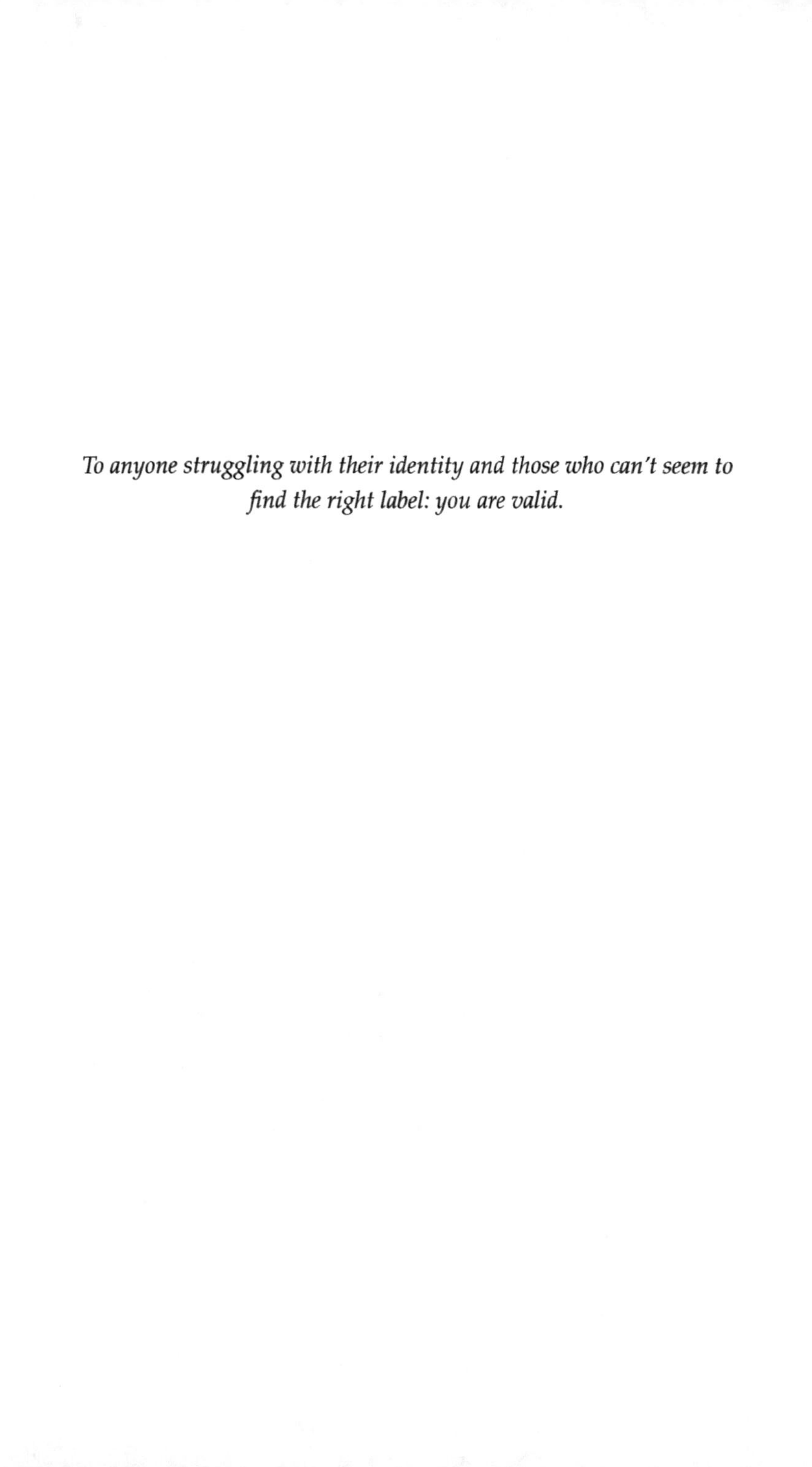

To anyone struggling with their identity and those who can't seem to find the right label: you are valid.

RAINN

Walking to work is fun. Especially in the snow.

Almost as fun and exciting as being told it will cost six hundred bucks to get a new alternator for my piece-of-shit car.

Yup. Today is just … fun.

Fun. Fun. Fun.

Whoever said positive thinking is the key to happiness has to be talking about a new party drug.

Because this is bullshit.

I would have taken an Uber, but I'm running late and it's quicker to walk the mile and a half from my apartment. I usually walk, but in this weather, it's easier to drive. You know, when my car is *working*.

If it was light snowfall, that would be one thing, but no. It's annoying sleet that hits me as it falls in pellets, stinging my face. I pull up my scarf, but it only helps a little.

My boots crunch the ice on the sidewalk as I trudge toward Church Street. I used to love the snow, the ice, and everything to do with winter. Now I crave summer.

Even though my shift at the bookstore started five minutes ago, I duck into the Maple Factory and order Harrison an apologetic tea and granola muffin. I grab an espresso to wake myself up and a hot chocolate to warm my frozen insides.

When I get to Vino and Veritas, I have my customer-service smile ready and flash it toward my boss.

He gives me a derisive look.

My face falls. "I know, I know. I'm late. I'm sorry. The car broke down."

Harrison's expression softens. "Again?"

I grunt. "New problem this time."

"You really need a new one."

All is forgiven when I hand him his coffee and muffin.

"I'd get a new car if I didn't spend my last five bucks on sucking up to my boss." My smile is genuine this time, but it's only because if I don't smile, I'll cry.

"Tanner might have some more hours for you in the bar if you're desperate." He points next door. "You can grunt at him. He'll grunt back. Bam, more shifts."

"Thanks, but I'm exaggerating." Sort of. I place my drink on the counter and take off my jacket and scarf, stashing them so I can get to work.

I can't say I thought working at a bookstore and wine bar would be my future when I was a kid, but it pays my bills. Mostly. It's good for rent and food. There's just no wiggle room for messed-up alternators.

"A shipment came in today, and because you've had a shitty morning, I'll give you a choice between stocking the shelves or customer duty."

"Oh, wow, how will I choose?"

"You could always do both."

I tap my chin. Tough choice. "I'll take customer duty. I'm trying this new thing where I think positively. If I pretend to be nice, it will eventually make me nice."

"Fake it until you make it." He slaps my shoulder. "Let me know how that works out for you."

A customer walks through the doors.

Time to work.

Mrs. Embry is a regular. She's in her seventies—at least—and I know exactly what she'll ask for.

"I've run out of men who can't find their shirts," she says, as predicted.

She thinks she's hilarious, and I have to admit, she is entertaining. She only reads romance novels with shirtless men on the covers, and she has to point it out every time.

"Right this way, Mrs. Embry." I lead her to the romance section.

"I was talking to my online book club, and they recommended …" She glances around the store as if we're being watched and then leans in and lowers her voice. "Something called MM romance."

I purse my lips to stop from smiling. "We, uh, do have those books, but, umm, do you know what MM means?"

When I started working here, I had no clue.

She whispers, "It's about the gays."

Do not laugh, Rainn. Do not laugh.

It's hard because her tone is so serious.

"We keep those books over here."

We move toward the gay romance section, and her little face lights up. "Ooh, what's better than one shirtless man on a cover but two?"

A chuckle finally escapes.

She reaches for a book, and my cheeks heat.

"That one is kind of … advanced."

"Oh, you've read it?"

"I read all the books that come through the store."

That's a lie. I haven't read every single book, but I make it a point to read this genre.

Both of my bosses are queer, and I work in queer spaces. I figured reading gay romance would give me insight into the

LGBTQ community, seeing as I knew next to nothing when I started here. I was worried about saying something homophobic out of ignorance.

I'd never do it intentionally—anyone can love anyone they want—but I'll admit to not being so aware when it comes to everything rainbow.

The books were definitely … eye-opening. I'll leave it at that.

Mrs. Embry flips through the book, pausing to read a few paragraphs. "What's a boy button?"

Loud laughter comes from behind me, but when I turn to glare at my boss, it's hard not to laugh with him. He's trying to contain it, which only makes his face look strained, and his cheeks turn pink.

He waves his hand and abandons his spot where he's putting the new stock out on shelves, no doubt retreating to the back room to compose himself.

"Uh …" I have no idea what to tell Mrs. Embry.

"Whatever it is, this man sure likes it being pegged. I'm sold." She hands me the book to ring it up at the cash register, and it takes a second for me to process what just happened.

"Are you sure you want this one?"

"This is good."

"All right." Can't argue with a sure woman.

I've definitely learned that through my dating life. My sad, pretty pathetic dating life, really.

As I'm making the transaction at the counter, a young guy steps into the store. Probably a college student.

He takes off his beanie and shakes out his light brown hair.

I give Mrs. Embry her book and a smile before making my way over to the new customer. "Hi, can I help you find anything in particular?"

His gaze meets mine, and I can't help noticing the different shades of hazel in each eye. One is a honey-brown color, and the other is a mixture of green and brown hues.

I try not to stare, because I'm sure he gets questions all the time. Like if he was born that way or got pushed into a vat of radioactive waste.

"I hope you can help me. The library doesn't have any in, and I've been looking online, but it won't get here in time, and I'm really hoping you have one in stock, and I realize this is probably the longest sentence in history, so I'll stop talking now."

I grin. "I might need the name of the book before you stop talking completely."

"Oh. Right. That would help. Uh, it's *Fundamentals of Agricultural Economics*."

"Sounds like a fun class."

Either he doesn't pick up on my dry tone, or he ignores it. "It is. In a constantly changing climate, sustainability in the farming sector is more unpredictable than ever before. Coming up with innovative ways to use natural resources— And I just realized you were being sarcastic. Sorry."

"That's okay. It's good to be passionate about something."

The passion I once had for life, for my future, *for everything*, was taken away from me four years ago, and I haven't figured out how to get it back yet. I'm twenty-six and don't know what I want to be when I grow up.

I had a plan. A smart person would've had a plan B. Now the thought of making any kind of plans makes me break out in hives.

"The agriculture section is this way if you want to start looking, but I'll go check the computer to see if we have it in stock."

"Thanks, man."

I'm halfway through typing the title into the computer when movement out of the corner of my eye catches my attention. The college kid takes off his thick coat, revealing a Burlington U hockey windbreaker underneath.

My fingers freeze on the keys.

Just when I thought this day was getting better, the universe takes a nice big sucker punch to my gut.

I fucking hate hockey.

"Rainn?" Harrison says, appearing next to me.

I shake out of my stupor and turn to him. "W-what?"

"Are you all right? You look like you've seen a ghost."

Yeah, the ghost of a person I used to be.

I glare at the offending jacket that's mocking me.

The guy's big hand runs over the bookshelf. He's taller than me but not by much, and he has the body of a forward. Sleek, muscular lines and not too bulky. He's built for speed, not enforcing. I immediately wonder what position he plays and hate myself for it.

Because I shouldn't care.

I hate hockey.

And if I say it enough times, I'll believe it one day.

"Want me to take over with this customer?" Harrison asks.

Is it being petty if I say yes? Probably, but I'm going to take him up on the offer anyway.

Harrison's staring at me with genuine concern, and my voice gets stuck in my throat.

"Found it." The hockey player slaps a book down on the counter, and I flinch.

"I can ring you up," Harrison says, taking the book. "Rainn, can you go finish what I started over there?" He points to the new display.

I leave them to it, but when the guy goes to leave, he stops next to me.

"Sorry, did that guy say your name was Rainn? As in Rainn Richardson?"

My face must answer for me, because his lights up.

"Holy shit, no way. This is so cool. You're, like, a hockey god on campus."

Was. I was a hockey god. I swallow hard.

"I remember seeing you play when I was in high school, and I was so bummed you were going to graduate the year before I could play on the same team as you. Though we play the same position, so it's not like we'd be on the same line or anything."

Center, then.

There are no words that could even begin to tell him to shut up without getting my ass fired, so I give him a curt nod instead.

"What are you doing now? Are you still playing?"

What does it look like I'm doing, genius?

"Your feet were like lightning, and your scoring record …" He keeps going, but it's all white noise to my ears.

"If you'll excuse me, I need to, uh …" I begin to retreat but stumble in my rush to get away. I bump into the display, sending books flying to the ground. "Damn it," I hiss.

I bend to pick them up.

He kneels to help, and our eyes meet. For a moment, I'm staring at someone I recognize. Someone I used to look at in the mirror. A young hockey player with awe in his eyes and excitement for the future ahead of him.

I almost hate to burst his bubble.

Almost.

"You want to know what I'm doing now?" I wave my hand around dismissively. "*This.* This is my life." Bitterness claws at my throat.

"Wait, this? Only this?" He glances around the store with a confused look on his face. "But—"

"I don't play anymore."

The excited puppy of a man finally loses his awed expression, as if I just told him Wayne Gretzky died. Slowly, but surely, it's sinking in that the guy in front of him is a has-been. A has-been who never got the chance to become a big thing in the first place.

I turn and put the books back on the shelves, hoping he'll drop the subject.

I'm not so lucky.

"What happened?"

Read the room, dude. I glare at him.

His face falls even more. "Oh. Sorry. Right. Intrusive and stuff. I should, uh … go."

I try my hardest to be polite as I say, "Hope that agriculture book works out for you. Have a nice day."

Too bad mine is shot to shit.

WHIT

I victory dance my way into the locker room, which is a talent in full hockey gear. I should get an award.

That is, until one of my teammates shoves me, and I fall flat on my face.

"I'm okay!" I call out.

Everyone laughs.

"Of course you are, Whit. You're used to falling while wearing skates," Jonah says.

The rest of the team snickers and lets out a collective "Oooh."

I jump back up in one swift move, and I decide my award should be for most graceful.

I don't point out I'm one of the only ones who actually scored on the ice during that game. Not that we needed anyone else to step up when our opponents couldn't find the net if we drew them a map.

"Celebratory drinks tonight?" Cal asks and slaps my shoulder.

I hesitate because I had other plans. I've spent years avoiding going out with the team or putting myself in any situation that would risk revealing my secret before I was ready, but now it's out, I should probably make the effort to bond with the team more. But not tonight.

There's a reason I've been the flaky goofball around these guys. I wanted an easy college experience and to focus on hockey and my degree without worrying about watching my back or causing issues on the team.

Living in Vermont, I've never felt scared to own my truth, per se. Moo U is progressive, and Vermont was one of the first states to legalize same-sex marriage. It was never society holding me back, but my own need to get through the other challenges in my life first—like juggling school, hockey, and working on my family's farm.

But this is my senior year, and my last season playing hockey, I realized I wanted to own who I am completely. So, during Christmas break, I came out.

First to my family, who were supportive. Maybe a little surprised but not all that shocked considering I've never had a girlfriend or spoken about girls. Dad had always thought I was a good boy who was focused on school instead of sex, but when I told them I'm gay, a lightbulb went on behind his eyes, as if he'd finally figured out my actions haven't exactly been the textbook definition of a het college guy.

After the break, I came out at school. My classmates from my agriculture study group were cool with it, and my teammates were accepting but quietly wary. Or maybe I'm reading into the team's reaction because, out of everyone, the testosterone-filled man-children are the most likely to have a problem.

I have made it a conscious effort to be the last in the showers since then. If anyone has a problem with me seeing them naked after all this time, they can cut their shower short.

I force a Whit smile, because they're what I'm known for. My smiles are all teeth and dimples. I've heard for years they have the ability to make all the girls swoon, but I wouldn't know anything about that. "I'm sitting this one out." I grab my towel.

"How new for you," Cal says. "Still going with the busy excuse, huh? I thought now that you were out, you'd stop hiding."

I feel the guys' stares, and I get it. I'm sure I'm not the only gay guy in the history of this school's hockey team, but I'm the only one on the current roster. The only *out* one, at least. I don't get any gay vibes from anyone else, but you can never tell. I'm proof of that.

"You're all welcome to come with me, but I don't know how comfortable you'll be in a gay bar."

There are some snickers.

"The boys couldn't handle all this," Cal says and does a ridiculous shimmy. He's probably my biggest ally on the team. He didn't even flinch when I came out.

"I thought *I* was the gay one."

Laughter erupts in the locker room, and I let out a quiet breath of relief. It's not always easy to drop the walls I'd spent so many years building.

While everyone starts making their way to the showers, Cal stops in front of me. "Seriously, though. If you want moral support or anything, I'm there."

"As tempting as it is to see you out of your element, I'm good. Thanks."

I don't have the desire to strike out in front of my teammates. I have no idea how to flirt with a guy, let alone proposition one. I'm half hoping my boyish good looks help with that.

Who needs to talk when I have this face?

In two months, I'll be a twenty-two-year-old virgin, and that's just … no. I've promised myself I won't let that happen.

So tonight, I plan to expand my newbie-gay-dude horizons. I'm going to check out Vino and Veritas. It's not technically a gay bar but a wine bar owned by a gay man that's welcoming to the queer community.

As I make my way into the shower block and take the last stall, I focus on the tiles in front of me and work the soap over my body.

With thoughts of tonight in mind, I contemplate giving myself a good scrub *everywhere*. What if Mr. Take My Virginity happens to be in the bar tonight and he's, I dunno, like only in town for one night? I can't pass up an opportunity like that.

A communal shower probably isn't the place to get my body sex-ready, though.

Ugh. Virgin for at least another night, then.

Which is a good plan. Maybe I should knock other things off the virgin list. Like, kissing a guy, having another man's hands on me, his mouth, feeling hard muscles caging me…

My cock gets excited thinking about it, and then I remember where I am.

Hockey!

I make a mental run through my scoring stats to rein in the anticipation simmering under my skin and finally manage to finish my shower.

After dressing in my post-game suit, I make my way to my car and drive toward town.

The closest parking garage on Church Street is a block away from the bar, so I find a spot and then walk to Vino and Veritas.

The combined bookstore and wine bar is relatively new, and as soon as I found out it was queer-friendly, I've been wanting to come check it out for myself.

The bar side was closed the other day when I was here, but I've been past it before when it's been open, and it looked like a chill place to hang out.

Which, of course, intimidated the fuck out of me. Because coming here … that would be owning who I am.

But now I'm ready. I think.

I've done the hard part. I already *came out* to my family and friends. This is where the fun part can start.

I run a hand through my hair, making sure it's parted on my right side, and then I try to flatten it so it's not sticking up at all different angles.

Adrenaline and nerves stir in my gut, and I can't tell if I'm trembling in anticipation or fear.

Suck it up, buttercup, and keep your eye on the W. You can't be a virgin forever.

I rush in so I can't change my mind, and in truest Most Graceful Award fashion, I run into someone like a bulldozer, and glasses of wine go flying.

Of course. Of fucking course.

My plan to sneak in unnoticed so I can watch for a bit before diving into the deep end has been smashed to pieces. It's scattered on the floor with shards of broken glass.

That's not even the worst part.

When the server straightens and turns toward me, his customer-service smile falls as soon as our eyes lock. Rainn Richardson not only works on the bookstore side of Vino and Veritas, he works on the wine bar side too. And … wait, does that mean Rainn Richardson is queer?

How cruel is the universe that the guy I completely embarrassed myself in front of, the guy who I think is one of the hottest men I've ever seen in person, might potentially be gay?

My memory of rambling at him in the bookstore flashes through my mind, and I wince.

Fanboying? That's not me. I've been to NHL games in Montreal and Boston and never once squeed over another player.

Rainn had been injured his senior year but had been drafted to the NHL. My teammates occasionally brought up his name, wondering what he was up to, but none of us realized he was still living here in Burlington and working at a bookstore and wine bar, of all things. Damn.

And now, as he scowls at me again, the same tongue-tied stupidity that hit me like a puck to the helmet the other day makes another takeover of my brain.

"I can pay for that," I blurt.

Rainn grunts.

Like last week, his jaw is unshaven and covered in dark scruff. His bright blue eyes are stormy. And fuck, even though he doesn't play hockey anymore, his muscles are … Nngh.

I may not have experience with guys, but I definitely know my type.

Rainn Richardson is my type.

"Don't worry about it," he grumbles and rushes off.

"No, wait."

But he's gone, and all eyes in the bar are on me. I'm used to being the focus of attention when I'm on the ice, but off it, I try to keep a low profile. When I'm not keeping to myself, I'm keeping the mood light and fun so no one realizes there might be something else underneath my carefree façade.

"The fun has arrived?" It comes out less confident than it normally would, but a few people laugh.

The bar is well-lit and cozy. It's got booths along the windows, tables in the middle of the room, a small stage at the back, and stools at the bar.

Rainn comes back with a small broom and dustpan and hands them to me.

"You're going to put me to work? Is that allowed?"

"Yup." He turns on his heel again and storms away.

"I guess that's fair," I mutter. It *is* my mess.

"I wouldn't worry too hard," a voice says behind me.

I spin to find a guy maybe in his early thirties who's wearing a saccharine smile.

"There'll be a lot of guys here who'll offer to do that for you for the chance to buy you a drink." His gaze rakes over me.

This is where I'm supposed to swoon or something, right? A nice-looking guy saying something flattering should make me weak in the knees, but nope. Nothing.

"Uh … thanks? But I have it. Thank you."

The guy doesn't look too disappointed. "Fair enough."

Even though I'm not interested, I do stare after him and check out his ass. It's a nice ass, but I still feel nothing.

Great start, Whit. You're, like, the smoothest guy ever.

I bend down to clean up the mess I made, and I'm almost done when feet appear in front of me. I get excited until a mop and bucket come into view.

"I have to mop too?" I look up and meet Rainn's eyes.

"No, I've got this."

What does it say about me that an interested-in-me dude with a cheesy smile and a nice ass did nothing for me, but the hardened features of one ex-hockey player will make my body buzz and my cock pay attention? Maybe I have an anger kink. That could be helpful to know.

I stand full height to find I'm taller than him by maybe an inch. A short inch. He's wider and hasn't lost his athlete's build.

"Where do you want me to put this?" I hold up the broom and full dustpan.

"Leave it by the bar over there, and then you can leave." He points to where the bar leads to a back room.

I frown. "You're kicking me out? Because I knocked over a couple of glasses?"

"No, I'm kicking you out because you're a hockey player."

I don't see what that has to do with anything.

"Are hockey players not allowed in here?" I glance around the bar to try to see what I'm missing.

"Are you lost? Do you know what type of bar this is?"

Realization dawns. "Ah. So, hockey players aren't allowed to be gay. Is that what you're saying? *You're* here."

"I work here."

"I'm so confused."

"Why are you here, Leighton?"

I pull back. "Y-ou … how … what?"

Rainn sighs. "I might have looked you up the other day after I was rude because I had contemplated apologizing."

"Only contemplated?"

"Yup. And then you came and made my job harder."

I rub my chin to cover my amusement. "My mistake was an accident. Yours was bad manners."

He scoffs. "I have bad manners? You were the one asking personal questions of someone you don't even know."

"Hmm, I guess that's true. I have an idea. Why don't you buy me a drink and we can call it even?"

"I'll buy you a drink, but we will be nowhere near even."

"That sounds promising." I turn on the mega-watt—mega-Whit, if you will—smile, but it falls as soon as Rainn starts laughing.

"Not in the slightest. I'm straight, but thanks for playing."

Just like that, my little baby gay heart shatters.

3

RAINN

Leighton Whitaker, Moo U hockey player, is gay.

Not that there's anything wrong with that, but hockey and queer don't go together often. It's not completely unheard of; I just wasn't expecting it.

Once we clean up what's left of the shattered glass and wine all over the hardwood floors, I lead him to a stool at the bar.

"What'll you have?" I was rude to him last week because I was already having a shitty day. Then his reminder of my hockey days might have pushed me over the edge.

Tonight, I accused him of not belonging here simply because he plays hockey. I'm so glad I read all of those gay romance books so I wouldn't offend any of the patrons.

Hopefully, the free drink will make up for it.

Leighton looks over the menu with a concentration line above his brow. A quip about being able to read is on the tip of my tongue, but I swallow it down. It's exactly the type of line I'd use on a teammate back in the day.

That is one thing I miss about the game. I mean, I miss a lot of things. The ice. The fast-paced play. The feeling of putting a biscuit in the basket. But the comradery between teammates was what had always given me a sense of belonging.

"Is there something other than wine?" he asks.

"Sure. Here's a full list of what we have. We've got local craft beers, cider—"

"I'll have a Shipley Cider. Thanks."

"Coming right up." I take a bottle out of the fridge and uncap it, sliding it in front of Leighton.

He smiles up at me.

I get hit with the same nostalgia I was sucker punched with last week. He looks so … what's the opposite of pessimistic and bitter? Optimistic and … happy.

I try to imagine what it would be like to have that kind of outlook on life again but can't see it.

"You're not going to check my ID?"

"I know how old you are."

"Oh, right, because you looked me up. Uh, where exactly did you look me up?"

"I noticed your hockey jacket last week. Went to the Burlington U hockey roster online. Leighton Whitaker, number fifty-nine."

"Whit."

"Huh?"

"Uh, everyone calls me Whit." *Whit* takes a sip of the cider and swallows hard. "So, you work here and in the bookstore."

"I do."

"And you're straight."

"Is it illegal for a straight guy to work in an all-inclusive estab-lishment? Isn't that what *all-inclusive* means?"

"Well, you said I'm not allowed in here because I play hockey, so I'm trying to work out the rules. I had no idea there were so many. It's, uh, my first time at somewhere like this."

It's almost endearing how his voice goes up at the end. Like he's unsure of his statement.

"Here's a tip for you." I lean on the counter. "Knocking drinks out of the bartender's hands isn't the best way to make friends."

His forlorn expression almost makes me feel guilty about giving him shit for it. *Almost.*

"Enjoy your drink and don't sweat the first-time thing. Our regulars are pretty welcoming."

Though the idea of any of them talking to Whit, who's clearly inexperienced, doesn't sit well with me.

I might hate his connection to hockey, but I have sympathy for the guy. It can't be easy being a gay player on a hockey team. That's if he's out to them at all.

He could be closeted and taking baby steps onto the gay scene, and that has to be daunting. Even in the most liberal communities, there are assholes.

I move to the other end of the bar and serve Jake, a regular and the guy who swooped in as soon as Whit was alone while I went to get the mop. The guy is a flirt, and I've worked out it doesn't hurt in the tip department to flirt back.

Is flirting with guys I have no interest in a morally gray area? Probably. But flirting is part of the bartender's code. Plus, my poor car and its broken alternator make my morals take a dip.

I give Jake a wink as he walks away from the bar. I'm putting his money in the till when I feel Whit's stare on me.

"Are you sure you're not gay?" he asks.

I laugh. "I think I'd know by now if I was inclined that way."

"Maybe. Maybe not. I've heard of guys in their forties discovering their sexuality for the first time."

I want to roll my eyes but hold myself back. I've never had any interest in men, and working here, I've definitely been propositioned enough to know.

"How did you end up working here?" Whit asks.

"I got a job at the bookstore first. One night they were short-staffed here. I needed the money, so I filled in. I pick up shifts whenever I can." Because I'm broke as fuck. I don't tell him that part, though.

There's nothing sadder than an old hockey hopeful who

everyone thought was destined for the Big Show turning out to be a bartender and bookstore clerk.

"Hey, so, umm …" Whit keeps his eyes on the bar in front of him as he talks. "I should apologize for all the shit I said last week."

"Forget it. I was having a bad day. I shouldn't have been rude."

"I had no idea. I thought …"

"Thought my injury wasn't career ending?"

Whit nods.

"Funny. The doctors thought the same thing. Spoiler, they were wrong. Buffalo didn't want to touch me after I'd torn my ACL for the second time. That doesn't scream longevity career-wise."

"Shit, I'm sorry."

I try not to think about it. "Two ACL surgeries before I was twenty-two. I was too high risk."

"Still sucks."

"Understatement."

Someone flags me down, and I'm thankful for the interruption. Talking about hockey turns me into an asshole, so I avoid it whenever possible.

A steady stream of drink orders keeps me busy for a solid half hour, but that doesn't stop me from noticing Whit moving around the room to flirt with guys. Ultimately, from what I can see, he strikes out and wanders back to me during a lull.

He sits at a stool and bangs his head on the countertop.

A laugh bubbles out of me. "I don't know how hygienic that is."

Whit's lips turn down. "You work here."

"Exactly."

"Eww." Whit wipes his forehead. "Is being gay always this hard?"

"I wouldn't know."

"I have to admit, this isn't exactly what I was expecting."

I lean my hip against the bar. "What were you expecting?"

"I dunno? For guys to see how hot I am and ask to blow me in the bathroom or something?"

A full-blown laugh falls from my lips this time. I have to admit, the dude is funny even if he's not trying to be.

"So glad my misery is entertaining to you."

"Sorry."

"Where are all the easy men who want all the gay sex and no strings or names?"

I purse my lips. "Maybe it's like that in big cities? The scene is low-key here. I mean, all bars by nature have that hookup culture, but if you're looking for boys in booty shorts and orgies, you're definitely in the wrong place. When Harrison opened V and V, he wanted to create a safe and queer-friendly environment that everyone could enjoy."

"Is everything about gay people in mainstream media wrong?"

"Probably."

He pushes his empty closer to me. "Can I get another cider?"

"Sure." I switch them out.

The night isn't super busy, but the work is steady. I leave him again to serve others but keep stealing glances at him. It's confusing. Objectively speaking, he's a good-looking guy. His intriguing eye color is a draw in itself, along with his dimples when he smiles. His suit doesn't make him look like your typical college hockey player. It's a mystery why he's striking out.

Jake reappears at Whit's side, and Whit's face lights up. Then Whit's mouth moves a hundred miles a minute, and Jake's eyes gloss over.

I can't hear what Whit's saying, but I think I've found the reason why he's not having any luck.

Jake turns his head toward me and mouths, "Help."

Super-bartender to the rescue. Not all heroes wear capes. I give Jake a new drink. "Whit here's too young for you."

Jake gives me a grateful look and moves away quickly.

"Oh, age isn't a big deal to me," Whit calls after him.

If possible, Jake moves faster.

Whit slumps.

"You don't want to date that guy anyway. He's in here all the time trying to score."

"Aww, that sounds perfect for what I need."

I cock my head.

"I can't be a virgin when I graduate in the spring. That's sad. I mean, ideally, I won't be a virgin by my next birthday which is in seven weeks, but I'm willing to be flexible."

Oh dear.

"This has been your opening line to guys tonight, I'm guessing?"

"Well … I told myself not to talk, but then, I don't know, isn't that something you should disclose? It feels like something you should tell someone. Because, they have to be, like, gentle and shit, and it's not like gay sex is something you jump into, right?"

"Again, I wouldn't know. But has anyone ever told you that you talk a little too much and maybe say things you don't need to put out there right away?"

"Really?"

"Well, we've only met twice, and oversharing and boundary crossing seems to be a common theme."

Whit groans. "I'm fucking this up."

"You really aren't. You're just coming on a little strong. You're hot—I mean, I'm guessing. Everyone keeps staring at you and checking you out. It's your mouth that's holding you back."

"So I just have to fill my mouth with something other than words."

His words make my straight cock twitch a little. Ah, blowjobs. Oh, how I've missed thee. I point at him. "That. Right there. Lead with that."

Whit glares at me, and I have to say his tough face is kind of laughable.

"Or every time you feel yourself rambling, take a drink," I suggest.

Whit's head falls to the bar again. "I'll die of alcohol poisoning."

It's not my fault a laugh escapes. Seriously, I can't tell if this guy is entertaining or plain sad.

He lifts his head. "You should be my wingman."

I should do what now? "As tempting as that is, I kinda have a job to do already."

"Yeah, but that's why you'll be good at it. You know people, and you've seen things."

"I'm straight, remember? I know nothing about gay hookups. I'd tell you to go on dates and make them feel special before trying to get them into bed."

"Is it against gay law to go on dates and make each other feel special?"

I throw up my hands. "I don't know. Which is exactly why I shouldn't be your wingman."

"Worth a shot." Whit finishes off his cider. He stands, and I think he's going to go back to mingling, but he takes his coat off his chair and puts it on. "Thanks for the drinks."

He slides a tip across the bar top, and I immediately feel guilty, but that doesn't stop me from taking it.

"You don't have to leave," I say.

"My ego's taken enough hits for one night." His smile this time is smaller, his dimples not making an appearance. "But ... I will be back. Maybe."

"You should come back." I find myself hoping he does.

WHIT

Sundays are my one day to sleep in, but my body never lets me sleep past eight. As the light streams into my bedroom, I wish I could return to the darkness of unconsciousness where my ego is still intact.

I'm never stepping a foot inside Vino and Veritas again. Nope, nope, nope, that's a hard pass.

That reduces my hookup options to dating apps, but there's something seemingly cheap and nasty about the idea, especially for my first time. Having said that, I'd prefer the anonymity of an app to scoping out any LGBTQ-focused events on campus. I'm out at Moo U, but there's a difference between people knowing I'm gay and seeing it, and while my reservations may be overly cautious, it has nothing to do with how others will react. It's about my comfort level.

I don't have much time to myself between studying, hockey, and working on the farm. I rise early to get morning chores done, go to class throughout the day, hockey practice is every night during the week, and games are on weekends. It leaves very little time to explore what I need to so I can get all these first-time experiences out of the way.

At the same time, something Rainn said last night stuck with me. When he said the only advice he could give me was to make someone feel special before trying to fuck them, I realized *I* want to feel special, or at least respected. I don't want to be seen as a hole or a dick to use, and I probably need to pay that same respect to whoever I end up sleeping with.

I'm not holding on to my virginity like it's some virtue or sign of purity or whatthefuckever all those religious people preach, but I want more than a hookup with a random person I might regret.

So dating apps are probably my only option if I refuse to go back to the bar, which I do. If I never saw Rainn Richardson again, it would be too soon. Twice now, I've embarrassed myself in front of him, and I won't let it happen again.

I take out my phone to open an app I downloaded ages ago but then buried in a random folder so no one could see it.

I have a half-filled-out profile that I abandoned when I'd decided I wasn't ready to be out and therefore not ready to take risks.

The information I filled in almost a year ago now is different from what I actually want.

I uncheck the box that says looking for a hookup and click "dating" instead. The relationship box is right next to it, and while I wouldn't mind meeting someone and having it turn into more, it isn't a necessity, so I leave it blank.

I fill in other details, omitting that I'm a student and that I'm a hockey player, because that part of my life is wrapping up with graduation looming.

A lot of the other profiles have pics of abs or chests, and only a couple have faces. I have no idea what to put on mine. Abs is suggestive, but I *am* looking for sex with a side of dating, so maybe I should do abs?

Will I care if anyone I know sees my face on a gay dating app? I assume most abs pics are posted for anonymity as well as marketing your best assets. Not too long ago, I would have cared about being recognized, but not anymore. Face, it is. It will send less mixed signals than asking for a date and then posting a pic of my half-naked body.

When all's said and done, and I switch my profile to live, it turns out I might have overanalyzed the photo thing. It takes thirty seconds to get my first DM, a few minutes to have ten, and after I check through all those, more keep coming in.

They're from everyone and everywhere. A guy in Connecticut offers to meet halfway before I've even said anything to him.

Face pics, abs pics, group pics, pics of guys with their dog, pics of guys from so far away I can't make out their features—all pop up with a message next to them.

The messages range from "Hey," to dick pics, to asking if I'm a top or bottom.

Thanks, random stranger, that's something I'd like to figure out.

One guy even offers to fuck my pussy-boy mouth. Whatever that means.

Nice to meet you too.

This is … no. It's too overwhelming. I throw my phone on my bed and ignore the constant vibrating of new messages coming through.

At least if I get desperate enough, I have options.

Yaaay.

I think I'm making this more complicated than it needs to be.

There's only one thing that will get me through this, and that's a vat of coffee.

Noise from downstairs filters up to my room, and the deep voices of my dad and brother let me know they've come back for a coffee break.

And, like every Sunday when I get out of bed and make my way down to the kitchen for breakfast, the usual ribbing starts.

"Hey, sleepyhead."

I give my brother the finger while Dad slaps the back of Campbell's head.

In farming, there are no days off, but Dad's lenient on me since I'm going to college, and to go to college on a free ride, I need to play hockey, which means lots of hours away from farm duties.

One day in the not-so-distant future, Dad's going to cut back his hours on the farm and then retire completely.

We sell hay and have dabbled in a few vegetable crops, but our milking cows are our main source of income. Dairy makes up seventy to eighty percent of Vermont's farming income, and it's unpredictable as hell. One year we can do great, the next we won't see any profit at all.

We've been trying to get Dad to build other sources of revenue for years, and finally he's starting to cave, but he's made it clear it's up to Campbell and me to make the decisions together. This farm is our future.

Mom always cooks big breakfasts for us and the farmhands, so I find the leftovers in the fridge to heat up and pour myself some coffee.

Dad's on his way out when I finally sit down, so it's just Campbell and me.

"You look like shit."

"Long night." Long, embarrassing night. "And thanks, by the way. It's always nice to hear how unattractive I am."

"Well, I have always been the better-looking brother."

"Whatever delusion helps you sleep at night."

Though, it's probably true. Campbell always had girls hanging off him. It's probably why they never paid me much attention. That, and my complete obliviousness to flirting. It's not only guys I have inexperience with. My friends in high school would laugh at me when I'd blatantly shoot girls down without even realizing they were flirting. It's not my fault I'm immune.

"Do you have any plans for today?" Campbell asks.

"Not really. Do you need a hand with something?"

"Nope, but you should have plans. Not long before you won't have your precious Sundays."

"I joined a dating app," I blurt.

My brother looks surprised.

"But I don't think I'm gonna use it. Everyone on there is so …" What's the word?

"Out?"

"I was going to say creepy."

"You should put yourself out there. Get it over and done with like ripping off a Band-Aid."

"I tried that last night at Vino and Veritas. Apparently all those years of keeping to myself also meant I never learned the art of flirting. I swear the guys couldn't get away from me fast enough."

Campbell tries to hide his amusement but fails.

"Why does everyone find my inadequacies funny?"

"Who else finds it funny?"

"The bartender Rainn. He kinda took pity on me."

"Ask *him* out."

I scoff. "He's straight. He was just doing his job. And besides, even if he was gay, *ooh yay, pity date*! No, thanks."

"Then maybe you should go into this app thing with an open mind. Weed out the creepers and go on a date for once in your life."

Damn it, he's right. I'm not going to admit that to him, though. His head is big enough already.

"Also …" He takes a sip of his coffee. "I need to talk to you about the wedding."

Oh, God, he's going to ask me to be best man or groomsman or something, but I really don't have the time—

"We've decided we're only having a best man and maid of honor, and I've already asked Gordo to be mine."

"Oh, thank fuck."

"Nice, little brother."

I laugh. "No, you know I'd do it for you in a heartbeat, but I have enough on my plate already, and—"

"I get it. And I did think of that when I made my decision. Christie thought you might be upset I didn't ask you."

"Nah, it's better this way. Best man should be a best friend's job."

"Awesome. It will also free up some time for you to get on that dating app. Maybe find a date for the wedding."

Ugh. Right. That.

Weeding out the creepers is harder than I originally thought. There are the quick dismisses—the dick pics, offers to drive a hundred miles for a fuck, and any mentions of pussy-boy mouths. And then there are the ones who start out nice enough and say, "Hey," and make small talk, and then suddenly it's all, "I'm waiting for your big fat cock right now," and "Can I come over?" and I realize I've wasted fifteen minutes of my life. It's not much time in the big scheme of things, but when it happens countless times, it adds up fast.

This is what I wanted … apparently.

It would be easy to take any of their offers, but something about it doesn't feel right, and I can't pinpoint why. I'm not excited about finding a guy this way, so it's hard to really want it.

I do find one guy who's nice to talk to. We haven't gotten into anything deep, but for six days, we message back and forth, and it seems like we're on the same page.

So when he asks me out to dinner on Saturday night, I'm vague about having a busy schedule and ask to meet on Sunday instead. He agrees, and then I sweat bullets until the date.

I can do this. It's a casual dinner. It doesn't have to lead to anything, but I'm prepared if it does. At the door of the restaurant, I almost chicken out, but thankfully the weather gods give me the push I need to get inside and out of the cold.

The lighting is low, and the romantic setting is a good first-date choice. My gaze sweeps over the restaurant as I take my coat off, trying to spot my date. I scan tables filled with couples and some families, and then my gaze lands on someone familiar. Someone I really don't want to see.

Rainn lifts his head, and instinctually, I dive to the floor because that's totally a normal and natural response.

The host rounds his station and stares down at me. "You okay down there?"

"Totally." My voice squeaks. "Uh, I'm here for, umm, a table for Kurt?"

"Ah. Blind date? Got one look at him and you're chickening out? Want me to tell Kurt you called the restaurant and couldn't make it?"

Is it weird that I'm strangely touched he's willing to do that? And people say chivalry is dead.

"No, it's not him I'm hiding from. It's someone else."

"Ooh, who?"

"Guy at the middle table along the wall. He's with a blonde woman."

Rainn must be on a date.

Damn, it sucks how I can't get the idea that he's gay out of my head just because he works at Vino and Veritas. Seeing him on a date with a woman is a slap of reality.

Why does he have to be so hot?

"You're seated on the other side of the restaurant if that helps," the host says.

"It does. Thank you. Is it safe to stand up?"

He checks for me. "Yup. I'll cover you. Stay on my left as I lead you to the table."

I smile up at him. "You're getting a big tip."

"Right this way."

The guy is shorter than me, so when I jump up, I crouch beside him and follow him toward my date.

Kurt sits facing us, so he watches as we approach.

I'm expecting a warm welcome, but he frowns, and then I realize I'm still hunched over.

I stand upright. "I walk normally, I promise."

The host laughs as he walks away.

"Okaaay," Kurt says.

"Moving on. Hi." I take my seat opposite him. "Nice to meet you."

"You too."

Kurt's relatively attractive, if a little … average-looking. His head is kinda small, his spiky hair twice as tall as his forehead. It's a lot more prominent in person than in the photos he sent.

I shake that thought free and reach for the water on the table. *He was the nicest one on the damn app,* I remind myself.

"Are you going to explain why you took a dive and then Quasimodo'd your way over here?"

I almost choke and then play dumb. "You saw that?"

"Am I not what you were expecting, or …"

"No," I say quickly. "It's nothing to do with you."

"I know you're out of my league, but—"

I reach for his hand on top of the table, a reflexive move that doesn't quite register until I'm doing it.

Holding hands. I'll check that off my to-do list.

"See the guy behind me on the other side of the room with the dark hair and permanent stubble?"

"Oh. Is he an ex? You're only here to make him jealous? So, you're using me. Right. Got it." He lowers his head.

Damn, this guy has some self-esteem issues.

"He's not an ex at all. I made a fool of myself in front of him last week … and the week before that. I kinda prefer not to do it again, so I don't want him to see me."

"Are you sure?"

"Definitely. I'm here for you."

He seems to believe me, but when I remove my hand, his face falls again.

I am so out of my element.

RAINN

Whit is the weirdest person I've ever met.

I have no idea what he's doing, but it looks like he's on a date. An incredibly awkward date.

Why did he dive behind the host's station and do this weird walk toward his table?

I want to know because who the fuck does that? He's walking proof that good looks don't always equal charm.

"Who are you looking at?" my blind date, Kelly, asks.

She seems nice, but there's no spark. I get the impression the feeling is mutual.

"No one. Just this guy I know."

Kelly puts her napkin on the tabletop and gets a serious look in her eye. "I think you're great, but—"

"But Sommer is the worst matchmaker ever?" I should've known better than to trust my cousin when she said she had an amazing woman to set me up with. She has the worst taste in men. Apparently, women aren't her strong suit, either. Not that there's anything wrong with Kelly. She's just all wrong for me.

Kelly laughs. "Sorry."

"I get it."

"Split the check?"

"No, it's my treat," I insist. I may only have twelve dollars in my bank account, but it's how I was raised. Men pay for dates.

"Thank you. Friends?" she asks.

Even if the gesture is empty, I take it. "Friends."

I don't have many friends anymore. Everyone moved on with their lives when they graduated. I'm still here in Burlington hoping something in my life will change without actually taking any steps to change it.

It's a real mystery why Kelly's not interested.

She has drive and ambition. She has spent half the night talking about her plans to move to a bigger city once she finishes her grad program to do … umm … something. I probably should've listened harder, but I've been distracted. Ever since Whit walked in, I haven't been able to pay attention to anything else.

He's like a train wreck. I don't want to see it, but I can't look away.

Kelly kisses me on the cheek as she leaves me to finish off the wine we ordered.

I give my credit card to the server and wince as I sign the slip.

Out of the corner of my eye, I notice Whit get up from his table and move toward the bathrooms. I have the sudden urge to follow and check in on him.

I was hoping he'd come to V and V again after his game last night. Every time the door opened, I glanced up from the bar and was filled with surprising disappointment when it wasn't him.

It got to the point where I checked his hockey schedule to see if he had an away game. Which he didn't.

And then I realized I was looking up *hockey schedules* for the first time in forever without feeling sick to my stomach.

There's something about Whit that's hard to process. There's a bond with him like I used to have with my teammates. And maybe that has to do with our hockey connection, but since my injury and finding out my dreams were shot to shit, I haven't wanted anything to do with that world.

It's why I never finished my sports management degree. It's why I don't talk about hockey, watch hockey, and avoid everything hockey related.

Except for Whit, it seems.

Maybe I'm taking pity on the guy. I know that if we had been the same age and went to college together, we would've been friends.

He's a wide-eyed puppy you can't help but find adorable when he trips over his big paws.

If I follow Whit into the bathroom, I have the chance to make two friends tonight. Though I don't actually think I'll see Kelly again.

I find him hunched over the restroom's sink, splashing water in his face.

"Bad night?"

He jumps at my voice. "Could be worse."

"Is it as bad as my date telling me the moment she finished her meal that she's not into me?"

Whit's mouth curves up at the edges. "That makes me feel a little better. My date keeps telling me I'm out of his league and better-looking in person."

"Oh, the horrible problems attractive people have," I say dramatically. "Wait, in person?"

"We met through an app."

My lips turn down. "We scared you off at the bar so much that you've resorted to *online* dating?"

"Hey, Mr. McJudgy, you're the one who told me I had to talk less."

I'm such an asshole. "That isn't what I meant. Well, it was, but I was trying to tell you that you should still be yourself. Not that you should stop talking completely."

"Well, now you're in my head, and all night I've been sitting there not knowing what I can and can't say."

"See what happens when I try to help?" I exclaim. "This is why I would make a shit wingman. Look, go out there and forget everything I said about not talking and calming down and whatever else. Because if they don't like you for who you are, then what's the point?"

"Not being rejected would be nice."

"True that. Though, the feeling with my date was pretty mutual."

Whit leans against the counter. "What was wrong with her?"

"Too ambitious."

"What a bitch," he says dryly.

"It's a great trait to have, but people like that need to be with other ambitious people or they'll get dragged down and held back."

"It sounds like you're speaking from experience."

"High school girlfriend didn't want me to move to Vermont for college."

"Where are you from originally?"

"Rhode Island."

Whit's brow scrunches. "That's not *that* far away."

"Four hours is far for eighteen-year-olds. She wanted to do the 'high school sweetheart, get married, and have lots of babies' thing. I wanted hockey fame and would do anything to get it. Even say goodbye to her."

"Why didn't you move back after your injury? Reunited high school sweethearts. That's a cute story."

I swallow down the truth to that answer. I'm too bitter to go back. I'm a failure. I stupidly thought I'd still finish my degree at some point, so I stuck around waiting for my ambition to come back. "I like Burlington."

Whit looks confused. "But your family's in Rhode Island."

"Yep. I have a cousin here. She went to Moo U as well and decided to stay when she graduated."

"So … you just … spend holidays and weekends with your cousin?"

"What? No. I get home occasionally. For major holidays." If I have the gas money. "They've come here a couple of times."

Though, if I'm honest with myself, I can't even remember the last time I called my mom.

When I had my second injury, I'd been drafted to Buffalo, but I never saw a contract after my surgery. Every time I'd talk to Mom, she'd spout the usual bullshit people try to convince you of when you experience loss. "It wasn't meant to be." And all that other fate bullshit.

Whit rubs his chin. "Huh."

"What?"

"I live with my parents, and I can't fathom spending a weekend where I don't see them."

My first response is to cringe, because I've been on my own since I left for my freshman year, but that closeness actually sounds … nice. Unexpected longing stabs at me.

I shake it off. Talking to Whit seems to bring back all the crappy emotions I've been pushing down for three years. "You should get back out there. Your date probably thinks you're in here taking a dump, and I'm not sure about gay relationships, but in my hetero experience, women like to pretend we don't do that. And if we do, they don't want to hear about it."

Whit smiles, but it doesn't bring out his dimples. "Is it bad I don't want to go back out there? How do you get out of a date?"

"Well, tonight I did nothing but be myself, so take whatever you want from that."

"Okay, so be you. I need to be a grumpy straight guy who tells people to stop talking. Got it."

"In my defense, I only ever told you to talk *less*. I let my date tonight talk all she wanted. Which was a lot, but still not as much as you."

"Wow. So helpful. Thank you. Really. Thank you so much."

His expressive, mismatched eyes tug at my sympathy strings.

I can't believe I'm about to say this, but it comes out anyway. "Do you want me to go say you don't feel well and are going home?"

Whit's face lights up. "Would you?"

"It's partially my fault for giving you bad advice that led to this date to begin with."

"Yes. Your fault. Let's go with that."

I chuckle. "Wait here."

I leave the restroom and move toward his table where the server is clearing the empty plates. A quick glance around lets me know Whit's date has left.

Well, shit. I'm not sure his ego could take this hit right now.

When I get back to him, I don't have the heart to tell him the truth. "All done."

"How'd he take it? Shit, I should've done it myself. He was so … unsure, and what if I've scarred him for life?"

Okay, would it be worse or better for him to know the dude abandoned him?

"That's a little dramatic," I say. "It was a first date. I'm sure he's fine."

Probably. Maybe.

"I should catch him before he goes and explain." Whit starts for the door.

I grip his arm. "Whit …"

He slumps. "He was already gone, wasn't he?"

It must be written all over my face. "I'm sorry."

He groans. "I'm going to be a virgin forever."

"That's *a lot* dramatic. Come on. I'll buy you a drink at V and V."

"So you can watch me make a fool of myself again? I'll pass."

"No, because I get a staff discount on drinks, and it's all I can afford. I'll help you in your quest to lose your virginity."

Whit blinks at me.

Then I replay my words in my head. "By finding you a guy. Not *personally*. Geez."

"Damn. Still straight, then?" He smirks.

"Last time I checked."

"Need a hand checking again? Because I volunteer as tribute."

Words are just words. They're meaningless. They hold even

less significance in the form of a joke. But for a split, miniscule second, my mind drifts to what taking Whit up on that offer would look like.

Despite the tiny interest, I easily dismiss it as fascination. Reading those books at the store might have piqued my curiosity, but not any more than stumbling upon some hard-core bondage porn one day. I watched it. It intrigued me. But that's all. I'm not going out to buy rope and handcuffs anytime soon.

"I'll keep that in mind," I say dismissively. "Let's get that drink."

Whit smiles. "You know what this means, right?"

"What?"

"You agreed to be my wingman. *Rainn Richardson* is my wingman."

I snort. "I don't think that's something to brag about. 'Gay virgin recruits straight man to get him laid.' Sounds like the butt of a joke."

"I like butts."

"Of course you do." I don't even know why, but my gaze lowers to Whit's ass as he walks in front of me.

Ah, hockey butt. I miss mine.

My ass used to be my best feature. Now I'm just an ass in general.

WHIT

"Okay, take me to where all the boys are at." My excitement might be hiding the irrational embarrassment of stepping inside Vino and Veritas again.

Hockey players are supposed to have game. Apparently gay hockey players have none. I'm basing this completely on my own singular experience and applying it as a huge generalization.

On the ice, I'm fast and smooth. My moves are as natural as working on the farm. My moves on members of the same sex? They're nonexistent.

Walking through the doors, we're met with a practically empty bar. That's good, because there are fewer people to witness the awesome talent I have of making every single person here uncomfortable.

"Welcome to Sunday nights when there's no open mic night," Rainn says as he rounds the bar. "Hey, Tanner, I thought you had the night off."

The man shakes his head. "Ned called in sick again."

"You could've called me."

"I knew you had a date, and I was told making you cancel would be mean."

Rainn grins. "Jax told you that, I'm guessing." He turns to me.

"Jax is the only reason Tanner doesn't grunt one-word answers to everything anymore."

Tanner grunts, and Rainn laughs.

"You should've called. Date was a bust," Rainn says.

Tanner leans against the bar. "Do you want to take over Ned's shifts? Because I'm this close to letting him go. It's one thing if you're like Molly, who has no idea what she's doing half the time, but at least she tries. Ned … He stopped trying a while ago. The only reason I've kept him on after all this time is not wanting to go through the pain of finding someone else."

Rainn responds even before his boss stops talking. "Yes, I'll do it."

"Is Harrison going to be okay with that? You might have to cut back hours in the bookstore."

"He told me to ask you for more hours when I complained to him last week about needing money."

"Consider it done. You'll start taking on extra shifts next week." With that, the boss turns around and gets back to work.

Rainn doesn't ask me what I want—he just grabs us both Shipley Ciders and leads me to a booth. He reads the bottle's label after we sit down. "This is made in Tuxbury."

"I know. I'm in a lot of the same classes as Dylan Shipley."

"Oh, cool. I've never actually had their cider before."

"You're missing out." The drink goes down smoothly.

Rainn takes a sip, and I can't help watching his throat work around the liquid. I sigh because that's sexier than it should be. Not only because he's doing a simple human action that shouldn't turn me on so much, but because I'm drooling over someone I could never have. I should stop that.

"What's your major?" Rainn asks, and I get the feeling he's making small talk to get me to stop staring at him like a weirdo. "Oh, wait, let me guess. Agriculture. You came in for that book a few weeks ago. Fundamentals of … economical farming … things."

"Yes. Economical Farming Things is the unofficial title."

He doesn't find me funny, apparently.

"My brother and I have plans to take over our family's farm when Dad retires, so we figured a degree in agriculture for me wouldn't hurt. Though, I don't think Dad will ever retire completely until he's dead. There's no way he'd sit by and watch us run things without his input. But eventually, it'll be mine and Campbell's."

"Wow, so you're not only close with your family, but you're super close. Like live-in-each-other's-pockets kind of close."

"Yup." I wonder if I should tell him that my brother and I are both in the middle of building our own houses on the family's property because we can't imagine moving far away. Campbell currently lives closer to town with his fiancée, but his house is almost finished, and I know he can't wait to move back.

Yeah, with the way Rainn is looking at me, maybe I should keep that to myself.

"That's …" Rainn looks like he's struggling to come up with the right word.

"Nice?"

"I was going to go with odd, but what do I know?"

"So you said. Aren't you … lonely?"

Rainn leans back in his seat. "Hey, I'm not the one here looking for someone to warm my bed. I do better on my own, I think."

"Being lonely has nothing to do with sex. I couldn't imagine not seeing my family all the time. My brother's engaged, and I can't wait for him to fill the farmhouse with a billion nieces and nephews. I'm built to withstand noise and chaos."

Rainn's eyes move toward the window, holding a sadness I don't understand. "That's a hockey player thing."

"You have it too?"

"Used to." He glances down at his bottle of cider. "Tonight, my date was talking about her future. She was excited and animated, and all I could think was that it sounds exhausting."

"Having a future is exhausting?"

Rainn takes a deep breath. "Plans are exhausting. And heart-breaking when they don't work out. It's why I don't make any."

"That's …" Depressing, pessimistic, and yeah, depressing. "You're a little too young to be at the 'Get off my lawn' stage of grumpiness."

"I live in an apartment. I don't have a lawn."

I pause. "You aren't close with your family, and you live in an apartment. I … I … Nope. Do not comprehend."

"Not everyone was born with acres of land to his name. I'm happy where I am."

"Are you, though?"

Rainn pulls a face I've seen on a lot of guys this past week.

I'm making him uncomfortable.

Note to self, talking to Rainn Richardson about his *feelings* is not welcome.

"You don't have to answer that."

His gaze moves behind me. "Someone just came in. He's around your age."

"*Our* age. There's only four years between us."

He rolls his eyes. "We've established I'm the equivalent of a grumpy old man. He's *your* age."

I turn to look, and Rainn kicks me under the table.

"You really need to learn to be subtle."

"I'm a hockey player. Subtlety is not my forte."

This time, I turn slower and catch sight of who Rainn thinks could be a potential suitor for me.

I deflate and face him again. "Pass. He's in a few of my classes at school."

"So?"

"I don't want the potential of running into the person I lose my virginity to every single day."

"You graduate in May, don't you?"

"No one from school. It'll be easier that way. Next target."

"For someone seemingly desperate to lose his virginity, you're certainly picky."

He's right, and I must look dejected or something, because Rainn's expression softens.

Pity isn't something I thought I'd ever appreciate, but I could do with some sympathy right now. I'm so out of my element I don't feel like I'm in my own skin. On the ice, I know exactly who I am. I'm a guy looking for the W. Off the ice, I've always known who I am, but I guess there's a difference between knowing it and *living* it.

"You should wait for the right guy," Rainn says.

"What?"

"I shouldn't have insulted you for being picky. You should wait for someone you're comfortable with. If that's someone you don't go to school with, then it's not."

My voice gets stuck in my throat, and I swallow hard. "It's probably stupid …"

"Nah. It's good to have standards. I should probably get me some of those."

"Right. Your standards are looking for someone with no ambition."

"Exactly. Maybe I should also add 'must be a train wreck' too. It will make me feel more accomplished."

It sounds a hell of a lot like he's preparing for disappointment, and I can't say I don't get it. The half of me that wants to trade in my V-card is eager to get it over with, but then the other part of me is holding back because I'm cautious about being disappointed.

"So, what are these rules of yours?" Rainn asks.

"Uh, well, so far I have no guys from school, no one who uses the word pussy-boy mouth, and no one who sends unsolicited dick pics."

Rainn rubs his chin as if in thought, but it honestly looks like he's trying not to laugh. "Those are all good qualities to look for in a partner."

"Not everyone can have high standards like you."

Rainn can't keep a straight face. "True that. I'm still willing to help you. With me picking up more shifts in the bar, I can play wingman whenever I'm working."

The question *"Why?"* fills my head, but I can't bring myself to ask it. Because Rainn may be as clueless as me when it comes to gay dating, but there's something about him that I'm drawn to.

Even though I've been embarrassed in front him countless times now, I can't help the way he makes me feel. My heart beats that little bit faster, and my stomach swarms with tiny butterflies. When his bright blue eyes meet mine, I freeze.

Maybe I should add humiliation kink onto the list of things I should try? No, wait, naked humiliation doesn't sound like something I would be into.

"Or not," Rainn says.

"What?"

"I said I can help you when I'm working, but then you screwed up your face."

"Oh. No, I ..." Was thinking about how kinky I might or might not be. Let's not say that and embarrass myself more, okay? "I was on a different train of thought." *The train that leads to you and me having sex.* "Like, sex thoughts. Don't mind me, I distract easily, and apparently the average twenty-something male thinks about sex, like, eight times a minute. I don't know if it's that much, but it's a lot. Especially for a virgin, but I mean, you would know this. You're a guy." Oh great, and now I'm mentioning Rainn thinking about sex. "This is one of the times when I should shut my mouth, right?"

Rainn's brows rise in surprise, and I swear I see intrigue in his eyes, but that can't be right.

"Hey, you're picking up on when you talk too much, so that's something." Rainn takes a large gulp of his drink.

I wish he wasn't so damn nice. When he's not grunting at me or getting mad at me for breaking glasses of wine or mentioning hockey, Rainn is a decent guy. He doesn't deserve me drooling all over him.

The way he swooped in and offered to end my date for me made me swoon like some teenager.

"If I'm taking over Ned's shifts, I'll be here five nights a week," he says.

"I really only have Saturdays after games and Sundays."

"Sundays are always this slow unless it's open-mic night. Saturdays will have more potential."

I force the words out. "It's a date, then." I need to move my interests to someone else before I begin to think what I feel for Rainn could actually be real. That would suck so hard, and not in the way I'm looking for.

"A date to try to get a guy to sleep with you." Rainn shakes his head. "Still weird, but I guess we're doing this now." He turns in his seat. "All right, let's see who else has potential."

I don't even look because I'm too fixated on the guy sitting in front of me. "I think I can only handle one rejection per night. I've decided that's another rule." I finish off my drink and stand. "Thanks for the drink. I'll see you next Saturday night."

All week, during morning chores, through every class, every hockey practice, my head is elsewhere. I can focus enough to get through everything, but my papers are mediocre and my playing is sloppy.

I can't stop thinking about a dark-headed ex-hockey player who has promised to help me have sex … with someone else. Because having sex with him is not possible.

Straight guys don't have sex with men. Which is a shame because the only guy I've been comfortable around since deciding to do this happens to be straight.

Ooh, yay, gay achievement unlocked—lusting after a straight guy.

I bang my head on the breakfast table, not realizing Mom is right behind me.

"What's wrong with you? Do you feel ill?"

My head snaps up at her voice.

Like the good mom she is, she kisses my forehead. "You don't have a fever."

"I'm fine. Just …" Way too old to be experiencing the first of what will no doubt be many unrequited crushes. "Tired."

The kitchen is empty because apparently, my mental capacity is limited to a single thought at a time, so that means I was late coming in from morning chores.

She takes the seat next to me. "I'm going to talk to your father about giving you a lighter load."

"Don't."

"Between studying, hockey, and the farm, you're working nonstop."

"It's not work, Mom. I promise."

"Oh, is it a boy?"

I rub my hand down my face. "I lied. It's totally work. Yup. Work."

"Leighton—"

"We really don't need to do this. If I were straight—"

"I'd be asking the exact same thing. Ask your brother. I hounded him with questions about Christie until he brought her around."

"Well, you won't be meeting this guy. I'm discovering the painful side effect of being gay."

She purses her lips. "Is this a sex thing? Because that, I don't need to know."

I groan. "No. He's straight, so he only wants to be friends."

"Aww, hon. I'm sorry. You should try out that gay wine bar in town."

I laugh. "That's where I met him."

"I'm confused."

"He works there, but anyway, I'm going back tonight because he promised to introduce me around to some guys who aren't straight."

"As long as you're safe."

I screw up my face. "Mom!"

"I meant don't drink and drive! Not …" It's her turn to screw up her face.

"Can we please pretend this whole conversation didn't happen?"

"Agreed, sweetie." She promptly leaves, and I know I'm going to spend the rest of the day not only trying to forget any romantic feelings for Rainn, but also about that awkward conversation with my mother.

It's funny to me that when I was in the closet, all I could think about was coming out. Now that I'm here, those small confining walls seem mighty appealing.

Campbell walks in as I'm finishing up breakfast. "One of the farmhands found a fence down on the northeast pasture. Want to give me a hand fixing it?"

"Sure." Anything mindless where I don't have to think is the most I can handle right now.

Fixing the fence takes most of the day, and by the time we're done, I have to shower and get ready for tonight's game.

I move on autopilot, from showering to driving to school and suiting up, it's all a blur. I'm exhausted when I hit the ice, but when I do, something ignites inside me. It always does when I'm playing. There's no gay or straight out here, no farm, no obligations other than getting that puck in the net.

Though my muscles are tired, my body knows what it's doing, and when I light up the lamp, I'm on a high nothing can bring down. That is, until I hit the adrenaline crash in the locker room after the game.

Games are exhausting, tonight's even more than usual. I'm dead on my feet, but I told Rainn I'd be there tonight. Then again, I'm not sure he'd really miss me if I went home and climbed into bed instead.

I still haven't decided what I'm going to do by the time I head for my car, but when I see a teammate run into his girlfriend's arms and kiss her hard, the longing I've had in my chest since hitting puberty rears its ugly head, and I want that for myself. But with a dude, obviously.

I steer my truck toward town and leave my car in the same parking garage as last week.

The bar is as busy as it was the first night I came here, and there are a few familiar faces who I know to stay away from, thank you very much. Repeat embarrassments are not on the menu tonight.

I head straight for the bar, but there are no stools available, and Rainn is busy.

I tell the disappointment to fuck off because I'm not here for him. He's here to point me in the right direction. That's all.

He acknowledges me by immediately getting me a drink.

I make my way through the crowd, and a group of four leaves a booth, heading for the exit as I get there.

It's selfish to take a whole booth for myself, but there aren't any other tables available.

And hey, maybe someone will ask for a seat, we'll hit it off, and I'll forget all about the dude behind the bar.

"Hey," a soft voice says.

See? My plan is flawless. I turn my head, and okay, maybe it has some flaws.

I never thought I'd be the guy who looks at someone and goes, "Nope." But … *nope.*

"Hi," I say anyway, because I'm not a rude asshole.

There's nothing wrong with the guy—he's attractive, probably around my age, and I don't recognize him from school. They're all good points, but he's pretty and twinkish. I'm attracted to muscles. That's been the type of guy I've always checked out and fantasized about. I like so much testosterone that my ideal guy would shave every day and still have a face covered in stubble.

Like someone I already know but should not be thinking about.

"Mind if I …" The guy gestures to the spot opposite me.

"Go for it."

"I'm Ian."

"Whit."

Amusement shines in his eyes. "Whip? That sounds promising."

"Whit. With a *t*."

"Oh. Shame. Is that your real name?"

"Nah, just something my friends call me."

I don't miss the way he checks me out while he takes a drink from his short glass. "What's your deal?"

I glance at Rainn behind the bar, and as if sensing my stare, he looks our way, checks out the guy opposite me, and gives me a thumbs-up. That pretty much explains my deal.

I have a brief memory of his advice—be myself but don't talk this guy's head off, but … Wait, what was the question again?

Ian laughs. "The talkative kind, huh?"

"Sorry. I've been told I talk a lot, so I'm trying to think of the shortest answer possible. I didn't know whether to say hockey or farm, and so I almost said hockey farm, and then I thought of a farm where they grow hockey players, and then I remembered people farms don't exist yet, but it could totally be a thing. Like Build-A-Bear but with hockey players. And now I'm doing the overtalking thing again."

Ian looks amused, at least. "If I've deciphered that properly, you live on a farm and play hockey. Or like hockey."

"Play. For Moo U."

"Ah, nice. I didn't go to college."

"What do you do?"

"Work construction."

I eye him.

He laughs again. "No one believes me when I say that, and I guess I can see why." He looks down at his small frame. "I work in the office of a construction company."

We talk some more, and the live music kicks in at some point.

Ian is nice and normal. He doesn't have self-esteem issues, and he isn't intense, but he's all blond and pretty and a little femme, which isn't my type at all.

Maybe Rainn is right and I'm too picky, but hey, at least this one is clearly into dudes.

We talk and listen to the music. He buys me a drink, and when I tell him it's my round, he insists he'll get it and buys me another one.

At one point, he invites me over to his side of the booth so I can see the musician play. I take a seat beside him, and he immediately begins to make the gap between us smaller and smaller.

Honestly, the guy playing his guitar onstage, the way his long fingers work the strings, the soft tone of his voice as he sings ... he's turning me on more than the guy next to me, and he's at least twenty years older than me.

I don't know what's wrong.

Then my eyes lock on Rainn again, and I realize exactly what's wrong.

I turn to Ian. "Have you ever had a crush on a straight guy?"

"Ah. So that's why you've been moving every time I inch a little closer. Good to know. I was thinking I'd lost my game."

"Nothing to do with you. I can't get this other guy out of my head, which is ridiculous."

"Been there. Done that. Have the T-shirt. My only advice would be to not get a crush on a straight guy, but I'm guessing that's a little too late."

I take another sip of my drink. "Way too late."

"I'm sorry, man. That's rough. But I think we've all been there at some point."

"How do I get it to stop?"

He gives me a sympathetic stare. "There are two ways. Time—"

"Which I don't have."

"Or getting under someone else. I can totally help with that if you want."

"Time it is."

"Ouch." He chuckles.

"Sorry."

He elbows me. "I'm messing with you."

I like Ian. Damn it. Why can't I be attracted to *him*?

And how long do crushes last?

RAINN

My gaze keeps gravitating toward Whit and the guy he's hitting it off with.

At first, I was happy he was carrying on a good conversation, with appropriate-looking levels of back-and-forth with a guy. But the longer they sit there, the more unsettled I become.

I can't figure out why.

The guy he's with has a nice smile, but I don't like the way he's looking at Whit. It's somehow predatory but inviting at the same time. Like he wants to take Whit home and do wicked things to him … or have Whit be the one doing wicked things.

The image of Whit pinning this guy down and fucking him invades my mind without permission.

I don't like it. But not for any reason that makes sense.

With every flirtatious touch the dude lays on Whit, the urge to go over there and tell him to back off grows stronger. Which is very *what the fuck* in my world.

I don't know where those thoughts are coming from. This is what Whit wants, and I promised him I would help. So why am I fantasizing about marching over there and kicking this random guy out of my bar?

They climb out of the booth, both smiling at each other, as

Tanner calls my name. I'm torn between turning to my boss and chasing after Whit as he makes his way toward the door.

Is he really going to give it up this easy?

"*Rainn*," Tanner says again.

I shake it off. "I have to do a trash run."

My boss looks at me with a confused expression because the bar is busy and now is definitely *not* the time for a trash run, but I escape too quickly for him to stop me.

After I throw the half-empty trash bags in the dumpsters out the back, there's absolutely no logical reason for me to round the building, but I do it anyway.

I'm not fast enough. I can't see Whit or his date anywhere, and a voice in my head tells me I'm too late.

Too late for what, I'm not sure.

It's not like I'd be volunteering to take Whit's date's place for obvious penis reasons.

This sudden protective streak came out of nowhere and is taking over me, but it doesn't make sense to be worried about this particular guy.

He was thin and small and pretty. Whit's a hockey player. He would be able to hold his own. So why am I standing here coatless in the freezing cold, trying to stop Whit from going home with him?

I don't know. But Tanner is gonna kill me.

When I walk through the front doors, yep, there's my boss scowling at me. Though, it might not be an actual scowl. The man has a serious case of resting bitch face.

My heart skids to a stop, along with my feet, when I catch sight of the brown-haired guy sitting on a barstool. Alone.

Whit … He came back?

I round the bar and try to ignore Tanner's stare as he approaches me.

I try on an innocent expression. "Umm, I accidentally let the door to the alley close, and I had to come around the front."

Tanner grunts and gets back to work.

I approach Whit and try to be sympathetic. "What happened?"

"Yo, can I get a Barclay Stout?" Someone squeezes between Whit and the guy next to him.

"Sorry," I say to Whit and serve the other guy.

Then a woman asks for a glass of merlot.

The bar is insanely busy, and I fear Whit will give in and go home before I get a chance to talk to him.

But he continues to sit there, slowly sipping his cider. I feel his gaze on me as I work, or at least I think I do. Every time I turn to look at him, his attention is on the drink in front of him, his head held low.

When the crowd begins to die down and everything isn't so busy, I finally get a chance to talk to him, but by that point, he looks exhausted.

"Rough night?"

His light brown hair flops into his eyes as he shakes his head. "Just long."

I lean on the bar. "What happened with the guy? You looked like you were going to leave with him."

He avoids eye contact. "Wasn't feeling it."

Huh? "But—"

"He wasn't really my type. I like …" His eyes rake over me, and I hold my breath. My chest puffs out on its own accord. Then he finishes his sentence, and I deflate. "Older guys. He was only twenty-one."

"You're only twenty-one. Are you saying you wouldn't date yourself?"

"Exactly."

I grin. "So, we're adding 'must be older' to the list? How much older?"

As I ask, Jon, the musician who's playing tonight, takes the stool next to Whit. "Hey, Rainn, can I please get a water?"

I go to get his drink, but not before I hear, "Hey, you were great up there."

I turn back to find Jon smiling at Whit, and ugh, ugh, ugh. I just saw one guy undressing Whit with his eyes, now Jon's doing it too.

And for some stupid reason, that protective urge is still there, even though I know Jon is a good guy. Jon's in his forties, so maybe that's my excuse this time. Whit may like older guys, but Jon is *too* old.

Whit's right. Finding someone suitable to lose his virginity to is hard work, and I'm not even doing the heavy lifting.

Again, images of Whit throwing someone against a wall and pinning them, him kissing them roughly and moving his hands all over them, fill my mind, only this time, I'm imaging Jon as the other guy.

There's a part of me that's super uncomfortable with that, but it's not the act or the image.

It makes me uncomfortable because I'm not exactly put off by it.

I could try to psychoanalyze it all night—that love is love and it's great to see people openly be themselves in this environment without fear. But that has nothing to do with me picturing what Whit would look like while hooking up with a guy in private. Why would I even think about that?

"Rainn," Jon calls out, and as I look down, I realize I've over-filled his water glass, and the excess is falling through the drainage holes on the bar.

"Fuck." I turn and hand him his very full water. "Sorry. I was distracted."

Jon takes it and guzzles it down. "Thanks." He angles himself in Whit's direction, and I hold in a growl. "It was nice talking to you."

Jon walks away, and Whit watches Jon's ass the whole way.

I snap my fingers in front of him. "You may be into older dudes, but that one is too old for you."

"Age is just a number."

"Yes, but you know how that meme goes. Is four dollars a lot?

No. Four murders? Yes. It's all about context. And a twenty-year age gap is too big. He's two generations older than you."

Whit studies my face, and I begin to think I've spilled something on it or missed a spot shaving, but then he smiles. "Two generations … he could teach me a few things."

"He has a kid."

"Ooh, yeah, I'm out. I don't need baggage at my age."

"I don't need baggage ever. That's one of *my* rules. No single moms."

"Why not?"

"Don't want to be tied down to one place."

His eyebrows rise, and my answer doesn't only surprise him. Even though I dropped out of college and I'm working two dead-end jobs, I haven't made a plan or a move to change anything.

I'm scared of being tied down, yet, I'm realizing I already am.

Well, shit.

"You okay?" Whit asks and takes a sip of his drink. "You look like you're having an epiphany. I had one of them once. It almost broke my brain."

I laugh, but it's forced. I need to change the subject, stat. "Why do you only drink Shipley Cider?"

He shrugs. "Support local businesses and all that. And it's good. It tastes like sex."

I narrow my eyes. "Like … sex? First of all, how do you know what sex tastes like? And second of all, how can a drink taste like sex?"

Last week when we sat at a booth across the room and had a couple bottles of cider, I remember it tasting nice, but … sex?

Whit's dimples appear. "Here. Take a sip. Now that I've pointed it out, you won't be able to stop thinking about it."

I take his drink and down a huge gulp of it, and— "Holy shit, that does taste like sex." It's hard to explain. Maybe the smell combined with the aftertaste, I don't know. Whit is right, though. I won't be able to drink it again without thinking about sex.

"Can you see why I'm so eager to get laid now?"

Images. So many more images. Why can't I turn them off?

I shake them free. "You're obviously not too eager if you let that pretty guy go tonight. Even if he's not your type."

"I'm discovering that I'm a little old-fashioned on the inside. It's embarrassing."

"That's nothing to be embarrassed about. At all. And maybe that's not being old-fashioned. Maybe you're not a hookup kind of guy."

Whit screws up his face. "Are you saying I might be ..." He gasps. "The monogamous type? Eww."

"Hey, there's nothing wrong with that, either. It means you want to be in a relationship to sleep with someone. That's admirable this day and age."

"I'm an abomination to the gay community!" he cries dramatically.

"And which gay community are you talking about? Because I'll have you know there are a lot of committed gay couples who come in here."

"Oh, the community that I've seen all over mainstream media. Are ... are you telling me that's all fake news? We're not all man-whoring slutbags? I am so disappointed."

"You look it too." I smile, but he doesn't. "You really look exhausted."

"Wow, you sound like my brother and my mom."

"Are you okay to drive home?"

"If I stop drinking now, I'll probably be all right by closing time. I didn't really plan ahead."

"Where do you live? Can you get a ride or—"

"Nah, it's too far. It's thirty minutes that way." He points east. "No, that way." Now he's pointing at the ground.

"South?"

"Yeah. That."

"I get off in thirty if you want me to take you home."

His eyes widen, and I realize how it sounded.

"You know what I mean."

"I do, and thank you, but I'll be all right."

Customers are beginning to disperse, and I have cleanup to do before I can get out of here. When my work is done, I find Whit again. He looks like he's falling asleep sitting up.

"I don't think I'm comfortable with you waiting another hour before driving home."

"Shit." He yawns. "I think the alcohol was keeping me awake. Ever since I switched to water, all I want to do is sleep."

I take his arm. "Come home with me. You can crash on my couch. You said Sundays are your day off, didn't you?"

"Yeah."

"Perfect. Then you won't be waking me at ass o'clock to get home. Come on." I pull him up, but he barely budges.

"Are you sure?"

"What are wingmen for?"

"Well, generally, to get someone for me to hook up with. You're slacking."

"It's been one week. You still have plenty of time to find someone."

"Right. Plenty of time." He doesn't sound convinced.

WHIT

Oh, this was such a bad idea.

Rainn is being super nice and a great friend, but my little gay heart is galloping a million miles a minute and reading into everything he says and does, hoping he means it all the way I want him to.

Like telling me that musician guy is too old for me and being concerned about getting me home safely. But it kinda sucks that him being decent only makes me lust after him more.

I groan as we hit the street. Going home with Rainn isn't going to help me get over this stupid crush. Maybe I can sleep in the cab of my truck and drive in a few hours.

"What's up?" Rainn asks.

"I … I don't want to impose." Look, I'm a good old farm boy with manners and everything.

Though I have to say, the thoughts running through my head about what I'd do to Rainn if he let me are anything but polite.

"You're not imposing, jackass. We're friends."

Eww, he went and used the F word. *Friends*. Even though it's what we are now, I guess.

"Where's your car?" I ask.

"Car heaven. May she rest in pieces. I need a new one, but my last car cost more money in repairs than it was worth. I couldn't keep sinking money into that lemon, and I'm terrified the next one will be the same."

I take out my keys. "Here, we'll take my truck. You drive."

He doesn't protest, and a short, *silent* ride later, he pulls up outside an old red house that's been converted into apartments.

Before we can climb out of the truck, I pull on his arm. "Are you sure? This isn't weird, is it?"

He pauses. "Is it weird for you? Have you never stayed at a friend's place before?"

"I have, but …" But I was never crushing on any of them. Ugh, I'm the one making this weird. "Never mind. Lead the way."

I follow him up the walk and through the front door. I shove my hands in my pockets because I'm trying to remember what I usually do to occupy my hands when I'm walking.

Rainn opens his apartment at the back of the building and gestures me inside.

The space isn't much. It has hardwood floors and a small kitchen. There's what I presume is the bedroom to my right, and in front of me is the "couch" I'll be sleeping on. The futon looks about fifteen years old and not big enough to hold my two-hundred-pound frame.

Rainn strips out of his oversized coat and beanie. "It's not much, but I can afford it. That's the main thing."

He's not wrong. Then again, I'm used to a large farmhouse, barn, and hell, even our livestock have more space than this.

"It's … cozy." Even I don't believe myself.

"That's a polite way of saying small, but hey, it's only me, so it's not like I need much more room."

"I'm guessing this is a rare thing, having a friend over."

He thinks about it. "I don't think any of my old friends have even seen my apartment."

"Aww, way to make a boy feel special."

Something happens to Rainn's posture. It tenses, but I can't tell if it's because he likes what I said or it makes him uncomfortable.

Of course it makes him uncomfortable, you damn moron.

He stares at me with such intensity that now I'm the one who's uncomfortable.

I clear my throat. "Do you mind if I get some water?"

"Not at all." He moves toward the kitchen, but I cut him off.

"I can get it. You've been serving me drinks all night."

"It's my job. And it's the social expectation for a host to offer food and drinks to guests."

"Ooh, you got food here?"

"Hmm, well, no."

I gasp. "But the gods of social expectation will smite you! You better run along and get me some pizza."

He ignores me and gives me the water.

"Fine. No pizza." I drink down the cool liquid. "Mm, tasty water. It's definitely better than pizza."

It's amazing how he can say so many things with one look.

I take another sip and sense him watching me as I swallow the rest. He's still watching me when I place the glass on the counter, and it makes me self-conscious.

"Uh. Thanks." I rub the back of my neck. "I guess we should …" I gesture to my bed for the night.

"Right. I'll get you some blankets." He pauses. "Unless …"

My heart picks up a notch. "Unless?"

"Unless you want to watch something first? I usually take a while to wind down from shifts at the bar."

"I could watch something. I might fall asleep halfway through it, but I'm down."

"I'll make it something you can't sleep through."

Honestly, he could put anything on the TV, and I probably wouldn't be able to sleep. Not with his presence right beside me on that tiny futon of his.

It's weird to think a few weeks ago, Rainn Richardson was a

campus legend in my mind, a hockey idol for Moo U, and now he's here with me. Or, I'm here with him, more specifically.

I glance around his small space. There's a typical entertainment center that's filled with a PlayStation and games, the futon, and a bookcase under the window on the far wall that is surprisingly full of books, but the room lacks personality.

I can't help wondering where all the hockey stuff is because Rainn Richardson *is* hockey.

Or … he was.

"You look like you're concentrating pretty hard over there. What are you thinking about?"

"Where's all your hockey stuff?"

His face pinches.

"I know you don't play anymore, but, I mean, you can't leave a sport like hockey with nothing to show for it."

"I assure you, you can." He sits on the futon and picks up the remote for the TV. "Okay, what are we watching?"

I sit next to him, making sure to leave a big enough gap between us so I'm not tempted to move closer. "Why do you hate talking about hockey so much?"

"You know, social courtesy also extends to guests not asking such nosy questions."

"Okay, fine, you don't have to tell me, but one day, you'll talk about it. I'll be too charming to resist."

Rainn tries to squash a smile. "How's that charm thing working out for you, *virgin*?"

I hold my heart. "Help. It hurts! It hurts so bad."

Rainn laughs. "You're too much."

"I've made a decision," I declare.

"Oh, have you?"

He probably thinks I mean I've made a decision about what we're going to watch, but it's nothing like that.

"I'm going to repay my debt to you for being my wingman by making you fall in love with hockey again."

Rainn scoffs. "Good luck."

I don't think I'm going to need it. He wouldn't have an aversion to hockey now if he hadn't truly loved it at one point. I may not have big dreams of professional hockey, but I live and breathe the sport, and any hockey fan understands the hype.

Rainn has to see that he can still have hockey in his life without playing.

I take the remote from him and begin to search for a movie. "I'm thinking we watch *The Mighty Ducks*. Ooh, or *Youngblood*."

"It's not going to work," Rainn warns.

"Let's try it."

I try to contain my victory dance as he chooses *The Mighty Ducks* to stream.

* * *

"Pfft. These stupid movies and their triple dekes. It's not even a thing."

This isn't the first time Rainn's made that comment. I've forced him to sit through countless hockey movies, from *Slapshot* to *Goon*, and now we're back onto the rest of the *Mighty Ducks* trilogy.

Our movie night has kind of become a routine, and it's crazy how quickly and easily we settle into a pattern. I live for Saturday and Sunday nights, whichever night I can get to Vino and Veritas to spend time with Rainn.

If I have an away game, I'll go on a Sunday night and not drink so I can get back home for morning chores, but my favorite nights are when I can escape to the bar after a home game and stay at Rainn's.

He sits slouched beside me in his usual spot, his legs spread wide as he rests his head along the back of the futon, and his usual, ever-present scowl is on his face.

Even though he claims to hate the movies, rips apart all the inconsistencies, and is his grumpy, grunty self when it comes to anything hockey, I know something is getting through to him because he never once says no to watching them.

I wish I could be deluded and say he does it so he can keep seeing me, but everyone with eyes knows that's not the case.

That crush I've been harboring? It might be getting out of hand.

Rainn turns his head to look at me. "Nothing to say?"

Nope. I'm too busy admiring his long torso in a shirt that's so tight I can see every definition and contour of his abs. I'm too busy *drooling*.

Ugh, this has got to stop.

"So what if there's no such thing as a triple deke? It's not like the rest of this movie is filled with complete accuracy. Just enjoy it, you big grump."

Rainn's shiny blue eyes narrow. "Just for that ..." His big body moves closer, and my cock twitches.

Not a night goes by where I stay here and don't have a hard-on. Luckily, Rainn keeps the bedding for this piece-of-shit futon handy. I can cover my lap with my pillow, but if I do that now, while he's moving closer to me, it won't only draw attention to my dick thickening in my pants, it will be a giant beacon telling Rainn, *Hey, my cock likes you.*

So I hold my breath as Rainn practically pushes himself against me.

I have no idea what the fuck is going on right now. This can't be happening, right?

"Uh, Rainn?"

His mouth is so close now his breath is on my cheek. Then his hand slowly comes up, and I swear to God he's going to touch my face. I realize too late what he's actually doing.

He picks up the remote next to me, grins, and then moves back to his side of the futon. "Thanks."

I blink, and then blink again. "You are an evil, evil man." My unrealistic fantasies about a straight guy becoming interested in a gay guy have once again been crushed, but that's not the reason I'm upset. "Stealing the remote is one of the biggest bro-code laws you could break. Other than sleeping with another bro's ex—

totally not a problem with us—or dating each other's siblings. And as far as I'm aware, you don't have a hot, single, gay brother."

"I don't. But I have a very married, pregnant sister in Rhode Island. You're welcome to her, though, if you want to steal her off my brother-in-law. Bros should be supportive of other bros and their love lives."

"Sometimes I wonder why we're friends," I grumble and subtly try to cover myself with the pillow.

"It's because I humor you into making me watch these dumb films because you hope they'll spark something inside me, and I'll suddenly go out and fill my apartment with hockey paraphernalia."

"Hey, just because it hasn't happened yet, that doesn't mean it's not working."

"Mm-hmm."

There is one thing, however, that I'm damn sure is not working —my plan to lose my V-card before my birthday. It's only two weeks away now, and I've wasted precious weekends spending time with Rainn. He's distracting and funny, and … I really like him. Ugh, I like him way too much.

My schedule is insane, but I realize this ugly thing called friendship between me and him is probably temporary, so I don't want to spend precious minutes with someone else.

Every time he points someone out at the bar for me to go talk to, I die a little inside, and my excuses for not approaching other guys are wearing thin. I label everyone as being either too short or too tall, not muscular enough, or has the personality of a fish.

He nonstop tells me how picky I am, but I can't tell him the truth. Which is that every guy has one huge flaw: they're not him.

I don't need to be told it's unhealthy. I already know that, but I can't stop.

All the warning bells are getting drowned out by laughing with Rainn and talking to him. With him, I feel like I'm being real with a guy for the first time. I've never let my teammates and friends see the awkward, unexplored side of me. Rainn has seen it, and more. It's easy to be self-deprecating around him. I can say things I wouldn't dare say to an actual date, and in a weird way, I love that he jokes with me about my lack of experience. It makes it seem less like the big deal I've made it into in my head.

Hanging out at Vino and Veritas has been helping too. I'm comfortable there now. I feel like I'm getting acquainted with an actual community, rather than standing around a bar guzzling brews and looking for someone to fuck me.

Rainn's always behind the bar or on the floor serving, and it feels like a home away from home.

What's even better, is the nights I do stay over, we wake on Sunday mornings and walk to the Maple Factory on Church Street for coffee and pastries.

My stupid body clock wakes me up long before Rainn, and I've started reading the thrillers he has on his bookshelves. Each week, I pick up where I left off the week before.

I'm engrossed in Stephen King one morning, when Rainn opens his bedroom door. I jump a mile and nearly fall off the futon.

He snorts. "That never gets old."

"This book is bad."

"Aww, is Whit a wittle scared?"

"No. You're scared. You shut up."

He runs his hand through his messy hair. "I'll hit the head, and then we can get some coffee."

"Let me finish this chapter."

Rainn approaches and stands in front of me, all tall and hot in sweats and a plain black T-shirt.

He's so damn good at distracting me, the book is already out of my hands before I can blink. "You said that last week and only put the book down when I got hangry."

I stand. "In my defense, I didn't know the difference between your usual grumpy self and when you were hangry. I still don't know if there's a difference."

Rainn pushes past me. "You're so funny."

"I think so."

"At least someone does. Hurry up. I'm hungry."

Yeah, I'm going to hold on to this friendship for as long as it lasts. Finding someone to have sex with can come later.

RAINN

Falling into a routine with Whit becomes so easy it takes a few weeks for me to realize we've never exchanged numbers. We've gotten into this pattern of friendship where he'd turn up at the bar, and I'd take him home after I finished my shift.

Today when I woke up with allergies and Tanner told me to take the night off no matter how many times I said it was because spring had sprung and I wasn't actually sick, I realized I didn't know how to contact Whit to tell him I wouldn't be at the bar.

For a college student, his social media presence is scarily absent.

I'm lying on my couch feeling sorry for myself when the buzzer for my front door sounds. I half roll, half fall off the couch onto my knees and slowly stand to get to the door.

I greet Whit with a sniff.

My eyes are still itchy, and my nose is like a faucet. "Did I ever mention how much I hate spring?"

"Your boss told me you were actually sick, not being a whiny baby."

"Wow, some friend you are. You're supposed to say puffy eyes is the new sexy."

Whit's mouth drops open. Then closes.

"Coming in?" I step aside.

"Only if you're up for it."

"Like I told Tanner. I'm not actually sick."

Whit enters and takes off his coat. "It's March. The trees are still bare."

"I swear I walked past a tree that sprayed its sex pollen all over me. It only takes one tree, Whit. I've been sneezing ever since."

"Sex pollen …" Whit blinks at me.

"That's what it is!"

"I will never look at trees the same way again. Does that make bees, like, nature's pimps?"

I laugh and then wince. Fucking sinuses. "Laughing hurts my head."

"Aww, poor baby. Can I get you anything? Do you have allergy meds?"

"Ran out."

"And you didn't go buy more because …"

"Who are you, my mother? I didn't get to the store. I had plans to, and then I hurt. So I sat down. And then I slept. It's a catch-22. To feel better I need to go outside, but to go outside, I need to feel better."

"Are you sure allergies is all it is?" Whit's hand comes up to try to touch my forehead, but I swat it away.

"It's *allergies*."

"Maybe it's a head cold." Whit winces and steps back. "Maybe it's the flu. I can't get that. Coach will kill me."

"It's not the flu, jackass, but good to know where your priorities are at. Hockey trumps our friendship. Got it."

"Are you one of those people who always downplays being sick or injured?"

Why, yes. Yes, I am. How do you think I ended up with a career-ending injury?

Whit keeps talking. "Like, say you severed your pinky while

cooking. Would you be the kind of guy to shake it off and say it's fine or run screaming to the hospital?"

"Who needs a pinky finger? I mean, really. Least useful finger of them all."

Whit grabs my shoulders and spins me toward my bedroom. "As I suspected. Okay, it's bedtime for you."

"What?"

"Bedtime."

The deep rumble of his voice sends a shiver through me. It was not at all a sexual remark, but for some reason my body takes it that way.

Or maybe I really do have a fever.

Maybe it *is* the flu.

Yes. Flu can totally make your dick twitch. His large hands on me have nothing to do with it.

My brain's all muddy with hay fever. That's it.

Nothing else.

"Rainn?" Whit's hands leave my shoulders, and he steps in front of me.

"What?"

"Bed."

I grumble, though I can't say I hate it. I can't remember when someone last took care of me like this. Probably my mother before I left for college.

While I get into bed, Whit moves around my apartment, opening cabinet doors in the bathroom and kitchen.

"What are you doing?" I call out.

"Trying to find some cold medicine."

"I told you, it's not a cold."

"And I told you, I don't trust your judgment."

He said that? "You did? When?"

"Oh. Maybe I was thinking it."

"You're mean when I'm sick."

He appears in my doorway. "Aha. You admit you're sick."

"No. You're sick. You shut up."

Whit shoves a bottle of NyQuil at me. "Drink."

"This will only make me go to sleep."

"Good. Sleep it off."

I reluctantly take the cold medicine and drink it down, but I'm confused when Whit comes to the other side of my bed and sits, using the headboard as a backrest.

"What are you doing?" I ask.

"I'm going to sit with you until you're asleep and make sure you have what you need."

"It's not the flu."

"I hope not. I better not catch whatever it is."

I close my eyes with a sleepy smile. "Just don't go kissing me, and you'll be fine."

He doesn't reply, and the air in the room suddenly feels thick. But I'm too busy falling asleep to ask about it.

I wake up with my head feeling worse than it did yesterday, so that sucks, and my brain is foggy with confusion about my surroundings.

I'm in my bed. It's my bedroom. Those are my black curtains to keep the sun out, though they're doing a piss-poor job because they're open. The light filters over my bookcase, my closet, the discarded clothes on the floor … I'm definitely in the right room.

But the arm draped over my stomach isn't mine, and the continuous light snoring is definitely not mine.

I turn my head and come face-to-face with a sleeping Whit.

In my bed.

Next to me.

It's not like I haven't shared a bed with another guy before, but this isn't middle school, and it's not a sleepover.

It is the first time I have cuddled with a dude. That one's new.

And it's not like we did it on purpose. At least, I don't think we did. Last thing I remember is falling asleep with Whit babying me.

Accidental cuddling. It's no big deal.

Neither is the giant hard-on I'm sporting. It's morning wood. It's *nothing*.

Nothing.

It's fine.

But … how do I get out of this without waking Whit?

I suddenly understand all those jokes about preferring to gnaw off your own arm than wake a one-night stand. Only, in this case, I'd have to gnaw off Whit's arm. Yeah, that's not going to happen.

Gently, and while holding my breath, I move his arm away from me so I can slip out of bed and go to the bathroom.

He stirs when I come back. With a soft groan, he rubs his eyes and sits up. "Shit. I fell asleep."

"It's all good." The rasp in my voice is unintentional.

"Are you still sick? You sound horrible."

I clear my throat. "Gee, thanks." At least I'm able to sound the slightest bit normal this time. "And fine. I'm sick," I admit. Allergies don't usually make my head all … unthinky.

Whit gets out of bed and stretches, his T-shirt riding up and showing a tiny sliver of skin underneath.

Stop looking at another man's V, Rainn.

"Want me to go get you anything from the store? More cold medicine?" Whit's eyes rake over me, and while I'm ninety percent sure it's because he's assessing how sick I am, my whole body flushes. Like he's looking at me in a way that's not just *friendly*.

But I don't say anything. Calling him out would be like being the straight friend who accuses the gay friend of being into him, which is conceited and stupid.

Whit knows I'm straight.

"Let's go," I say.

Whit approaches and pushes me toward the bed. "No, no, no.

You're not going anywhere but back to sleep. I'll go get you whatever you need, and then I'll go home and bathe in sanitizer."

"It's a cold."

"Uh-huh, and last night it was allergies."

Touché.

Whit asks where my keys are so he can let himself back in and returns in no time at all with a bag full of meds. Maybe I did fall back asleep because it felt like he was gone for a minute.

I take the pills, cough syrup, and more NyQuil off him. "Thank you."

"Now, give me your number."

I cock my head. "Huh?"

"Your phone number?"

"You want my number," I say flatly.

"Yeah. So if you're sick again, you can give me a heads-up."

"Oh. Okay. Give me your phone." I hold my hand out for it, punch in my number, and then give it back.

The way his face lights up makes my stomach flip.

Maybe it's a stomach flu I have.

"I promise I won't text you, like, all the time," Whit says. "Even if I get sent videos of adorable kitties doing cute things."

"Good. I'm not really a cute kitty type of guy."

Whit bites his lip. "I'm trying really hard not to make a pussy joke."

I laugh and begin to shake off the weirdness of this morning.

"I would stay and look after you more, but I've already been too exposed, and I can't be hacking up a lung on the ice."

I wave him off. "It's fine. You've already done more than anyone else ever would."

Even though we leave everything on normal terms, I can't get waking up next to him out of my head.

The heavy arm draped across me was different than I'm used to, but it wasn't awkward. I think … I think I liked it.

Clearly, I've gone so long without a serious girlfriend that I'd lean into any affection. A hug from a cactus would be appealing to me right now.

The warmth of *any* body would have the same effect.

Maybe I should try to get out there and date again, but the thought of sitting through job-interview-like dinners has no appeal. Funnily enough, bartending bookstore clerks aren't in high demand on the dating market. I can't imagine why.

The week progresses, and, as promised, Whit doesn't message me random shit. He does message me about a car he saw for sale out near his place. The fact that he thought of me kinda kills me, but I have to pass on seeing it because of my stupid cold's impact on my savings. After missing three days of work due to sickness, it will be a stretch to pay for rent and food.

The closer I get to seeing Whit on Saturday, the more I think about him and what happened the last time I saw him. What if he stays at my place again? He usually takes the couch, but now that he's been in my bed, will he assume he's welcome there? Would I welcome it?

There's no doubt that I liked it, but guy friends who cuddle doesn't sound … normal.

Not that it's *not normal*. For other people.

Ugh.

I don't think I've overanalyzed something this hard since my injury where I was constantly asking, *Why me?*

I'm a mess by the time Saturday night rolls around. The temptation to call in sick is strong, but Ned got fired because he used the I'm-sick excuse too often. I can't afford to lose this job.

Tanner's behind the bar when I get there, looking as grumpy as ever.

"Hey," I say. I put my phone and keys under the counter for safekeeping while I work.

"Your college boy coming in tonight?" He speaks in his usual gruff tone, and his expression stays grumpy. I'm not sure why he's asking.

"Probably. Why?"

He steps closer to me. "You've got to be careful with that one."

"Huh?"

"He's got major love hearts in his eyes for you."

I scoff but practically choke trying to make the noise. "Bullshit."

"No bullshitting. Just, let him down easy, okay? Don't be the straight asshole and ridicule him for getting a crush."

I frown. "I wouldn't do that. We're friends."

"No, you're friends with him. He's like an animated puppy sniffing out a bone."

My heart starts beating faster for some reason.

I rub my chest. "Don't think so."

Tanner leans against the bar. "Think about it. How many guys has he spoken to or hit on since he started coming here?"

"Lots."

Tanner laughs. "Nope. He sits on that stool right there, orders cider, and talks to you every chance he gets. Then you go home with him."

That feeling is back. The unease in my gut. Though, is it unease or is it butterflies?

I can't be sure.

When Whit walks through the doors a few hours later, I'm surprised by the warmth in my chest. But as he takes his usual seat at the bar, orders the same drink he does every week, and doesn't even look at other customers, I realize Tanner might be right.

I don't know what to do with that.

WHIT

Rainn is acting weird, and I have a feeling it has something to do with me falling asleep next to him last week, but it's not like it's my fault. I was on a comfortable bed, and with my schedule being as crazy as it is, I'm always tired. Give me a chance to fall asleep, and I will.

When he first woke up, I thought he might have felt weird about it, but everything was fine when I left him last week.

Right now, I'm guessing that impression was wrong.

The bar is always busy on a Saturday, but tonight Rainn seems to have no time for me at all. He avoids eye contact, and when he does bring me a new drink, he's so speedy I don't even get a chance to ask how his week was.

At one point, his boss pulls Rainn aside to say something to him, but I can't hear what it is. Directly after that, Rainn approaches me. "I'm going on break. You want to come with me to get something to eat?"

I don't have a great feeling about this, but I down the rest of my drink and stand. "Sure."

On our way out, I spot Ian at one of the booths with a couple of guys, and he lifts his beer toward me. I nod back, but when he smirks, I get the feeling it's at me, not with me, and it's probably because of my stupid crush on the straight bartender who I've been lusting after for weeks now.

Rainn takes me to the Church Street Marketplace to a little kabob shop. "You want anything?"

"I could always eat. I'll have whatever you're having."

"Ah, the appetite of a hockey player. You better watch it come graduation. You'll end up like me." Rainn rubs his stomach, drawing my attention to his filled-out form. And by filled out, I mean amazingly hard and toned.

"There's nothing wrong with you."

"No, but I used to be all lean like you. Stop all that cardio, and the slimness goes away."

"You're forgetting I work on a farm. That's all physical activity." I show him my guns to prove my point and see the small smile trying to break through on his lips.

"Put those things away before you hurt yourself."

We get our food and go to the small bench seat by the window, and I have the distinct impression Rainn wants to tell me something. He makes no move to say it, so we eat in silence.

"Thanks for the food," I say when I'm done, wiping my hands on a napkin.

"No problem." He swallows hard. "That's what friends do for each other."

I know that's what we are, and yet the word somehow hurts, which is ridiculous.

"So, listen …" he starts, but then his mouth closes.

I hold my breath. For some reason, I picture Rainn telling me about a life-changing sexual identity crisis he's having. *Oh, naïve little baby gay heart.*

"My boss has this crazy theory that you're into me, and—"

"Your boss said that?" Shit. Okay, did someone squeeze my balls to make my voice go that high-pitched?

"Yeah." Rainn averts his gaze. "And while I told him he's

wrong, I just … I mean … God, this is going to sound so conceited, but, like … I wanted to make it clear that nothing could ever happen."

Yup, there's the sound of my shattering heart. It's followed quickly by a quake of guilt. Rainn looks upset, like he's done something wrong.

I act unfazed. "Rainn, I'm not delusional or waiting around for some straight guy to suddenly realize my abs are hot and my cock is even better."

He huffs a tiny laugh.

"Straight guys aren't into dudes. I know that." I shrug, but it's stiff.

His mouth opens and then closes like he's changed his mind about what he's going to say. "Why …" His lips press together.

"Why what?"

"Why have you stopped trying to find a guy at the bar?"

Ah.

That broken heart of mine thumps hard. "That has nothing to do with you."

Rainn's blue eyes narrow.

"I guess … I've been chickening out. Hanging out with you while you work has been a good comfort, and … yeah, I guess I'm nervous about putting myself out there."

It's not a *complete* lie.

His sexy-as-fuck mouth purses, and damn it, I hate not telling him the truth, but if I do that, he'll run the other way, and then I won't even have him as a friend.

"Are you sure? Because I don't want to be an asshole here and lead you on or—"

I hold up my hand to stop him. "You're not leading me on. I mean, you're hot, but what idiot gay guy would fall for his straight friend?" *Yes, what gay idiot, indeed.*

Rainn's lips quirk. "I'm hot, huh?"

"For someone who's a grump, yeah."

His grunt only makes me laugh and fall for him a little more. Damn him.

"I promise you, I'm still looking for someone, and I'll prove it." I stand.

"How?"

"I'm going to take someone home tonight." I cover it well, but my gut twists at the thought. Still, I feign confidence. "Or, actually, I'll let them take me home. My place is too far."

"Great." Rainn's tone is light, but it looks like he's gritting his teeth.

"But first, drinks for courage."

Lots and lots of drinks.

I'm going to do it. After weeks of putting this off and making excuses—holding out for a guy who will never be into me—I'm going to do it.

I slide off my designated stool, and okay, I'm going to do it as soon as the room stops spinning. Fusing my eyes shut, I wait for my equilibrium to return, but I may be a wee bit drunk.

The Shipley Cider wasn't enough, so I switched to the hard stuff, and that's how the bar lights became blurry and my face became happy. Even if it's heating up.

"Whoa, there, big guy." Rainn rounds the bar and puts his hand on my shoulder to push me back down to the seat. "You're a bit wobbly."

"Did I tell you I never drink hard liquor?"

"No. You neglected to tell me that while I kept feeding it to you."

I wobble on the stool. "I haven't since freshman year when I was at a party. I got so drunk I almost blurted my sexuality all over everyone. That wouldn't have been good." I shake my head. Or maybe the room shakes and I'm completely still. Probably the former, but it could so totally be the room.

Room is a funny word.

"I'm going to get you some water."

"I'm going to get me some." The room is less spinny now when I stand, probably because I'm on a mission. I'm laser focused, like a cheetah stalking its prey.

Why is my conscience talking in David Attenborough's voice suddenly?

"Ian," I bark a little too loudly when I get to his table.

He and his friends flinch.

"Oops. That was loud," I whisper.

Ian smiles up at me. "Can I help you?"

"Yep. If your offer's still good, I'm ready."

His smile widens as he leans back in his seat. "Oh, really?"

"Yep. Totally."

"How drunk are you? Touch your nose for me."

The guys at his table snicker while I roll my eyes. "Fine." My finger hits its target but barely. "I'm not drunk-drunk. I know what I'm doing."

Ian slides out of the booth, but a big bartending hand pushes him back down.

"No, he doesn't," Rainn growls.

"Yes, I do," I whine, and I know I sound like a petulant child, but I really don't care.

Rainn drags me away. "It's not going to happen this way."

"Last time I checked, you don't get a say."

"I do when I'm the one who gave you all the alcohol I thought your hockey body could handle. How are you such a lightweight?"

"Only when it comes to liquor. Did I ever tell you I don't drink it, ever?"

"Twice now, but more warning beforehand would've been nice." He pushes me back down on the stool I usually sit at. "Now, you're going to drink this water." He slides it over to me. "And then you'll drink another. No hooking up tonight, and please, for the love of my job, don't do anything stupid while you're this intoxicated. It could get me fired."

I glance up at his beautiful blue eyes that give away the nice guy under the grumpiness. "Aww, we can't have that. If you get fired, I won't have anything pretty to look at every week."

"Buttering me up won't change my mind. You're too drunk to do anything tonight. You're coming home with me as soon as I can get out of here."

This is why it's so hard for me to find someone—because the guy I want is too fucking nice, and instead of letting him go, I'm holding out for a miracle that he'll wake up one day and really see me.

I honestly believe that anyone has the potential to fall for anyone. Yes, I identify as gay, but maybe I'm pan? I mean, I've never found women attractive, but can I truly say I never *could*?

Isn't it what's on the inside that counts?

I don't understand how physical attributes can override everything else. I've met some truly ugly people with a pretty exterior. It doesn't make them any more attractive than a swamp monster who eats babies.

Eating babies is bad.

My thoughts don't make sense.

I want there to be a social experiment where gender isn't a construct. I guarantee there would be same-sex connections. Because what is a connection? Really?

Common goals and common interests. Bonding moments. Rainn and I have that up the wazoo, but it just so happens that I have a dick.

I laugh out loud.

"What's so funny?"

"*Wazoo.*"

Rainn looks at me weird.

"It's a funny word. So is dick."

"You're so drunk, dude."

Maybe I am.

I shift in my seat. "Hey, I have an idea for a reality show."

Rainn humors me. "Yeah?"

"Yeah, so, like, you put a bunch of people in chat rooms and stuff, and you take gender out of it. Like, no one can say what they look like physically or what they might be packing down there. Or not packing. Genderless Love. Ooh great title, right?"

"O … kay?"

"Hear me out. Sexuality is an ever-changing thing. It's a spectrum."

"It … is?"

"I thought I was straight growing up because heteronormative narratives dictate modern society even though the concept is outdated and stupid, and so is the construct of gender."

Rainn stares blankly at me. "Are you always this philosophical when you're drunk?"

I keep going. "Physical attributes have nothing to do with gender. If you take that out of the equation, people would be able to connect on a deeper level. That's all I'm saying. Thank you for coming to my TED talk."

"That's all good and well, but say you were one of the contestants, and you found yourself talking to … another hockey player for instance."

My ears perk up.

"You talk about plays, you talk about the thrill of putting a biscuit in the basket, you bond, and then the next thing you know you're talking about your life's ambitions and getting to know them on that 'deeper level.' And then when you meet in person, she's a gorgeous, leggy blonde woman who plays for the women's team. Are you telling me the big boobs and the hourglass figure aren't going to put you off?"

"Not if she's the same person I fell for before knowing she identified as female. Though, why does she have to have big boobs? Don't be boobist. Little boobs deserve love too."

He has a point. To a degree. Masculine bodies are sexy as fuck, and yeah, they're what gets me hot, but I still think if the perfect person was out there for me, I wouldn't care how they identified.

"I just think personality negates everything else," I say, my tone defeated.

Rainn slides another glass of water my way. "Drink up."

RAINN

Whit does as he's told for the next hour while I work. He sits there and drinks his water, but I can't get his words out of my head.

Earlier when he'd told me Tanner was wrong and that he's not stupid enough to have a crush on me, I was weirdly … disappointed.

Which is selfish because, what? I want him to want me, even though I know I can't return the same feelings?

Then he was rambling on and on about how gender is an outdated construct, and I'm trying to wrap my head around that too.

I love hanging out with Whit, but everything is becoming too … I don't want to say uncomfortable because that makes me sound like a dick, but he's pushing me to think outside my comfort zone. That's difficult for me.

Whit's words make sense. Probably more than I want to admit. The protectiveness I have over him, the jealousy and hatred I have for that guy who's been sniffing around him, the disappointment over Whit not having a thing for me—it all points to one glaringly obvious conclusion that I'm not ready to admit to myself yet.

And I am more than willing to live in my denial while I drive Whit's truck back to my place with his drunk ass beside me.

Though, I'm not entirely sure how drunk he is now. He's quiet, and that's a rarity for him. We're silent as we enter my apartment, and he's less wobbly than he was back at the bar.

He flops down on his usual spot on the futon. "I was really going to do it tonight."

"I know you were." I try to keep the condescension out of my voice.

He has wanted this since I met him. He's been desperate for it, even. But something has been holding him back, and I don't know how I can help him if I don't understand it.

"Maybe you're just not ready. That's okay. No one can tell you when you should be ready for sex, and it doesn't matter how old you are. Twenty-one isn't old."

"I'm twenty-two on Wednesday."

"Twenty-two isn't old, either. It's older than average for being a virgin, but sometimes I think teenagers shouldn't be allowed to tie their own shoes, let alone have sex. Or vote for that matter."

Whit sits up, leaving a space for me next to him.

When I join him, he turns to me.

"The thing is, though, I'm so ready. I've been ready since I came out, and that was months ago. I thought the closet was what was in my way, but now I'm thinking it's *me*."

"There's nothing wrong with you. If I hadn't stepped in, that creepy Ian dude would've taken advantage tonight. I don't understand why you thought you had to get so drunk to go through with it."

Whit sighs. "I almost did it. Almost had my first kiss. But I was lip-blocked by my straight friend who's straight."

I try to make sense of what he's just said. "Wait. First *kiss*? You told me you were a virgin, but I at least assumed you'd made out with a guy."

"Nope. Haven't kissed a girl, either. Unless we count, like, fifth grade peck on the lips. That was gross, by the way."

Whit has never even kissed someone. That's umm ... Wow.

"Okay, well, that's your problem," I say. "You've built this up in your head, and now it's this monumental thing. You've just got to do it. Rip off the Band-Aid. Then you can move on to thinking about sex."

"Sure. And who do you suggest I rip this Band-Aid off with?"

Me.

Wait … what?

"I tried tonight with Ian," he says. "But according to you, he's creepy. Do you really think he's creepy?"

No, I'm just insanely jealous of the guy for reasons I'm fighting to understand.

"What about him is creepy? He's not exactly my type, but there's nothing off-putting about him. He's cute, but yeah, he is kinda small …" Whit's doing that rambling thing again. The more he talks about Ian, the more frustrated I get.

My leg bounces, and my mouth wants to tell him to shut up.

"I should be attracted to him. He's a guy, and I'm gay …"

He's still talking, but I'm fixated on the idea that he's never even kissed someone before.

The more I think about it, the more it makes sense. He only recently came out. He went from being a closeted college hockey player to suddenly trying to put himself out there. It has to be an adjustment.

I want to give him something he can hold on to. A good memory or at least a tiny nudge in the right direction.

He looks contemplative as he keeps talking. "Maybe my whole gender theory is right, and I would be more attracted to the busty blonde woman you were talking about. Maybe I'm not gay at all."

All those confusing feelings, my body's responses to Whit, and everything I've been trying to ignore bubbles to the surface, and I seize a chance. A chance where both of us could get something.

He gets his first kiss out of the way. I get to try to figure out what the hell is going on with me.

Suddenly, leaning over and kissing him seems like the best idea I've ever had. My stomach flip-flops.

"Fuck it." I cup his face.

"What are you doing?" Whit tries to pull back, but I follow.

What am I doing? I have no fucking clue, either.

I press my lips against his, feathery light.

It makes no sense. Yet, for the first time in weeks, everything isn't muddied in a haze of confusion.

Every nerve, every twitch. It's all been leading to this.

His mouth fits against mine, and I try not to think about how we got *here* because I know that it was all me.

He was talking about another guy, and *I* kissed *him.*

I put my mouth on *him.*

It's soft. No tongue, but not one of those gross middle-school pecks, either.

Whit's the first one to pull away. "Oh, I am so gay—so very gay—but you're definitely not, and—"

The voice that comes out of me is not my own. It's gentle and soft. "Rip off the Band-Aid, Whit."

My hand still lingers on his cheek.

Our breaths mingle, because I can't move away. I can't be the one to kiss him again, even though everything inside me really wants to.

The next move needs to come from Whit.

He's stunned for a moment, completely frozen by the switch in mood. But then he takes the opening I've given him. His mouth comes back to mine, only this time it moves ever so slightly. Just enough for the roughness of his stubble to sting the top of my lip and send a jolt of want down my spine.

That's not even the craziest thing. The craziest part is it doesn't freak me out. It doesn't make me think, *Oh, shit, I'm kissing a guy.* All it makes me think is, *I'm kissing Whit, and I want more. Give me more.*

As if reading my mind, Whit's mouth opens, and I follow his lead.

I'm the one who's experienced in kissing here, but he's the one teaching me new things. Like the power behind a man's mouth.

Whit's tongue parts my lips as it seeks entrance, and I let it inside.

A needy moan comes from the back of his throat, and fuck if that doesn't turn me on.

The surprise doesn't come when my cock hardens in my jeans. It doesn't even come when our tongues tangle or when my moans match his. The surprise comes from the neediness inside me to keep this going.

But Whit doesn't give me the chance.

He pulls back. "Fuck, I'm so sorry."

"Don't be," I murmur and try to kiss him again. *Just don't stop this. Not yet.*

"I can't …" He pulls back. "Sorry, I—"

"You what?" My lips are swollen, my eyes heavy-lidded.

"It shouldn't be like this. I'm not … I …"

Wow, so he's really not into me, then. Tanner was way wrong.

I make my way back to my side of the couch.

Whit runs a hand through his shiny brown hair. "I shouldn't have done that."

He didn't, though. That's all on me.

I messed up. "I kissed you. Technically."

"It was a favor to me."

He's talking as if my motivations were purely selfless when they aren't. I wanted to kiss him. It may have been disguised as something else, but it was definitely not a selfless act. And now he's sitting there feeling guilty when it's me who has done the wrong thing.

"It wasn't that," I say, but can I really tell him the truth?

That I've developed some confusing obsession with his love life? And the thought of him going home with Ian tonight made me want to do everything to stop it?

It had nothing to do with how much alcohol he had. It's just that when he'd told me he had never kissed another person …

Fuck, I'm an asshole. "I shouldn't have done that. I shouldn't have taken that from you."

Whit averts his gaze and refuses to look at me.

"I really am sorry." No matter how hot and enlightening that kiss was.

I'm not scared of the kiss. I'm scared of what it means. What it *could* mean. And it's not so much the label that scares me, but that everything I've thought for twenty-six years isn't at all the reality.

It's the notion that there has always been this unknown thing inside me waiting for the right person to come along and show it to me.

Or I could be blowing things out of proportion and am jumping to conclusions for no reason. If that's the case, I can't rely on Whit to help me figure it out.

Even if it does sound kind of perfect. He gets some experience, and I explore … whatever the fuck it is going on with me.

I couldn't do that to Whit, though. He's become important to me. A great friend. Something I haven't had in a long time.

Whit leans forward and puts his head in his hands. "Oh my God, my first-kiss story will always be about a straight guy. I can hear the *awws* of sympathy and pity now."

"Don't think of it that way," I say, and finally, he pierces me with his gaze. "Your first kiss was with a good friend who respects the hell out of you."

Truer words have never been spoken, but that doesn't mean kissing him was right.

We sit in awkward silence, and I hate what I just did to him. At the same time, I don't want to take it back. "If it makes you feel any better, you're a really good kisser."

Whit laughs. "Good kisser for a guy, you mean?"

"No. Gender is an outdated construct. A smart hockey player told me that once."

"Smart hockey player. Isn't that an oxymoron?"

"You're an oxymoron … hold the oxy."

Whit shoves me, so I get the cushion he uses as a pillow and hit him in the side of the head with it.

Just a small snippet of normal is all we get before the air between us tries to stifle me again.

I wring my hands. "Are we cool? This didn't fuck everything up?"

"Of course. Totally cool." The way his tone hitches gives me the impression he's lying.

"Well, uh, I should get to bed."

Whit nods. "I should sleep off this alcohol-induced haze."

That makes me feel worse.

But not as bad as waking up the next morning to find Whit gone.

I'm more confused than ever, and now he's running.

WHIT

My alarm goes off, and I curse myself for not turning it off before going to sleep.

Happy birthday to me.

I roll over in my bed and stare at the ceiling because today is the day I have officially become a twenty-two-year-old virgin.

But hey, I got my first kiss out of the way. My first ever pity kiss from a guy who felt sorry for me for being so inexperienced.

The embarrassed groan flies out of me.

I left Rainn's apartment the other night as soon as I was sober enough to drive, and I haven't spoken to him since, because it's too humiliating.

Sitting there while he told me things couldn't happen between us because his boss noticed how infatuated I was with him was bad enough, and then I had to go and make him pity me, acting like I'm such a sad-ass gay man and can't find anyone to kiss me, that he probably felt like he had to do it for the good of the queer community.

Thanks for taking one for the team. Love, every gay man out there.

And that kiss was the worst thing that could've happened because my teeny, tiny little crush? It's morphed into full-blown pining now.

I rub my hand over my jaw and touch my fingers to my lips, swearing I can still taste him.

My cock twitches in my sleep pants, and I reach into the waistband to adjust myself, but the smallest of contact, my fingers wrapping around my shaft, feels so good on my tightening skin.

The only thing worse than pining after a straight guy is jerking off to thoughts of him. I've resisted this long—weeks and weeks of passing thoughts about big arms enclosing around me, Rainn's mouth on mine—and now that I know what those lips taste like, I don't think I'll be able to hold out anymore.

Rainn's sexy blue eyes fill my head, along with that one loose curl of dark hair that falls across his face when he sweats.

I have to bite back a moan as I stroke my dick.

I have no idea what time it is, but I can hear movement downstairs.

It's my birthday, so they're letting me sleep in, which means no one will interrupt this. I just have to be quiet enough for them to think I'm still asleep.

I can't wait for my house to finish being built so I can jerk off whenever I want without worrying about my family overhearing. Getting time in this house alone is rare, and it's even rarer to be able to do this in the morning.

I stroke slowly, trying to draw it out, but I've been spreading myself a little thin lately, and I haven't even had the energy to make myself come, so I'm surprised I'm not blowing my load already. Especially since I'm indulging in a fantasy of what would've happened if I hadn't stopped that kissing session.

Logically, I know he would've ended it and things wouldn't have gone any further. Straight guys don't decide to take a walk on the gay-sex side just to be a good friend.

Then again, I wasn't expecting him to kiss me, either, but it's my fantasy, and I run with dreaming of what could've been.

Would he have pinned me down on his uncomfortable, lumpy futon?

With his heavy body laid out on top of mine, would he have ground against my erection?

I imagine his hands moving all over me, exploring, and then because this is my fantasy, our clothes would magically disappear, and then his hands would be on me again.

His mouth would track every inch, moving all over my body while I called his name over and over again. I'd spread my legs for him, and his fingers would find my entrance and push inside easily.

I wince as my fingers try that right now. Unlike fantasyland, I need actual lube. I spit on my fingers and then tease my hole, imagining it's Rainn and not me.

God, the things I'd let that man do to me. Sure, I haven't experienced any of it with anyone else, but I've been dreaming of stuff long enough to experiment with my fingers. I would've ordered toys if I had a place to hide them.

The thought of taking something bigger than my fingers has precum dripping onto my stomach while I stroke my aching cock with my free hand.

I've become an expert at getting myself off, but the need for something more is getting too hard to ignore.

I'm ready, *so ready*, to share my body with someone, but when I close my eyes, it's always Rainn Richardson I imagine fucking me.

I picture his big arms holding me while he takes me from behind. I bet that dark scruff on his face would be rough as he dragged it along my skin.

Just like that, my cock erupts all over my stomach. I stroke harder and grit my teeth while I convulse through my orgasm.

The guilt and shame don't take long to kick in after the high fades, and then I'm lying there, in my bed, a sweaty mess of cum and bad decisions. It really only reiterates one thing: I need to keep avoiding Rainn.

After I check the hall and duck into the bathroom, I shower even though it'll be counterproductive once I get to work and get covered in dirt, more sweat, and cow shit, but I'm not going downstairs covered in the result of Rainn fantasies.

I finally head downstairs and find my mom in the kitchen with a plate of pancakes in her hands.

"Happy birthday!"

Ugh, don't remind me.

"Thanks, Mom." I kiss her cheek and take the huge stack of pancakes from her.

"Eat up fast. Your father and Campbell are heading out to the houses today."

My gaze flies to hers. "Really?"

"The guys are putting the finishing touches on Campbell's house."

I do a little shimmy because once they're done with his house, mine's next, but my dancing almost makes me lose my breakfast.

With quick hands, I save the pancakes from hitting the floor. "Oops."

"We prefer food in mouths in this house. Not on floors." Mom's pretend stern look is cute. "I thought hockey players were supposed to have soft hands."

"And lightning reflexes. I saved them, didn't I?"

"Hurry up and eat."

I'm so excited. The houses we're building are on another part of the property, far away from the main house. We'll be neighbors instead of living on top of each other, and as much as I love Mom and Dad and love living with them, I want to be on my own. I need privacy and a place I could actually take a date without being embarrassed by my family being … well, them. It would be all good-natured ribbing, but please, I can make a fool of myself on my own without their help.

Mom and Dad have been saving for this ever since we were born, and along with the business loan we got to expand the farm, it's finally happening.

After I shovel the pancakes into my mouth and practically swallow without chewing, I meet Dad by his truck.

"Happy birthday, son."

If I hear that again today, it will be two times too many. "Thanks."

"Let's go." He slaps my shoulder. "Campbell's already down there."

Dad pulls out onto the road and drives the half mile to the makeshift driveway the construction guys have been wearing into the grass.

"I remember when you used to talk to us about doing this when we were little," I say.

"We never wanted you boys to go far."

Mom and Dad give us so much love and support. It's been a constant in our lives, and I find myself thinking about how Rainn had said he doesn't have much to do with his family.

That has to suck. I couldn't imagine not seeing my parents frequently. I mean, sure I could probably go a few days, a week maybe, but we're a family unit who thrives on each other's support.

It's been a while since I've been to the construction site, because I've been too busy, and as Dad pulls up outside Campbell's house, my eyes widen.

The wooden frame now has walls, siding, and a roof. The navy shutters framing the windows and brick chimney rising from the roof are charming, and it looks like a smaller version of my folks' white clapboard farmhouse. Campbell and Christie's place is bigger than mine will be. They're already planning to fill their home with kids. I'm going to fill mine with … me.

I'm impatient to have my own place but also sad. I'll be completely alone, and I know I'd be more excited about the move if I had someone to share it with, like Campbell does.

"You okay?" Dad asks.

I plaster on my Whit smile, showing dimples. "I'm perfect. The house looks amazing."

"Yours is next."

"I'm in no rush."

Sadly, I really mean it. It turns out I don't just want to lose my virginity after all. I want *everything*, but the guy I want it with …

Damn it. I need to stay away from Rainn so I can get over this crush.

Even as I make the decision, my phone chimes, and I find a message from him. *Happy birthday.*

It's bad enough he remembered, but him being nice will make it hard to keep my distance. I close the app on my phone and pretend I didn't see it.

13

RAINN

Whit doesn't reply to my birthday text, only cementing that kissing him was the wrong thing to do.

He's avoiding me now, and I don't like it. Not only because I fear I've fucked everything up, but because … because *reasons*.

How much I liked kissing him is the main one.

I liked it a hell of a lot.

But that doesn't matter in the big scheme of things because we're in different places.

I think he's been putting way too much pressure on himself, and no matter how hard I try to help, I go and fuck things up more.

What we have—our friendship—I need to fix. So I get out my googling fingers. I may not have a lot of money to buy Whit a birthday present, but I can give him something better.

Only, I don't take into account that he won't make his typical weekend appearance at V and V. I checked his schedule online and saw he was at an away game on Saturday. I figured he'd do his usual thing and show up on Sunday night.

I spend my entire shift watching the door, much like I did those first couple of weeks he started to come see me.

If he spent the weekend with his family for his birthday and was busy, he'd at least text me to say he wasn't coming. No, this is very much him avoiding me because I made it weird between us.

I need to see him, but I don't know how. Well, technically, I know exactly where to find him during the week, but going to him would demand a visit to a place I've avoided for almost four years.

My newly found friendship with Whit means a lot to me, but that much? I mull it over for a couple days, and when my night off arrives, I make a decision.

I grab Whit's present and force myself out of my apartment. And then I start walking.

Numerous times, I change my mind, and I must look like an idiot pacing the sidewalk.

Fuck it.

I charge toward campus. It's about two miles from my place, so not far, but I take the long route because I'm still not sure if I can go through with this.

My left leg aches the way it did right after it was injured. Rubbing doesn't help the pain, because it's all in my head.

Living so close to the place I'd suffered my life's biggest failure kinda sucks. But I never could bring myself to leave Burlington.

I've always had thoughts of going back. Of finishing my degree. I just haven't gotten there yet.

If I'm honest with myself, I'm not sure I could handle it.

But here I am, at least setting foot on campus again.

For Whit.

I can't ignore the big-ass revelation that I might have feelings for Whit that aren't strictly platonic anymore. Not after this. Really, I probably shouldn't have been able to ignore it after I kissed him, but the denial over that was easier to swallow than coming back here.

I have to see him so I can make things right with him, even if that means facing the ultimate failure in my life.

When I get to the hockey facilities, I almost turn around and go back home again. But the thought of Whit keeps me moving through the familiar doors, down the hall that infuses my senses with scents, sights, and sounds I'd once known as well as my own body. Muscle memory kicks in, and my feet take me right to Coach's office.

His face lights up when he sees me, and he leans back in his big chair behind his desk. "Rainn Richardson."

"Coach Keller."

He stands to shake my hand. "You're not one of my players anymore. You can call me Bart."

"Yeah, that's so not going to happen."

He laughs. "To what do I owe the pleasure?"

We take our seats, and fuck, it feels like four years ago when we'd have meetings in this very office to discuss my future. Or lack thereof in my senior year.

"I'm actually here to see one of your players."

"I think I would've been told if you were scouting for an agent or team."

"No, no. Nothing like that. I'm a bartender now."

Coach's face falls. "You're what?"

I huff. "A bartender. I'm living up to my utmost potential as you would put it."

"Please tell me it's until you get your degree or … is that why you're here? Are you coming back?"

"Nope. I have a birthday present for Leighton Whitaker to drop off, and then I'll be on my way."

A frown line forms on Coach Keller's forehead. I remember the expression well. There's nothing more shattering than seeing the disappointment on his face. Even if he's being polite and trying to hide it.

"Are you still skating?"

It's not that I'm not allowed. The doctors said my leg would handle it. But I haven't ventured onto the ice because it hurts that I'll never be as good as I once was no matter how much training I put in. My leg is weaker and always will be.

"Nope."

"Can you tell me why?"

I let out a loud breath. I knew it would be hard to face Coach's questions.

I don't want to relive the ugly emotions—anger, grief, mourning, and hopelessness. There's a reason I decided to hate hockey. Or pretend to hate hockey.

The loss of it hurts too much.

I shrug at my old coach. "I haven't had anything to do with hockey since ..." I pat my knee.

Coach Keller sighs. "It's such a waste."

I love hearing that the only thing I was good for was playing hockey. Then again, have I done anything to prove that theory wrong?

"I really am here for Whit, not a life lesson. Thanks, Coach."

"Nah, I don't accept that."

My eyebrows shoot up.

"You're one of the most talented skaters I've ever coached." He stands. "Lace up. You can help me run today's practice. It might do some of these kids some good to skate with someone who's actually made it to a Frozen Four final."

Whoa, whoa, whoa. I did not sign up for this. "I ..."

"What's it going to be, Richardson? Is your plan really to be a bartender for the rest of your life?"

"Well, I'm not going to be an NHL player, so ..."

"And hockey is the NHL or nothing, is it? My job here is meaningless, then?"

"Well, no, but—"

"A play isn't just about getting a puck inside that net. It's good defense, quick offense, and working them together."

Gee, where have I heard that before? "Your point?"

"Life isn't always about the end goal. It's how you get there that's more important."

"Deep, Coach, really." But fuck, if it doesn't ring true.

Could I really do this?

"What's it going to be? You in or out?"

I get the feeling this is one of those moments where there's a clear right move, and if I don't take it, I will regret it.

My inner bitterness is telling me to walk away, but I don't.

I stand. "I'm in."

WHIT

I'm eager to get on the ice today. Our practice sessions leading up to the semifinals are grueling, but I need it. I need the busywork and to keep distracted from thinking about anything but Rainn and that kiss.

For once, I'm not only happy for my busy schedule, but I'm reveling in it. Because the more I have to do, the less time I have to fantasize.

This practice, though … What the fuck? As soon as my skates hit the ice, my feet almost fall from beneath me because standing with Coach Keller is someone I'd never expect to see here wearing skates and a nervous expression.

Rainn is here? As far as I know, he hasn't been back since his injury. He hasn't wanted to come back. Rainn hates hockey.

I turn to my teammate Cal. "Was there something in the news about hell freezing over or perhaps the four horsemen of the apocalypse appearing somewhere?"

"What?"

I shake my head. "Nothing."

Rainn's gaze finds mine, and I almost fall again. Skating is hard, okay.

Coach gathers us around. "Everyone, this is Rainn Richardson, former hotshot on this campus."

Rainn winces but covers it well, probably from being called a *former* hotshot.

There are some cheers and enthusiastic greetings from the team. Most of them hold an expression of awe—similar to what I probably looked like when I'd first seen Rainn at the bookstore.

"He's here to see what you all can do," Coach says, and I can't make sense of that, either. None of this makes sense.

Did Coach and Rainn run into each other somewhere and Coach forced him here against his will?

I want to tell Rainn to blink twice if he needs rescuing, but at the same time, I want to keep ignoring him and pretending this electric charge between us isn't there. I didn't go to the bar last weekend for a reason. We need breathing room. No, *I* need breathing room.

During practice, I keep my head down and try to concentrate on whatever task is thrown my way, but my mind is never far from Rainn. I watch him with the other guys, torn between wanting to skate up to him to say hi and staying on my side of the ice.

When Coach splits us into two lines for a passing drill, I go to Coach's line instead of Rainn's. It's immature, maybe, but I think it will be better for both of us because I need to get over him before we can be friends again.

My plan backfires when Coach blows his whistle as I get to the front of the line.

"Sloppy! Richardson, show 'em how it's done."

Rainn's eyes widen as they flit between me and Coach. "Sir?"

One of the freshmen offers Rainn his stick, but he's too stunned to take it.

"You and Whit have some trust already from being friends. Show these boys what soft touch means."

First, Rainn told Coach about us? And second, thinking about Rainn and any sort of soft touch is not a good idea.

Rainn pushes off on his skates with too much grace for someone who's had a four-year break. I skate opposite him, my stick ready to accept his pass. The puck finds my blade as if they're magnetized, and I pass it back to him where he shoots and scores.

The play is fast but smooth, and it's exactly what Coach is looking for. "That's how it's done."

Rainn gives me a wide smile, and though I try to give one back, I know I fail when a small frown line appears above Rainn's eyes.

Coach skates by Rainn and slaps his shoulder. "Still got it."

"Like riding a bike," Rainn says, but there's no energy behind it.

I just fulfilled one of my high school dreams—to be on the same ice as Rainn Richardson—but it's tainted by everything that's happened, my need to stay away, and my concern for him being back here when he struggles with anything to do with hockey.

When practice is over, I take a longer shower than I usually do and dress in my jeans and flannel shirt, trying to wait it out until Rainn leaves.

I don't want to have to explain that I can't be around him without feeling like a lovesick puppy, and yay for humiliation number eight hundred and sixty-seven in Rainn's presence.

Once I've made sure my cubby is neat and tidy—it's so very important to perform a sudden spring clean—I grab my gear bag and leave the empty locker room.

All the other guys ran out of here as fast as they could to get to their girlfriends or whatever midweek party they're going to.

Rainn and Coach Keller are in the hallway talking when I take my exit. Obviously, I didn't take long enough.

"Give this guy a call," Coach is saying. "Promise me."

Rainn takes a card from him. "Promise."

Then they notice me.

"Thanks for coming in," Coach says and shakes Rainn's hand.

I'm tempted to run away, but that won't look suspicious or anything. When Coach walks off, I adjust the bag on my shoulder and stare at the ground.

"You didn't come to the bar," Rainn says.

No shit. "You could be a cop with that kind of detective work."

Rainn's smile is weak. "I … I got you a birthday present."

He what?

"You … present … me."

"Don't get too excited—it's nothing big, but I was hoping … Could I take you to dinner to give it to you?"

"You want to go to dinner. With me."

"I wouldn't have endured that"—he points down the chute toward the ice—"if I didn't care about you. I was planning to give it to you when you came to the bar. But you didn't."

"Wait … you came to practice and skated again just so you could give me a birthday present? Is this a guilt thing? About the …" God, I can't even say *kiss* in front of this man.

"It's not a guilt thing, but I shouldn't have kissed you."

"Right. Because you can't like me like that. You're straight."

"Can I take you out for your birthday?" he asks.

"I … I don't think that's a good idea."

"You said what happened didn't fuck everything up, but now I get the sense you're avoiding me."

"I need to," I snap.

"What? Why?"

"Because …" *The only way I'm going to get over this juvenile crush is if I don't see you for a while.* "I just can't right now, okay?"

The right words fail me. Telling him I have feelings for him will make this even weirder, and there's no point. It will make him even more uncomfortable.

Rainn glances at the wrapped, rectangular package in his hands and holds it out for me. "Here. This is for you."

I swallow hard. "Thanks."

With an awkward nod, he says, "I hope we can move past this." He starts off down the corridor toward the exit, and I'm ashamed to admit that as soon as he rounds the corner, I tear into my present.

I may want space and time to get over him, but any little piece of attention he gives me, I'm going to take.

When I pull out the stapled-together papers, I'm confused for a moment, but then I start reading. It's pages and pages of printed-off online magazine articles, all of them about people who didn't lose their virginity until they were older and the unnecessary pressure they felt to get it over with.

There's another one about how the whole virginity concept is outdated because *sex* isn't defined as penetrative sex between a man and woman anymore. I skim one about a thirty-one-year-old who still hasn't lost his virginity and doesn't even care.

I stare down the corridor where he disappeared. He did this so I'd feel better about my situation and realize I'm not alone. Not by a long shot.

It's weird how such a simple gift can mean so much.

"Fuck," I hiss and take off after Rainn.

I find him outside the arena on his phone. "Rainn, wait."

Bright blue eyes meet mine. Despite the dull glow of the streetlights, his gaze still has that piercing shine.

"You can take me to dinner," I say.

He looks confused. "But you said—"

"I know what I said, and I still think it's a bad idea, but this—" I hold up the articles. "I can't pretend this wasn't the best gift I got this birthday."

A small smile breaks out on his usually stoic face. "Where do you want to eat?"

"The same place you rescued me from my horrible date?"

"Sure. You can drive. I walked here."

"You really need to get your own car," I say on our way to the parking lot where I left my truck.

"Sure. I will buy it with Monopoly money. Car dealers accept that, I'm sure."

"You work two jobs."

"I do, and with the extra hours in the bar, I'm putting some money away, but unless I'm going to buy another clunker that breaks down every few weeks, it will be a while before I can get something decent."

"Fair enough." Though, something about his words doesn't ring completely true.

I've known Rainn a while now, and it seems any big decisions or anything that involves big plans are always future things to deal with.

He puts off making decisions—like going back to college.

I've asked him why he hasn't gone back, and all he says is there's no point when his future isn't in sports, so finishing a sports management degree would be useless, but I don't know why he can't go back and study something else instead.

The drive to Church Street is short, and the whole way I coach myself that I can do this. I can have dinner with Rainn and pretend I'm not sulkily pining after him, but when we enter the restaurant, I know I'm well and truly fucked and this was a horrible idea.

We're led to a table and take our seats opposite each other, and in this kind of atmosphere, and Rainn being … well, Rainn, I have to remind myself this is a nice dinner for my birthday. It's not a date, and it never will be a date.

I'm flooded with that painful ache in my chest reminding me that this is all I can have with him.

The server takes our orders and fills our water glasses, and I watch as Rainn takes a sip. No, I stare at the way his throat moves as he swallows, and I hate how sexy he looks. Always.

I sigh, but it must be louder than I intend it to come out.

"What?" Rainn asks.

"Nothing."

He arches an eyebrow at me.

My neck sweats, and I adjust the collar of my shirt. "It's just … since the kiss, you look good doing every-fucking-thing." And long before that, but let's pretend it was the kiss.

"All I did was take a sip of water."

I shrug. "Apparently, I like that. As well as watching you on the ice tonight. You're still amazing, and seeing you skate up close was something else."

Rainn chews on his bottom lip. "Want me to try to make myself as unappealing as possible so you can forget the kiss that never should have happened?"

My heart twinges.

"I'd like you to at least *try*." I try to keep my tone light even though I'm dying on the inside.

He looks contemplative. "Okay. Shaved head it is. I'll go to the barber tomorrow."

I gasp. "Don't you dare. You can't shave your head. Your hair is all shiny."

"What about inner ugliness? Will that help? Truth bomb: I have spoken to my mom only a handful of times since my injury because she always wants to talk about it, and it drives me crazy."

"Wow. Hitting where it really hurts, right off the bat. I can't even fathom not seeing my mother all the time."

"*Mama's boy*," Rainn sneers.

"Actually, I'm close with my dad too."

"Family … boy." Rainn screws up his face. "That doesn't have the same negative connotation."

I laugh. "Sure doesn't. Also, even being called a mama's boy isn't offensive to me."

"Of course it's not." Rainn taps his chin. "Hmm, I never give to charity."

"You have no money. That makes sense."

"I hate people."

"People can suck."

"Whit," he complains. "You're supposed to be judging me, not taking my side."

"Oh, sorry. Right. Uh, you … suck?"

Rainn leans back in his seat. "Okay. Here's the real deal. Coach Keller told me tonight to call this guy he recently met. He's planning to create a hockey camp for underprivileged kids. They'd learn skills that might give them a chance at a collegiate-level hockey scholarship and a degree, and maybe even the chance to get drafted."

"Really? That's amazing. Why would that make me dislike you?"

"Because my first thought when he told me that was 'Why would I want to help other kids steal my dream?'"

I wince.

"See. I'm selfish." He hangs his head, knowing his reaction is wrong which immediately cancels his point. He's not a bad person at all.

It's an amazing opportunity and something he definitely shouldn't pass up, but the slump of his shoulders and his tone of voice—yeah, I already know what he's thinking about this chance.

"I don't think you're selfish," I say. "I think you're heartbroken."

RAINN

I think you're heartbroken.

I don't know how Whit can read me the way he does, but I hate it.

His words may be the biggest truth I've ever been hit with, and the admission hurts.

Our food is delivered, but I'm too busy staring at Whit to even thank the server.

See, selfish.

"You looked at home on the ice tonight," Whit says as he shovels food in his mouth.

Being on the ice, part of a team again, it *was* fun, and it surprised me how much I enjoyed it from a watching and helping perspective. When I was out there, I felt like I was breathing properly for the first time in four years.

But my high didn't last. The crash came when I returned the skates I'd borrowed to Coach, and I had to acknowledge that I wasn't coming back. That part of my life is over. The weight sat on my chest, and sucking in air became hard all over again.

"It was fun," I say blandly.

"Come on, it was more than fun."

"You have to understand I lost hockey a long time ago, so it's hard for me to see past that."

"The NHL isn't *everything* when it comes to hockey."

"You sound like Keller. But you're biased. You never even entered the draft. Hockey has never been your future."

"But I am still a hockey player. I understand the love of the game."

Not like me, I want to say but refrain. Instead, I try to give him some perspective. "Just say something came along tomorrow and wiped out your entire farm—"

"Hey, whoa, why are you putting a jinx on me like that?"

I roll my eyes. "Guess you are a true hockey player, after all, with superstitions like that. Knock on wood"—I tap the table —"and all that hocus pocus. My point is, what if the future you've been looking forward to and working toward your entire life was ripped away from you?"

"I'd be upset for a while and then come up with a plan B."

That answer is so ... Whit. All optimistic and shit.

"Easy as that?" I ask.

"Easy as that. I wouldn't sit around for years thinking about what was taken from me but what I could do to be happy again."

I purse my lips. It really does sound simple when he puts it that way. But my only goal in my entire life has been hockey.

"I'm not saying you have to put a time limit on grieving, but you're still in stage two, and it's been four years."

"What's stage two?"

"Anger."

"Are you saying if I go Zen, the world will open a million opportunities up to me?"

"Maybe not a million, but this guy with the hockey camp might be a good start."

I huff. "I could see me yelling at the kids for not taking it seriously enough and being ungrateful little shits."

"Oh, I had one of those coaches in high school, and it was

horrible, but I don't think you'd be that bad—you were great today."

"Yay, I passed a puck."

Whit shakes his head. "No, you did so much more than that. Just you being there gave the team a boost in morale. They wanted to impress you. If you were a nobody, why would they look up to you?"

Whit's words are so sincere, so touching, that I might forget who I am for a second.

I reach over the table and lay my hand on top of his. "Thank you."

Whit cocks his head. "For what?"

"Perspective, I guess."

"Oh. Then, you're welcome, but, uh, along with being a selfish jackass, 'no hand-holding' might need to go on the list of things you need to do so I can forget that kiss."

I reluctantly take my hand back, but my skin tingles, wanting to touch him again. I want to keep feeling that connection that keeps happening between us. I want to feel the scruff on his cheeks against my lips again—to experience that burn I haven't been able to forget. I want to explore my cravings for Whit, but I'm not sure how fair that is.

I take my time eating my dinner because I want to draw this whole night out.

"Want to order dessert?" That will keep us here longer. "You have to have birthday cake."

"Coach will kill you, but I can never say no to dessert."

Dessert only buys me another twenty minutes.

When Whit wipes his face with his napkin and leans back in his chair, I hold on to anything I can. "Want to come back to my place and torture me with whatever hockey movie you haven't made me watch yet?"

Whit hesitates.

I hold my breath.

Please say yes. Please say yes.

"You still haven't watched *Youngblood*."

"Only for your birthday."

I'm lying. I'd watch anything he told me to if it meant tonight wasn't over. I want things to go back to how they were before we kissed, and hanging out like this is the only way. That's the lie I tell myself as we head back to my apartment. We're going back to normal. We're not going to hook up. I'm definitely not going to act on the confusing feelings I've been having about him.

I'm not.

I throw my coat on the tiny circular dining table at the entry, and Whit does the same. My keys jingle as I place them on the hook near the door, the single sound echoing through the small apartment.

Whit stands a few feet away from me, refusing to even look in my direction. No, his gaze is laser focused on the futon where we kissed.

"Drink?" I ask.

"Whiskey," he says quickly.

I cock my eyebrow, and he glances away.

Whiskey, it is.

There's no doubt in my mind he's picking up the same nervous energy I am, and I can't tell if it's coming from him or me.

Can he read my mind and see the millions of different scenarios I've got going on up there?

Whit seems intent on staying at least six feet away from me. Every time our eyes meet, he immediately glances away. What the hell are we doing?

I move toward my kitchen and pull down the whiskey. I pour some in a glass and throw it back and then pour some for him to do the same.

He takes the glass, and for the first time tonight, he doesn't look away when our eyes lock. As he drinks the honey-colored liquid, he watches me.

Then he swallows hard and puts the glass down between us.

"More?" My voice is unintentionally raspy.

"I better not. Last time I drank too much, I apparently thought it was a great idea to attach my face to … well, your face."

My lips quirk. "It is an amazing face."

"Thank you."

"Hey, I meant *mine*."

Whit gives me a playful shove.

I step toward him so I don't lose balance, but now we're so close I'm just a breath away. Our chests have only an inch of separation between them.

Whit's playfulness fades.

My throat dries.

The urge to wrap my arm around his back and pull him against me is almost overpowering. I don't know if I'll be able to contain it if he doesn't move away soon.

As if he knows what I'm thinking, he steps back. "Movie."

His lips are slightly parted, and I wonder what it would be like to move my tongue over them. For once, I don't try to shake the thought. I don't want to this time.

"Rainn?"

I blink out of my stupor. "Huh?"

"Movie?" Whit gestures to the couch.

The couch where mistakes happen.

Maybe I can make another mistake.

"Right. Movie. I just …" I glance at the whiskey. "More alcohol."

Whit steps far enough away to take a seat, and I can finally breathe, but that doesn't stop me from downing another shot. It makes my insides warm and dims the buzzing in my veins.

Whit's sitting on his usual side of my couch, his legs spread wide while he flicks the TV on with the remote. He seems focused on the screen, but as I get closer, I notice those eyes on me. Watching me.

I have the urge to stand between his legs to see how he'd respond. Would he run his hands up the back of my thighs?

Would he pull me down on top of him?

Jesus H. Christ, get a grip, Rainn.

I take my seat next to him, maybe a little closer than normal. Apparently, I can't help myself anymore.

The menu for my streaming service is on the screen, but the selection isn't moving.

I turn my head to find Whit staring at the screen blankly.

"We watching *Youngblood* or—"

Whit suddenly stands. "This isn't going to work."

"What's not?" I stay where I am, worried if I make the wrong move, he'll leave faster than I can come up with a way to stop him.

"I think you know," Whit says. "I can't … We can't go back to normal after that kiss. At least, not yet. I need time."

No. That's the last thing I want.

I stand too, but slowly, so I don't make him run for the door. "What if we don't go back to normal?"

"What does that even mean?"

I'd like to know too.

My hand trembles, wanting to reach for him. "What if …"

What if I kiss you again?

The words refuse to leave my lips, so instead, I step toward him.

"What if we forget about labels for a second? All labels."

He looks confused. "Okay …"

"You're a person and I'm a person."

"Can we be penguins instead?"

"No."

"But you said—"

"We're not fucking penguins."

"Well, that's good. I don't think you'd be let into SeaWorld ever again if you fucked a penguin."

I glare at him.

"Did you know that, at a zoo, there were these two dude penguins who fell in love? Apparently penguins mate for life, right? And during mating season, this one male penguin thought this other dude penguin was a female. Now they're all bonded and shit."

This is getting way off topic.

"What the fuck are you talking about?"

"Penguins," he says, like that answers my question. He composes himself. "Sorry. I'm nervous about what's going to come out of your mouth next. I'm trying to deflect."

"Kiss me again," I blurt.

His eyes widen. "What?"

Instead of repeating myself, I press against him.

"Rainn, what's—"

"Kiss. Me."

There's a split second where neither of us moves, and I think he's not going to do it. But then, all at once, he's in my space, his lips on mine, and everything confusingly makes sense again.

The small doubt, that fluctuating idea that this might not be as good the second time around, disappears completely when his mouth tentatively moves against mine.

This is even better.

He's not drunk, and I'm not surprising myself.

I want this.

It goes from soft and slow to wanting in the blink of an eye.

Whit grips my shirt in an effort to bring me closer, but we're already flush up against each other. His tongue enters my mouth, and a needy sound comes from the back of my throat. I never imagined kissing a guy could feel this amazing.

I never imagined kissing *anyone* could feel this connected. It's not just our mouths, but *us*.

I'm conscious about going too fast while trying to tell myself to savor it. Explore it. Find out if this could be something more substantial than curiosity.

As Whit moves a hand into my hair, shivers run down my spine.

For someone who's never kissed anyone before, he knows what he's doing. Or he at least knows what buttons to push.

Right now, that might be every button.

I'm used to being the one in the lead—the one to take charge—but the way Whit pulls me against him and holds me, the way his tongue tries to battle mine to be in control, it creates this push-pull between us, and the fight is completely new.

I thought I knew everything there was to know about kissing. How to make a woman feel needed and treasured. How to make them feel wanted. Being on the receiving end of that opens up a whole new world of possibilities.

Whit pulls back and whispers, "Is this okay?"

I'm unable to find words. He should be able to tell how okay it is by the way my cock is pressed against him. How hard it is.

It's more than okay.

It's consuming.

"Couch?" I croak.

"Bed."

A jolt of want goes through me, but caution makes me pause. "I can't promise I'll only stick to kissing if we go in there." I tip my head toward my bedroom.

"Trust me, I've slept on that thing you call a couch—FYI, a futon is not a couch—and it's uncomfortable as fuck."

"Then why did you keep staying here?"

He runs his thumb over my cheek. "Because I got to spend time with you."

"Fuck."

Whit makes me feel wanted in a way I never have before.

"Okay, bed, but I'm not … I mean, I don't think I'm ready for—"

"We'll take it slow." Whit's reassurance settles everything.

Slowly, I work my hand down his chest and hard abs to hover above his waistband. It's not like I'm new to a dick. I have one. But I've never given consideration to another man's or what might get off a different dick.

"I'm not saying no to more. Just not … all the way."

"You're looking a little unsure."

"Not unsure. Just new to this. Little-known fact about me— I've never done this with another man. You might have forgotten that, seeing as you haven't called me *straight* in at least two minutes."

"That's what you are, though."

"Nope. We're still in No-label-ville. It's right next to Confusion-land and Denial-town."

"Sounds like a horrible place to be."

"It's not horrible. Not at all. Not if it means I can do this again." I lean in and press my mouth to his.

Whit pulls me close but breaks away from my lips. "We definitely need the bed."

He takes my hand and leads me toward my bedroom.

"Will it be like the blind leading the blind?" I ask. "Is it really smart for a gay guy to hook up with a straight guy for experience?"

"Is it really smart for a straight guy to get first-time gay experience from a virgin?"

"Touché."

We reach my bed, but I don't push him down on it yet. I step back and toe off my shoes and then ditch my socks while Whit does the same.

When he stands upright, we stare at each other. By nature, it's normal to be nervous, for both of us, like it is with any new partner, but this is different.

I tug off my long-sleeved tee and undershirt, leaving my chest exposed.

At first, Whit doesn't do anything but roam his gaze over me.

He reaches for me but pulls his hand back before he makes contact.

I step closer and take hold of his wrist. "Touch me." I place his hand on my chest, and he runs his fingers over the smattering of dark hair there.

"Can I ..." Whit pulls back and lifts the hem of his shirt, and I nod. Miles of skin appears as he takes it off and drops it to the floor.

Unlike me, he has no hair on his pecs or chest, just smooth and hard muscles.

I want my hands on him. My mouth. I want his hands and mouth on *me*.

"Fuck, I need you on top of me." I can't resist pulling Whit down on top of me as I fall back on the bed.

My head hits the pillow, but Whit doesn't try to kiss me. He stares while he hovers above me.

I lift up so our mouths meet, and the sensation of the spiky scruff around his lips and jaw catches me off guard. I wonder if it's something I'd ever tire of—if it's possible to become desensitized to it. I hope not, because it turns me the fuck on.

Not much makes sense when I'm kissing Whit, but when I can focus on the roughness of his mouth, his commanding tongue, and the little groan he makes, I don't care if I never figure him out. Or myself.

Whit pushes me so my head falls back onto the pillow, and he adjusts himself on top of me. That tiny bit of movement causes friction between us that almost makes my cock explode.

I break apart from his lips. "Holy fuck."

"What?"

I lift my hips, replicating the sensation. "That."

Whit shudders on top of me. "Feels good."

"Feels fucking amazing. Keep doing it."

"With pants or without?"

"No pants," I say and begin wriggling to try to get mine off.

If it's this good with layers of clothing between us, I can't even fathom what heights it could take me without them.

We wrestle out of our jeans but keep our underwear on. I don't want to push too far tonight. Him or me.

I want Whit to take his time and experience everything, and I'm still trying to make sense of this. Of us.

It's not a rush to the finish line.

This time when Whit lowers himself, with only the thin material of our boxer briefs between us, my eyes roll back and my whole body trembles.

Whit moans, adding to the sensory overload as his cock rubs against mine and his big body moves on top of me.

Being boxed in by his masculine physique isn't as weird as I thought it would be. It's different, and there's something about the power of it that's a little unnerving, but not in a scary way.

With his mouth back on mine, his tongue doing wicked things, the best kind of shiver runs through me. My skin flushes, breaking out in goose bumps, and when he moves against me, my senses take over, and all I want to do is feel. His dick—so hard as it thrusts against mine. My cock and briefs are damp, soaked in precum. Every breath is a struggle, but I don't care.

My hands run down the hard muscles of Whit's back, and they contract under my touch. I grip his ass and push, making Whit move faster and harder.

"Oh, God. Oh, fuck." He's panting now as he breaks away from my mouth to take in gulps of air.

I lean up and kiss his neck, loving his needy response.

He reaches between us, but I can't work out what he's doing until I glance at the small gap between our bodies. Whit tucks his underwear under his balls, exposing the deep red tip of his hard cock. His hips rotate, dragging that dick along mine, which is still confined in my boxer briefs.

I can't tear my eyes away, but then he says, "Rainn, I ... I think I'm gonna ..."

I look up in time to see Whit's face contort. It's the hottest goddamn image I've ever seen.

"Do it," I encourage.

Whit lets go, his body giving out and leaning on me heavily through his release.

His cum hits my stomach. I thought that would weird me out, but it doesn't. I've had cum on me before. Sure, it was *my* cum, but it's no different with Whit. Although, it might be a little hotter. Like he's leaving his mark on me.

I'm close but too distracted by Whit's orgasm to think about my own. I want to puff out my chest with pride like some caveman. There's something about having actual physical evidence of his pleasure on my skin that feels like an accomplishment.

He shifts to his side so his body is half on the mattress, one leg still over mine. "Can I …?" He shoves his hand down my boxer briefs and grips my cock.

I throw my head back. "Fuck. Yes. So much yes."

He strokes lightly, as if testing it out, but I'm too keyed up for that. I wrap my fingers around his fist and give a hard pump. "I like a strong grip. Like in hockey."

Whit laughs and lays his forehead on my shoulder. "I can't believe you brought up hockey while my hand is on your dick."

"Hockey is—"

He gives a firm stroke, and I almost black out.

"Is what?" he taunts.

"I was going to say *life*. Hockey is life, but I might have to change that to handjobs."

Whit's confidence grows as I squirm and mutter obscenities under my breath. He jerks me off, and I can't remember a time where someone else's hand has been this good.

When you're a teenager, it's all about the handjobs and maybe blowjobs if you're lucky, but as an adult, it's easy to bypass all that and go straight to penetrative sex.

Whit's fingers are long, his palm big and strong. He encircles my dick with a grip that feels more solid than anyone else's, even my own.

I'm on the edge with just a few strokes, and as I turn my head and meet his mismatched eyes, I find myself begging. "Please keep kissing me."

I don't have to ask him twice.

With his tongue in my mouth, and his hand on my dick, I come on a muffled cry. More cum joins his on my skin as my body uncoils and all the tension leaves me. His strokes continue until I'm completely wrung out, and I have to swat his hand away when it becomes too much.

Whit slumps, half on top of me, and then the reality sinks in that the moment's over.

We lie in silence, breathing heavily, until Whit eventually chuckles against me.

"Oops?"

I smile. "Regret it?"

"Not one bit."

WHIT

"I could fall asleep," I say against Rainn's shoulder.

"First shared orgasm will do that." Rainn's deep, rumbling sex voice is sexy as fuck, but his words also make me realize something.

I lean up on my elbow. "Does this mean I'm only part virgin now?"

"You know, if you'd read more than a couple of pages of the articles I gave you, you might've found a whole article on what virginity really means versus what society deems it to be. It's entirely up to you to determine what constitutes sex." His hand moves slowly over my back.

I pull back. "You … you read those articles?"

Rainn turns his head and meets my eyes. "What, do you think I googled virginity stats, hit Print, and that was it? I had to make sure I wasn't printing off shitty articles implying older virgins are all incels."

"What's an incel?"

"It stands for involuntarily celibate, usually due to having a horrible, misogynistic, and creepy personality. It's *not* you."

"Of course not. I'm delightful."

"Sure you are." Rainn wraps his arm around me.

It's surreal to lie here pressed against his body. My head fits in the crook of his shoulder, and all the thinking about this, the wanting this, the fantasizing about how it would feel—it doesn't compare to the intimacy of actually experiencing it.

We're lying here sticky and mostly covered in cum, but I don't want to move.

A part of me is waiting for him to say, "Totally straight. Thanks for playing."

Though I don't know if a totally straight guy would get off with another guy. He can't still think he's straight after that, right?

"Uh-oh," he says, and I hold my breath.

"Uh-oh, what?"

"You're overthinking. Stop it."

I nudge him. "Am not."

"You okay?"

"Better than okay." If this had happened with an out-and-proud gay guy, I'd probably be worried he was done with me as well but for reasons unattached to his sexuality.

Doubt is normal after fooling around with someone, isn't it?

"We should get cleaned up," he says.

My arm tightens around him, but I force myself to pull it back. "Uh, okay. I can get going if you want me to."

He rolls over to face me. "I don't want you to, but I'm not going to hold you hostage if you need to go home. You work in the morning on the farm, don't you?"

I groan. "I should go back to the farm tonight, but ..." I don't want to.

"Well, is there much difference between driving home now or setting your alarm to make it there in the morning?"

"I could leave it up to future me to be responsible."

"That sounds like a completely foolproof plan that will definitely not backfire." Rainn leans over and kisses me. "I don't want to be selfish by asking you to get up early just so I can have more of you."

"You can have as much of me as you want."

"I like the sound of that." Rainn gets out of bed and leaves the bedroom, smiling at me on his way out.

The shower starts in the bathroom, and I contemplate joining him, but that might be pushing things. I get out of bed and grab a tissue from a box sitting on the bookshelf under the window.

I'm wiping myself down when a book catches my eye. I don't recognize it, and it's not one of the thrillers that fill his living room bookshelf. The cover catches my attention because of the rainbow theme. Picking it up, I read the blurb on the back, and my lips quirk.

Rainn reads … LGBTQ fiction?

I start reading but don't get far.

"You going to shower, or …"

I didn't register the shower turning off, and in a panic, I jump and drop the book. "Umm …"

Rainn's wearing only a towel and holding another out for me. "Ah. Found my hidden collection, huh?"

"Is this because of me?"

Rainn shakes his head and looks away. "I read them when I started at V and V. I figured a little knowledge about the community would be useful if I was going to work in it."

I purse my lips. "Did you enjoy them?"

"They were … okay. I guess I didn't really connect to them, like they weren't relatable to me." Rainn shrugs. "Maybe I should read them again now. I might see them from a new perspective."

"Your perception has changed?"

Rainn hums. "It's definitely one of those things where I had to experience it myself to really understand."

"And do you? Understand it?"

"Not even fucking close." He grins. "You want a shower?"

"Uh, yeah. Thanks." I reach for the towel, but he doesn't let it go.

Instead, he pulls me closer and kisses me again. It's soft and slow, a lot more tender than the needy way he was kissing me before.

I'm definitely not going to leave now. I want his lips on me as many times as possible tonight, while he's still into this.

The way he's acting, kissing me and saying he wants more, chances are he won't change his mind tomorrow, but I think until he really figures himself out, I will always have that doubt. Maybe I don't need him to label it, but I do need him to say this isn't experimenting or doing me a favor to get my virginity out of the way. That it's not chasing a good feeling merely because it's new and a novelty.

I force myself to pull away but then shower super fast, worried Rainn will be asleep when I get out, but he's not.

He's in bed, still shirtless, and my gaze gets stuck on his broad shoulders and hard pecs. The dark hair on his chest isn't a forest or anything, but that tiny bit might be making drool fall from my mouth a little.

My cock tents the towel wrapped around me, and I'm majorly disappointed when Rainn leans up on his elbow and the sheet falls below his waist, showing off that he's wearing sweats. There's a folded pair on the end of the bed too.

"They for me?" I ask.

"If you want them. I figured your boxers are … messy."

I snort. "Yeah, they are."

I hesitate before dropping the towel. After what we just did, I shouldn't be self-conscious, but I am.

Rainn smiles. "I've seen a million dicks before, dude."

"This isn't a locker room."

"Would you like me to close my eyes?" he taunts.

"No, I'm good." I'm just going to be completely naked for the first time in front of a guy I hooked up with.

Achievement unlocked.

I drop the towel and get dressed probably quicker than is considered normal, and Rainn chuckles as I climb into bed next to him. He's on his back, his arms held out to pull me close. As I curl into his side, I can't help thinking how natural this is.

I lick my lips. "Can I ask you something?"

"You can ask me anything."

"You ... you seem pretty comfortable with this."

"Orgasm."

"Oh. Okay."

He pulls away so he can stare down at me. "Was that the wrong answer?"

"I thought maybe it was a good sign, seeing as I'm a guy, and ... you know."

Rainn kisses the side of my head. "I have some pretty crazy news for you. Shocking, even."

"Mm?"

"Cuddling with you is really not that much different than cuddling with a woman."

"Hey. I'm a big, masculine hockey player."

Rainn laughs. "That's not what I meant. This doesn't feel like some Big Gay Experience™. It's like anyone else I've ever been with. And that's ... surprising. It's not living up to my expectations in an unexpected way."

"So, no freak-out?"

"Not yet."

Yet.

That's the word that scares me the most.

***

Dragging myself away from Rainn's warm body at dark o'clock in time to get home is difficult, and it's only made more difficult by Rainn refusing to acknowledge I'm leaving.

He's a fucking heavy sleeper.

It's way too much like a walk of shame trying to sneak out without waking him, so I find a pen and paper in his kitchen and write him a note.

Tried to wake your lazy ass up, but you're dead to the world.

See you this weekend? –W

I hesitate before leaving the note, but, eh, if he wants me to stop showing up at the bar, it's up to him to tell me. I drop the paper on the pillow and lean over the bed to kiss his cheek.

He doesn't even stir, and I'm jealous. I wish I could sleep like him … Wait, unless he's pretending to be asleep. That would suck.

I examine his relaxed features, from his soft eyes to his five-o'clock shadow under slightly parted lips, and then shake my head. I have to stop thinking like that, or it will only drive me crazy.

The thirty-minute drive home is filled with telling myself that this is what it is. Maybe it will turn into something, or maybe Rainn will go down in history as my first heartache. Who knows.

Maybe I'll lose interest. Not likely, but it might happen.

I'm not going to Whit-out on him—that's a new verb I invented. It's where I overanalyze and think too hard about something to the point reality warps.

I will not do that with Rainn. Okay, realistically, I'll *try* not to do that to Rainn. I can't pressure him or hound him about what happened, and while that's good in theory, I know it will be hard.

Another thing I didn't think of when agreeing to stay last night? That I'll be walking to a farmhouse full of family and farmhands who have known me since birth.

Staying out on a worknight is new for me. In fact, I've never done it before.

Even freshman year when everyone was partying most days a week, I did mine on Saturday nights only.

And the second I step through those doors, the whistles and hollers start from the dining room.

Everyone's there—Mom, Dad, our farmhands who are like uncles to me, my brother, and his best friend, Gordo, who's been working for us since he was a kid, basically. They're drinking their morning coffees before we get to work.

I pour myself a cup. "Calm down. I stayed at a friend's place after practice."

I'm definitely not going to go into the details with Mom and Dad here. Or the farmhands, for that matter.

"Oh, boo," Gordo says. "Here we thought we could celebrate the little guy becoming a man."

My brother punches him in the arm hard for me.

"Who are you calling little, Mr. I Need A Stepping Stool To Saddle A Horse?" I taunt.

Gordo gives me the finger.

"Nice."

Campbell stands. "Ready to head out there?"

"Let me change my clothes first." *Considering I'm not wearing underwear because they were covered in dried cum.*

"Just a friend, my ass," Gordo calls out as I turn to go head upstairs to my room.

"Don't want to hear about your ass, Gordo," I call back to more snickers.

I run upstairs and change as fast as I can. In the mudroom, I shove my feet into my boots and sling on my jacket. When I charge through the back door, my brother gets in my way.

"We're going for a ride."

I frown. "A … ride?"

"Dad said we could. He and the others are doing morning chores. Unless … there's a reason riding will be uncomfortable for you after last night?" Campbell doesn't even try to hide his amusement.

I shove him. "No reason at all, dickhead."

"Sure about that?"

We walk toward the stables.

"It's disturbing that my brother is asking about my sex life. My butt virginity is still intact, thank you very much, but uh … other stuff might've happened." My skin flushes, damn it.

"Aww, my baby bro is all grown up."

"Shut up. Why are we getting out of morning chores?"

"Can't a brother want to spend quality time with another brother?"

"No."

Campbell laughs. "You're right about that, but it's a surprise. And we don't get out of morning chores completely. We just get a time-out first."

"Oh, so this is a punishment?"

"Nope. You're going to love it."

I drop it. Most people don't like surprises, but I'm like a kid in a candy store. I get all giddy about what it could be.

We enter the stable, and my boy, Arlo, huffs and sticks his chestnut head through the small window of his pen.

"Hey." I give him a gentle pat. "I know I haven't come to see you for a while."

This farm has been in our family for countless generations. These stables used to house working horses back when our fields were full of crops instead of dairy cows and hay fields. Now, they house our pets. Normal kids get toys at five years old, but farm boys get horses. At least in this family.

We saddle up, and I follow Campbell, who's on his mare, Roxy.

Arlo becomes overeager when I steer him past his day meadow, and he suddenly thinks it's okay to move into a trot before I tell him to. I pull back on the reins to get him to slow down, which he does immediately.

"Good boy," I whisper. "I know you're excited to be out."

Campbell leads us to the neglected part of our farm—the part we have big plans for.

The unused land is overgrown with tall grass, but hopefully soon we'll be putting in a long driveway leading from the road to a future farm stand and visitor center. We want to make an attraction for families to bring their kids while they also pick up fresh produce.

Fruit picking, tractor rides, and homemade delicacies sold on-site.

We wouldn't be the only farm in Vermont to offer those things, but, like we keep telling Dad, we need avenues of income other than dairy if we want the farm to be sustainable.

The sun's early morning light dances over the acres of land that was once crops a long time ago.

Campbell pulls Roxy to a stop, and Arlo and I join him.

"So what's the real reason we're out here?" I ask.

My brother looks out at the expansive meadows. "We got the approval to build out here."

My eyes widen. "Really?"

Campbell nods. "It's happening. As soon as the guys are done with your house, they're getting started on the farm stand and greenhouses. You ready for it all?"

"So ready."

"Come graduation, it'll be balls-to-the-wall busy."

I breathe in the cold Vermont air. "I have to wait until May before I can really start thinking about it. I've still got the playoffs to get through, finals, graduation ..." *Rainn.* I stop myself from saying that last one aloud.

My phone burns in my pocket, and I'm tempted to take it out to see if he's woken up yet or texted or ...

Deep breaths, Whit. Play it cool.

"About that," Campbell says.

"About what? My crazy-ass schedule?"

"Yeah, that. You're going to have to add watch your brother get married next month."

"Next *month*?" I shriek.

Campbell's whole face glows. "We were looking at summer for the wedding, but there might be a little issue with Christie being able to fit into her dress."

"Holy shit, really? *Really*, really?"

"While I'm at it, I'm going to have to ask for time off in early fall, but the good news is, the next farmhand is coming into the world."

"I suggest waiting until your baby is at least three before putting them to work."

Campbell smiles. "Already spoiling your niece or nephew."

It's all falling into place.

"Ready to head back and get to actual work?"

I stare out at our future. "Five more minutes."

With superhuman strength I didn't know I possessed, I make it through morning chores before I check my phone.

My heart skips a beat at the simple message. *See you this weekend.*

17

RAINN

I so shouldn't be here.

I definitely shouldn't have asked for the night off from the bar so I could go see Whit at his away game against CU at the campus in Colchester.

This wasn't a spur-of-the-moment thing, either. I had to plan shit.

Me. *Plan.*

Hell, I even borrowed a car for this. When I'd asked my cousin to borrow her tiny-ass Fiat 500 to go to a hockey game, she'd looked at me weird but didn't ask too many questions.

It's not that I don't think Whit is worth it, but I am wondering how he'll take it.

Whit knows how I feel about hockey, so he might consider my attendance tonight as a more-than-friends gesture—maybe even a boyfriend gesture. And, damn, I need to figure out how I feel about that label, before I let Whit see me here tonight.

It's been so long since I've been to any hockey game, but the atmosphere feels more amped than usual. The buzz in my veins and the heavy thumping of my heart is something I typically got when I was *on* the ice and not just watching it.

I chose to come to his away game because I'm not sure I could face one at my old stomping grounds. Honestly, even being here at a different school is bringing back enough memories to bring me down, but I remind myself I'm here for Whit.

The teams are announced, and as they enter the arena, my gaze immediately seeks the name WHITAKER on the back of one of the green-and-white jerseys.

Like at his practice the other night, his skating is flawless and so smooth, and that's just during the warm-up skate. When the game picks up, he's rotated in often. He's not first line, but he should be. He has so much fucking talent, and I can't take my eyes off him.

The game is tight, but it's a high-scoring matchup. Both offenses are on point, and while the D-men on each side are fighting to stop them, bullets keep getting fired at the nets. No matter the outcome tonight, the goalies will end up drinking together by the end of it. They're both getting hammered out there.

Whit hits the ice for another shift, and I cup my mouth and let out a loud *whoop!* Pride and awe fill my veins as I watch him move on the ice. There's no doubt I miss playing this game, but watching Whit is giving me little pieces of my old life back. He's on absolute fire and sinks two goals by the time the final buzzer sounds.

I leave with the mass of people making their way outside and then find myself hovering by the back doors where the team will exit because I have to tell him how amazing that was to watch.

He's one of the last players out the door, and when he clears the exit, a group of people approaches him, with hugs all around. That's when I notice the resemblance and realize his family is here for this too.

My feet stall, and I shuffle awkwardly. *Abort! Run away!*

I'm so not ready to meet the parents.

Whit's eyes lock on mine, and even as his brow furrows, his dimples appear. "Rainn?"

I slowly approach, my gaze flicking between him and his family. "Uh, hey. I, uh …"

"You came to see me play?"

"I did. I, uh …"

He turns to the people behind him. "Can I get a second?"

They agree but watch with fascination while Whit leads me away.

"Umm, hi," I say.

Whit smiles. "Hi."

God, I want to lean in and kiss him, but I refrain.

"Can I drive you home?" I blurt.

He glances at his family and then back at me. "Sure. I already got permission from Coach to go home with my family instead of the team bus, but I'll go tell them I'm going with you instead."

Why does my throat suddenly feel thick?

"Family, huh?" I figured as much, but my heart pounds hearing it for sure.

"Yeah." Whit points to the guy who's about his height, but who's a lot more rugged and hairy. "That's my brother, Campbell, his fiancée, Christie, and the old people are my mom and dad."

I scratch my ear because it suddenly feels hot. "You can go home with them if you want."

Whit waves me off. "I see them all the time." He starts to walk away, but I stop him.

"Wait."

"What?"

"Do they know? Uh, about me?"

Whit rubs the back of his neck. "Kind of? I mean, coming home the other morning was a big clue there's a guy, but, I mean, they don't know you or your name or anything like that."

"Oh. Okay. Did … you … I mean, did you want to tell them about me?"

"Is there really anything to tell? We're friends who have hooked up once."

It hurts that he sees me that way, even though I've given him absolutely no indication we're more than that. Hell, I don't even know if I want more than that.

"Fair enough."

"If it were up to me, I'd march you over to them right now and introduce you, but I didn't think you'd be okay with that."

I'm not. Not really. But I also don't want to make a bad first impression with Whit's family. Even if we don't figure out what's going on between us, he's still a friend first and foremost.

"Maybe you could introduce me as a friend, and then when we work out what this is, they won't be all 'Oh, your boyfriend is that guy who blew us off at your game?'"

Whit cocks his head. "You think *boyfriend* could be a future label?"

Oh shit. That did not just fall from my mouth, did it?

I fan my face. "How is it this hot in March in Vermont?"

Whit laughs. "Come on. I'll introduce you as my friend … for now."

Yup, I think as we head over to his family. *Definitely having a March heat wave. Totally a thing. Yup.*

"Hey, guys," Whit says. "This is my friend Rainn."

Whit's family are all warm hellos except for Campbell.

"Rainn, huh?" Campbell eyes Whit. "The bartender? That Rainn?"

"Uh-huh." *Wow, real articulate. Way to go.*

"So, uh, I was thinking of driving home with him instead," Whit says. "Maybe go out for a drink."

"If that's what you want," his dad says.

Whit's mom steps forward to give her son a hug. "Go have fun, sweetie." When she pulls back, she lowers her voice, but I still hear it. "Can we expect you home tonight or late tomorrow?"

There goes the notion of introducing me as a friend.

"Uh …" Whit struggles to answer.

Before I know what I'm doing, I take Whit's hand. "Late tomorrow."

"Drive safe" is all she says.

Whit's stare burns into me as I lead him away. "I can't believe you just did that."

Neither can I, but it's done now. "It's obvious they knew something. It's up to you to tell them what we are … or aren't."

"Okay, then."

What is wrong with me? Two steps forward, a giant leap back.

"I'm shit at this stuff," I say.

"What stuff?"

"I've been told by girlfriends in the past that I'm not good at expressing myself and that I'm hard to read. And I know I'm probably sending you mixed signals, but I'm trying not to."

Whit stops walking and tugs on my hand to pull me toward him. "You're not good at expressing yourself, but I *can* read you. You want to explore this with me, you want more, but you're terrified."

"I'm not terrified—"

"Let me finish. You're terrified you're going to do or say the wrong thing and I'm going to get hurt, so you're trying to keep my expectations low. I, in turn, am trying not to get my hopes up. I'm in a rush to the finish line, but you're showing me how to pace myself. And though it's more for your benefit than mine, I appreciate it because I am the type of person to jump in heart first and think later. I'm good with where we're at, and I never expected you to want to meet my family, let alone basically tell them we're sleeping together. I'm trying to take this one night at a time."

"Me too. I want more, but—"

"You don't know what the limits are yet, if there are any, and I understand, okay? I'm just excited that I get to spend tonight with you. Touching you … kissing you …"

I lean in and kiss him softly. "Like that?"

"Exactly like that."

"Okay, then let's go."

The only parking spot I could get was on the other side of campus, and on the way past the hockey entrance, a guy in a suit waves to Whit, and Whit nods back.

"Who's that?" I ask.

"Eh, no one. He was there to watch one of the guys from CU who's been drafted by Pittsburgh."

"An agent?"

Whit's mouth opens, but there's a few seconds' pause before the words come out. "Nah, he's with the team. He introduced himself to me on my way out."

"He's interested in you?"

Whit shakes his head. "Have no idea. He just asked a few questions and gave me his card."

Excited butterflies swarm in my gut. "Are you going to call him?"

"No point, is there?"

"Why not?"

"Pro hockey has never been my future, and besides, he's probably interested in making me their towel boy or something."

When we get to the car, Whit bursts out laughing.

"Whose car is this?"

"My cousin's, why?"

"I can't wait to see you fit behind the wheel of this thing. Do you have to fold yourself in half? Shit, can my hockey gear even fit in the back?"

"It, uh, was a bit of a cramped drive here."

"This is going to be fun."

He's right. By the time we squash his gear bag into the car and then climb into the front, we're both laughing uncontrollably.

I start the car and put it in Drive. "Don't say I never do anything for you."

"Never. You drove this clown car for me. I'm touched."

I want to tell him I'd do a hell of a lot more for him, but I think it's too early for that.

● **18**
———
WHIT
———

One night at a time. I can do that.

Even if my heart's pounding from excitement that Rainn came to one of my games. He's still bitter about hockey, but he showed up anyway. Then facing my family? It makes the overexcitable part of me, the part that is moving from crush to real feelings at a hundred miles an hour, go into overdrive, and it's getting harder and harder to shove that down. I have to try really hard not to get ahead of myself.

He asks again about the guy from Pittsburgh, but I shut it down by changing the subject.

The truth is the guy was interested in talking to me about the affiliate AHL team. He wants me to go skate with them, with potential for a possible ATO contract.

I'm not interested, and I know Rainn won't understand that.

I don't love the sport like he does ... or did, I should say. It's obvious that love is still inside him, but it's been misplaced.

Hockey is amazing, but I love the farm more.

Hockey is Rainn's passion, and farming is mine. End of story.

"You should've been made MVP of that game," he says.

"I doubt it. There are much better players on the team than me."

"I wasn't watching any of them. My eyes were glued to you the whole time."

"That's because I gave you an orgasm last time I saw you. It's the orgasm effect."

Rainn smiles. "It was a pretty powerful orgasm."

Now this is a topic I can get on board with.

"I want to know if I can make the next one even more powerful. With my mouth, maybe?"

Rainn almost loses control of the car. "Never tease a man about a blowjob."

"I'm not teasing. Are you kidding me? I've been thinking about giving head for *years*. What it will feel like, what happens if I gag, things like that. I'm excited to find out."

Rainn palms the bulge in his pants. "You're not playing fair."

"You're the one touching your dick, and *I'm* not playing fair? I don't think so."

"I'm tempted to pull over just to take the edge off."

"In this shoebox? If I lean over, my head's going through your window."

Rainn laughs. "Good point. Fuck, home is so far away."

It's really not—we're about five minutes away—but I like getting Rainn riled up and hot for me. The other night, he didn't appear to have any control over what he was doing.

I want to make him lose it again. "Question? How many orgasms have you had in one night with a person?"

"What? I'm not answering that."

"Why not? Is it just the one? You have a long refractory period? Is that it?"

"No. It's … personal."

"When I first discovered gay porn, I made myself come four times one night, but when I was with you, everything was amplified. I don't think I could've come again if I tried."

Rainn groans. "Whit, why are you doing this to me?"

"Because it's fun."

"You're sadistic."

The second he pulls into a parking space on his street, he's out of the car.

I unfold myself and climb out, but Rainn's already at his door. "Uh, you parked kind of crooked," I point out.

"It's good enough." Gripping my suit jacket, he pulls me down the building's hallway like he's on a mission.

Rainn pulls me to him and kisses me while fumbling in his pocket for his keys and stumbling toward his apartment.

As soon as he lets us inside, everything is unceremoniously messy.

I took my tie off as soon as I got in the car, so he doesn't have to fight that, but he is fighting with the buttons on my shirt.

I force myself to step back and break away from his hot mouth. "The thought of you ripping off my buttons is hot, but I kinda don't want to explain to my mother why she needs to sew them back on."

We separate to ditch our clothes. Shoes and socks go flying, my jacket is flung in the general vicinity of the kitchen, but unlike last time, where I was the one hesitating to get fully naked, it's Rainn's turn to pause when he gets down to his underwear.

"I've seen a million dicks before, Rainn," I tease. "That's what you said the other night, right?"

He huffs. "Okay, fine. You might've had a point. This is different than a locker room."

I get down to my boxers and slowly approach him. "I'm nervous too. Probably even more nervous than you."

"How do you figure?"

"I *know* I like dick. What if you're down there getting all up in my business and you're like, 'So. Dicks are gross. I like you, but your dick, not so much'?"

Rainn laughs, and I mean, he should. I am joking—like … fifty-five percent joking.

The big wall of hairy chest moves closer as Rainn pulls me against him. "You know what I thought was the hottest part of us hooking up?"

"Please say my dick, please say my dick," I chant.

Rainn's hands wander over my chest and down my abs. "It was seeing you come unglued. I loved how you fell apart on top of me." His fingers dip into the waistband of my underwear, skimming above my cock.

Rainn Richardson is a tease.

"Yep. Like that." He presses his bare chest against mine, his lips land on my neck, and he whispers against my skin. "You don't need to worry about me not liking your dick, because if touching it, sucking it, anything else you want me to do with it makes you look the way you do right now, I'll do whatever it takes."

He finally puts me out of my misery by wrapping his long fingers around my cock and giving me a hard stroke.

I tremble in his arms.

"I want to make you feel good," Rainn rumbles.

I thrust into his hand. "Keep doing that, and I'll feel too good too soon, and it'll all be over."

Yet, I don't stop, and neither does he.

"Didn't you say something about four times in one night? I may not be a hockey player anymore, but I'm still competitive as fuck, and I want to break your record."

I breathe heavily. "There's no way I'll be able to come five times tonight."

"Maybe. Maybe not. But we can at least get number one out of the way."

He jerks me off confidently and fast. It's embarrassing how quickly I spill into his hand.

My orgasm rocks through me, first in tiny bursts and then all at once. My knees almost give out on me.

"Fuuuck," I let out. Cum fills my underwear, and now I'm regretting not taking them off. "I'm going to have to start doing my laundry here if we're going to make a habit of defiling our boxers." I peel them off, use them to wipe up the rest of my cum, and drop them to the floor.

Rainn chuckles, but I don't feel as exposed as last week when I was completely naked in front of him.

I'm still panting when I say, "You're really good at that."

The smirk on Rainn's face is adorably conceited. Somehow. "Well, not to brag or anything, but I've had sex with my fist so many times I've lost count."

The breathy laugh that falls out of me sounds foreign to my ears. "I'm jealous of your fist."

"When you get the chance to catch your breath, I'm cashing in your promise to me," Rainn says. "I remember something in the car about your mouth on my cock."

"Ungh."

"Is that a good ungh or a bad ungh?"

"Just, ungh." I stand up straighter and square my shoulders. "Okay. Blowjob. I can totally do this."

Rainn's needy expression morphs into something softer. "Nervous?"

"Excited nervous."

"You can't really do anything wrong except with the teeth. Just don't bite me, and we'll be fine."

"Wow, your dirty talk is soooo sexy."

Instead of giving me a smart-ass retort, Rainn takes my hand and leads me to stand next to his futon. Without taking his eyes off me, he drops his boxer briefs to the floor.

I swallow hard.

His cock stands tall and hard, and even though I had my hand wrapped around it the other night, it looks bigger than it felt.

He takes a seat and tilts his head toward his feet, indicating he wants me on my knees. This can't be real, because this shit is what fantasies are made of.

When I sink to the floor, Rainn widens his legs.

The hair from his ankles to his thighs stands out against his light skin. I run my hands from his knees up to his hips.

He eases forward on the futon, bringing his cock closer, and it gives me a sense of power I could easily get used to. I haven't even put my mouth on him yet, and his body trembles. It's intox-icating.

Lowering my head, I keep my eyes on him while I take my first taste. Just a small lick.

Rainn sucks in a sharp breath and holds it, while a bead of precum spills out from his tip. Here's the real test. I close my mouth over the head of his dick and drink up the salty flavor.

My cock twitches but is still essentially down for the count.

Orgasms with Rainn are more than orgasms. They're a life experience. Fuck, they could become my religion.

Focus, Whit.

I close my eyes and try not to overthink this, remembering not to suck him too deep. I've always figured deep-throating is an art you learn over time, and I'd prefer not to gag and choke. Not this time, anyway. One day, though, I'll want him to fuck my mouth until my eyes are watery and I can barely breathe.

I cup his balls and lightly squeeze them while I work him over with my mouth. He feels so heavy on my tongue.

"That feels so good, Whit." His encouragement gives me confi-dence, making me feel as if I know what I'm doing, even though I have no clue.

All that's running through my head is *no teeth, watch the teeth, oh shit, where are my teeth?* I need to calm down and let go.

Rainn told me that watching me fall apart turned him on more than anything, and I want to reverse that experience. I want to watch him while I bring him pleasure, I want the name he calls out in the middle of coming to be mine, and I want to enjoy this through his reactions and responses.

When I'm not overthinking, I let myself get lost in his soft moans and heavy breathing.

I alternate between sucking him while I bob my head up and down and licking his swollen tip.

All those times fantasizing about doing this. All those times I watched porn and thought about what it would be like. How it would feel.

It's nothing like the real thing. It's better because you can't taste porn, you can't smell it, and when you imagine someone running their hand over your head while you suck their cock, you can't feel them actually do it.

When my jaw begins to get tired, I use my hand to work the base of his shaft.

Rainn reaches for me, his thumb trailing down my cheek. "I take it back. The hottest part isn't you losing control. It's watching you drawing out my orgasm with those fucking lips that look so good wrapped around my cock."

Now that dirty talk is sexy, and I could definitely get used to it.

So could my dick. It's full mast now, wanting round two. I try to ignore it and only concentrate on the feel of Rainn's tight, velvety skin moving in and out of my mouth, but it doesn't help.

My cock aches to the point I have to reach for it for some relief.

"Yes," Rainn hisses. "Touch yourself while you suck my dick. I want to watch that."

My hand is no replacement for Rainn's, but when I look up with his dick in my mouth, my hand on my cock, the expression of pure lust in Rainn's eyes has me coming again.

It's not as forceful as before, but it seems to go on forever.

Waves of pleasure shoot through me, and it takes all my strength to keep my mouth open wide for Rainn's thrusts. The muscles in his thighs tighten and release, tighten and release.

"I'm close …" he warns.

Maybe I shouldn't try to swallow my first time, but I'm dying for it. I want him to give me his all. I hum around his cock, and he lets go.

Warm spurts of cum fill my mouth and my throat. There's so much of it, I can't take it all at once, and some dribbles out the side of my lips. Rainn squirms as he convulses over and over again.

If I thought my orgasm was long, it's nothing compared to Rainn's. When I think he's done, his hips lift off the futon again, and more salty taste covers my tongue. That's when his body finally goes slack, and he pulls out of my mouth.

I take a deep breath and rest my head on his thigh while we both recover.

"Bedtime?" Rainn eventually asks.

I nod against his thigh, but as he helps me up and we stumble toward his bedroom, I have to ask. "What happened to five times?"

"Power nap. If you're lucky, I'll wake you by returning the favor. You won't even know if I'm shit at it, because you have nothing to compare it to."

I laugh. "True."

Rainn offers me a tissue before climbing into bed. His eyes track me while I clean myself off for a second time tonight.

I fall into bed next to him when I'm done. "Why did I wait so long to do this stuff?"

The question was rhetorical, but Rainn pulls me close and lowers his voice to ask, "Did … did you have a hard time coming out? Is that why you didn't do anything with a guy before?" His arms are as good as a warm blanket wrapped around me, and I sink into them so easily.

"That's not what I meant at all. It feels so good, and I'm stupid for waiting. I should've propositioned you years ago when I saw you play in college."

Rainn scoffs. "Yes, because very straight, college Rainn so would've been a goner for teenager Whit."

"What were you like when you were a student? Big man on campus, I bet."

"Pretty much." The cockiness that should be in that statement is missing.

"Banging a different girl each week? Partying hard?"

"Not quite that level, but I was popular. The reality hit really hard when I had my injury. Suddenly I was no longer Rainn Richardson, future NHL star. Kind of showed who my true friends were. Then when I did finally get back on my feet, I got sick of the sympathy stares from those who did bother to ask how I was, so I lashed out at the only ones left until they were all gone too."

"Shit, I'm sorry."

He squeezes me tighter. "Not your fault."

"No, I mean for bringing it up. We should talk about fun stuff."

"What kind of fun stuff?"

"Well, blowing you was pretty fun."

"Agreed."

"Dancing is fun."

"Disagree."

I roll my eyes. "How surprising. I wouldn't have guessed someone as upbeat and enthusiastic as you can't dance."

"Hey, I never said I *can't* dance. It's just not fun."

"Maybe you're dancing wrong, then. You might have to give me a sample so I can make an informed decision on that one."

Rainn kisses the top of my head. "Maybe later. Sleep now. Blowjob later. Dancing tomorrow."

I let out a content sigh and close my eyes. "Sounds good."

I'm out like a light a second later.

RAINN

At some point during the night, I wake up and follow through on my promise, giving Whit what I'm sure is the worst blowjob known to man.

Giving is a whole lot different than receiving. Not that it's all bad. The faint salty taste isn't as overpowering as I thought it would be. And even though it feels awkward at first, as soon as I look up into Whit's eyes, all of my hesitance disappears because he gives me that look.

He looks at me as if I'm someone he respects and admires. So to avoid ruining the moment by telling him he's wrong, I focus all my energy on trying to get him to come so hard he can't remember his own name.

It's so hot watching him fall apart, I practically hump the bedsheets and don't even care when I come all over them while Whit shoots his load down my throat.

We both pass out quickly after.

The next time I wake up, the sun is trying to peek through the crack in my blinds, and I'm alone.

The apartment is quiet.

I strain to hear the shower or Whit moving around the kitchen, but it's dead silent.

My immediate response is to wonder if my blowjob skills were so horrible that Whit decided to run out of here while I was asleep. He did come, though. I can still taste him on my tongue.

Hmm, maybe I should get up and brush my teeth. But … the bathroom is all the way across the apartment, and I'm under a warm blanket. Ugh, I should get up and find my phone to text Whit and check in on him.

I don't need to. A moment later, the door to my apartment opens, and then Whit appears in my bedroom doorway. He's wearing my beanie, my jacket, but he has his suit pants from last night on, and damn, he looks good. "Finally awake? I tried to tell you I was leaving, but you grunted and then passed out again."

"What time is it?"

"Early. I was hungry. After three orgasms I needed sustenance, so I went and bought us breakfast."

"Mm, food sounds good." I stumble to get out of bed and stretch.

Whit watches and licks his lips as his gaze travels down to my sleep pants.

My lips twitch, along with another part of my anatomy. "Actually, that sounds like a better idea."

"I didn't say anything."

"The look on your face said it for you."

"There is no way I could come again because I need food first, but I can totally take care of you." Whit steps toward me.

My stomach rumbles. "I might need something to eat first too."

"I guess we wouldn't want your coffee going cold."

"Coffee is coffee no matter the temperature."

He doesn't get out of my way as I move closer. Instead, he wraps his arm around my back and pulls me to him. His lips are soft as they touch mine.

"Good morning." Whit's deep rumble makes me want to pull him back to bed and take him up on his offer.

But no. Food first. We sit at the table. He passes me my coffee and then pulls a bagel and a breakfast sandwich from the bag. "Which one do you want?"

"Which one do you want? You went and bought it, so you choose."

"I like both, but I got the sandwich you like."

I take the sandwich with a smile. *He knows what I like.*

I like sharing my space with Whit.

Then again, I'm liking a lot of things I've never experienced before.

And this breakfast thing. That's good too.

"So, uh, last night was fun," Whit says.

"A lot of fun," I agree.

"I'm ticking off a lot of my virgin boxes."

It's really hard not to make a joke right now, so I sip my coffee.

Whit's tone shifts. "How are you handling it?"

Nope, can't hold it back anymore. "Your virgin box? You want me to handle your virgin box?"

"So funny. I guess …" He starts to look uncomfortable. "I guess I'm asking if you're freaking out yet, or if you want more. Or less. Or if you want me to shut up in general."

The poor guy looks like he's holding his breath.

I reach over and take his hand. "I'm not freaking out. I don't think, anyway. I'm having fun. Lots of fun. I want more, but not … *more.*"

Whit frowns. "What does that mean?"

"I like what we're doing, and I know you're in some rush to go all the way, but … I'm not there yet. I don't think I will be until I … figure some things out."

He looks a little disappointed, but he doesn't fight me on it. "Sorry. One night at a time. That's what I promised."

I squeeze his hand and then go back to my food.

When we're finished, Whit stands. The panicky part of my brain thinks he's getting ready to leave, but then he walks over to the couch and takes his usual spot.

"You totally got out of watching *Youngblood* last week, so we're watching it today."

"Fine. Though, I do have to say what we did last week was a way better idea than a stupid hockey movie."

Whit mock gasps. "Stupid and hockey do not belong in the same sentence. You should know that by now."

I roll my eyes and down the rest of my drink. "Get the movie started. I'm going to hit the head and brush my teeth."

After finishing my business, I find Whit lying on the couch. "That's how it's going to be, is it?"

"You snooze, you lose. But I will let you be my pillow." He lifts his head for me to slide in beneath him.

"Wow, you're so generous." I glance at the screen which is still on the opening credits of the movie. "I told you to start it. I have seen the movie before. It's not like I'll miss anything."

Whit settles his head in my lap. "No. You need the full experience for my evil plan to work."

"It's cute you think it's working at all."

"Hey, I've gotten you back on the ice and got you to come to an actual game. My plan is ahead of schedule."

I run my hand through his hair. "Whit, that has nothing to do with the movies we watch and everything to do with you."

His eyes meet mine, and I lean down to kiss him, but when he arches up, all he gives me is a peck.

"I told you. You're not getting out of this one. Pay attention."

And I do. Just, not to the TV. My hand continuously plays with his hair while I watch *him*. He gets excited during a few scenes, which is adorable, and without a doubt, he's way more interesting to me than the movie.

Sitting here like this with Whit, our whole situation seems simple. We're two guys who like each other.

I like him a lot. Why is it so hard to put into actual words? Why can't I tell him that this could have the potential to be so much more?

I focus on the way he smiles, anticipating a funny moment in the movie and the way his lips move along with the dialog. I think about how he approaches so many things in life this same way—anticipating the good stuff that might happen.

I don't want to take away any of his smiles. I don't want to hurt him, ever.

What if I go all in but then something makes me realize this was some psychological bullshit where I've attached myself to the first friend I've had in years?

I don't see that happening, but I also didn't see me having sex with a guy. That came out of nowhere too. We can't go back to being friends now, but I'm scared to ask for more.

Whit glances up at me, and I think I've been busted, but all he does is ask, "What movie do you want to watch next?"

I lift my head. The credits are rolling. Did I really spend almost two hours getting lost in thoughts about Whit?

"Umm, whatever you want to watch."

"I've got the perfect one." He does a search for *The Cutting Edge*. "It's technically not a hockey movie, but it does have an injured hockey player who goes into figure skating instead. Maybe you should try figure skating. Ooh, or ice dancing."

I poke him in the ribs. "I already told you. No dancing."

"You promised me dancing. You could be the real-life Doug Dorsey and not know it."

"I'm pretty sure I'd need full use of my knee, even for ice dancing."

Whit huffs. "Fine, but we're still watching this anyway."

That's fine with me. Again, it's not like I'll be able to focus on the movie.

"Are you coming to the bar tonight?" I ask.

Whit yawns. "I should probably get an early night and catch up on sleep since someone kept me up half the night giving me orgasms. That bastard."

"Sounds like an asshole."

"I can come tomorrow night? After I finish classes, I have a study group and practice, so it will be late, but I can be at the bar after that?"

"Can't really blow you while I'm working, though."

"It's definitely not *that* type of bar, I agree, but coming to see you isn't about the sex. I like sitting there on my stool and watching you work."

I kinda hate that his simple statement makes my stomach flip-flop all over the place.

Whit starts the next movie, but I'm right when I say my focus won't be on the TV again. Only, this time, I'm taking his focus with me too. Because soon I'll have to get ready for work, and he'll be going back to the farm.

As my hand trails down Whit's chest, those mismatched eyes meet mine. And when I pop the button on his pants, he doesn't fight me on it.

I reach into his pants and stroke his hardening dick. "I know you said you're down for the count, but I'm thinking we should at least try to match your four-orgasm record."

Whit lets out a sexy little whimper. "You know what Coach always says …"

Together, we quote Wayne Gretzky. "You miss one hundred percent of the shots you don't take."

"We have to at least try." Whit leans up and captures my mouth with his.

Yep. Definitely not watching the figure-skating movie.

The time to drop off Whit comes way too fast. As we pull up to his family's farm, he directs me to a group of trucks parked outside the large farmhouse.

He hesitates to get out, and I bet it's because we look ridiculous in the Fiat next to trucks three times its size.

"What's up?"

"I don't know the rules," Whit blurts.

"Rules?"

"Yeah, like … in public? Last night in front of my family, you held my hand. But can I lean over and kiss you goodbye? Or is that too big a risk for them seeing—"

I close the small gap and press my lips to his. "Does that answer your question?"

"No. You might need to do it again so I really understand."

This time, I push my tongue into his mouth.

When we break apart, his cheeks are flushed. "Okay. I understand now."

"The really good thing about me being a bitter asshole for the last few years is that there aren't a lot of people in my life whose opinions matter to me. There's my cousin, but I already know she's cool. And I work in queer spaces. I don't have huge … closet doors, I guess. I'm lucky in that way."

"I didn't mean you'd have to come out, or—"

I wince. "That term honestly feels so foreign to what … I am. I know that makes no sense at all."

"You're still figuring stuff out, and that's okay. I meant you don't have to tell people about us. You can do that whenever you're ready. Hell, it took me about five years of knowing for sure that I'm gay before I came out, so I can't really talk, but I need to know your hard lines so I don't cross them. Knowing I can kiss you around my family is enough for me."

"You can kiss me whenever. I mean that."

Whit does it again just to prove my point.

I have to practically shove him out of the car. "Okay, go, before we do a whole lot more in front of your family."

"Okay, okay." He gets all his hockey gear out of the back and gives me a wave.

I have a ridiculous smile on my face the whole way back to town. It's still there while I fill up the Fiat's gas tank and when I arrive on my cousin's doorstep to return the key.

Sommer opens the door with a scowl on her face. "Why are men such dicks?"

My face falls. "Umm, I'm sorry for my species as a whole?"

"You mean gender?"

"No, no, I think it's pretty clear we're a completely different species."

She scoffs. "No arguments here." She's in a tank top and sleep pants with a blanket wrapped around her. Her dark hair is in a messy bun, and when I say messy, it's a bird's nest. Her nose is all red, and her eyes are puffy like she's been crying.

"What happened?" I ask.

She steps aside to let me in. "Coffee?"

I check my phone. "I have some time." There's still an hour before I need to be at the bar for my shift. "What did he do? I want to say … Tim?" That old saying, changing boyfriends more than underwear? That's my cousin in a nutshell. It's hard to keep track.

She huffs. "Thyme."

I purse my lips. "Like as in the clock or the herb?"

"The herb."

"Was it always Thyme, or was there a Tim in there somewhere?"

"Rainn," she complains.

"Sommer," I whine back. "You should know the rules. Never date someone named after herbs or spices. Anything food related, really. Kale especially. The food is as evil as anyone who's named after it."

"Yes, well, people could say the same about us. Never date people named after the weather."

"We're spelled differently," I argue. "Though, that is a fair point. We're both kind of fucked-up. What were our mothers thinking?"

"In their defense, I don't think it's our names that make us fucked-up."

I snort. "True."

Our families have a relatively normal level of dysfunction, and our childhoods couldn't have been more cookie-cutter. I guess my issues popped up around the same time as my injury, but I don't know why Sommer struggles so much.

"Speaking of fucked up, how's my car?" she asks.

"Tiny."

"I mean, were there any problems? I'm not going to find a major dent the next time I drive?"

"Nope."

"Good."

"And thanks. I should be able to get my own again soon." I take a seat at her kitchen counter while Sommer flits around to make us coffee.

"So what was so important about some hockey game last night?"

Before, when I told Whit that my cousin was cool, I didn't really think about how I would actually tell her that I'm seeing a guy. And now that the moment is here, I can see why so many people struggle to come out.

It's not so much the words, or what they mean, but how I'm supposed to say them.

She pours me a cup and hands it over.

"I'm ..." I croak. Nope, that didn't come out right. I take a sip of coffee and try again. "I'm kinda dating someone on the team." Dating, hooking up ... same thing.

I can't really say Whit and I are dating when we haven't had an actual date. Then again, I think back to all those nights we'd watched movies at my place. The dinner I took him to for his birthday. Friend dates. Do they count?

"You went to a woman's hockey game?"

I subtly shake my head. "Uh. No."

It takes her a few seconds, but then her eyes widen. "Really? No ... really? When you took the job at Vino and Veritas, I thought you were being progressive and cool."

"Hey, I am progressive and cool. I, uh, didn't think I'd actually meet someone I'd connect with while working there."

"I have to know everything," she gushes. "What's his name?"

"Whit."

"Okay, you can't judge me for dating a guy named Thyme."

"His actual name is Leighton, but his last name is Whitaker."

She pauses. "Wait. Campbell Whitaker's brother?"

"Uh, yeah. You know Campbell?"

"I'm friends with his fiancée, Christie."

"Small world." Getting smaller by the minute.

"Are you going to the wedding next month?"

"Umm, Whit hasn't even mentioned it."

"But you're dating him?"

"We're …" Umm … A label would come in handy right about now, but I've got nothing. "*New*." Yes, that works. "Everything is new."

"Oh, then I'm sure the invite is coming. Or not. Who knows with guys? Now that you're dating men too, we can trade horror stories."

"Man. Just one man, and so far it's been awesome. *He* bought *me* breakfast this morning."

"Well, wait, because that never lasts long." She's too young and pretty—messy hair not withstanding—to be bitter.

"I'm sorry again," I say. "Men are all sucky."

I'm not lying. Whit and I have definitely been getting sucky, just not in the way she's thinking.

WHIT

It turns out the walk of shame is even more embarrassing when my mother is the only one to witness it. Not because she watches me from the porch with her coffee in her hand and a knowing look on her face, but because of the questions she wouldn't dare ask in front of anyone else except maybe Dad.

"So … Rainn …"

I hold up my hand. "We're not official, it's completely brand-new, and I don't want to jinx anything by talking about it."

"I take it I'm not allowed to ask when we're going to meet him officially, then."

"Definitely not. We're nowhere near that." And I think if I were to ask Rainn over for family dinner, he'd run away screaming.

"Sit. Tell me about him, at least."

I drop my gear bag and take the seat next to her, because I know my mother, and she will not let this go if I don't. "There's not much to tell." I can't exactly tell her he's straight, or thought he was until me, because that will make her protective instincts come out. And I don't really want to mention the hockey thing, because it's a sore spot for him. "I technically met him at the bookstore, but we became friends when he saw how terrible I was at flirting and felt sorry for me, so he said he'd find me a guy to go out with."

Yes, Mom, *go out with*. Not fuck. Nope, not at all, I will not be mentioning that.

Mom smiles. "And he fell for you instead? That's sweet."

Again, I hold up my hand. "Slow down there. We're … dating." I try not to wince on the word because it's not exactly what we're doing, is it?

As much as I want it to be, it's not the truth. Rainn turning up at my game last night was surprising, and even though it was a total boyfriend move, I can't let myself think that way. We haven't had an official date or anything, and we've hooked up twice. Although, technically, I have come four times in the last eighteen hours or so, so is that one hookup or four?

Sex math is hard.

"But you like him?" Mom asks.

"I do. I like him a hell of a lot." Probably more than I should.

"Well, good. I hope it works out and you'll be comfortable enough to bring him home for dinner one night."

"I hope so too."

Dad comes out the front door, probably looking for Mom to join her on their usual coffee date in the late afternoon.

They do it most days, and it has always made me see my parents as the kind of love story to look up to. Every day, they sit out here, sometimes talking and sometimes not. They enjoy each other's company, even silent company.

"Hi, son. How are you holding up after last night?"

I blanch and then realize he means after the game, not after … Shit, I need to get my head out of the gutter.

"Good. I meant to tell you all last night that a scout found me afterward. It was surreal, but pretty cool."

"A scout?" Dad asks.

"Yeah, from Pittsburgh. Well, technically Wilkes-Barre/Scranton, but that whole organization. From what I know, they drafted a player from the other team, and I guess he's about to graduate and they're trying to figure out contracts and where to send him, but anyway, this guy saw me, and he invited me to check out the farm team."

"You have to do it," Mom says.

"What?"

"This is an amazing opportunity," Dad says. "You can't ignore it."

"Yeah, I can. I'm not interested in moving to Pennsylvania and playing for the AHL. I just thought it was cool they even considered me."

"You scored two goals last night," Dad points out. "Of course they'd consider you."

"Hockey was never the plan."

"Sometimes plans change," Mom says.

"True," I murmur. Sometimes not by choice, but this *is* my choice, and I don't want to go to Pennsylvania.

Dad leans against the balcony railing, but I stand, vacating his usual seat.

"All yours, and I'll leave you to it."

Dad takes his seat, observing me as I pick up my gear bag. "You should at least think about it some more before you make a final decision."

"I will." But I already know what my decision will be.

"What are your plans for the rest of the afternoon and evening?" Mom asks.

Oh, you know, catching up on sleep because I'm exhausted after Rainn pulled four orgasms from me.

"Not much. I'll probably head to bed early because I have a big day on campus tomorrow."

Mainly, I can't wait for classes and practice to be over so I can see Rainn again.

I can't get away from practice fast enough.

When I walk into Vino and Veritas, Rainn's dropping off drinks to a table, but his eyes immediately find mine, and he lifts his chin with a bright smile.

I'm about to take my seat when he meets me there and surprises the shit out of me by leaning in and kissing my cheek.

"Hi," he says like it's a completely normal greeting we've had a thousand times over.

"Uh, hey …"

He rounds the bar, putting his tray back in place, and then serves the person waiting for his attention. He looks like Rainn, he's acting like Rainn, but when he glances at me, he doesn't seem like the Rainn I've come to know. He looks … happy.

He passes me a cider with a wink.

"Did you win the lottery or something?" I ask.

"What? Why?"

"You're … chipper. It's freaky."

Rainn laughs.

"Stop that. Stop that right now, you pod person."

"Are you sure you're not the pod person? You make me laugh all the time."

"Yes, but usually because I've done something funny. You're smiling for no reason. Stop being creepy."

His smile doesn't drop. "I told my cousin yesterday."

"Told your cousin what? That her taste in cars is crappy and how she expects two guys our size to fit in it, you'll never know?"

"No. About us."

Oh. Okay, I was not expecting that. "Umm, how did she take it?"

"She was surprised, but apparently she knows your brother and Christie, so she approves."

I take a sip of my drink while I try to process that.

"I'll be right back," he says and serves more customers.

He told his cousin. Technically, he *came out* even if he doesn't like that phrasing. That's … amazing and crazy and … shit, why does that feel kind of pressure-y?

Someone takes the barstool beside mine, and before I can turn to look at them, they're in my personal space.

"Uh, did I see the straight bartender kiss your cheek?"

I turn toward Ian with a smile. "You did."

Instead of looking, I don't know, *impressed*, he looks like I told him my dog died.

"Oh, honey, you didn't, did you?"

"Didn't what?"

"Sleep with the straight guy."

"How straight can he really be if I slept with him? Which I'm not saying happened, but—"

"Bad move." Ian glances over at Rainn, who's serving a customer at the other end of the bar. "Most 'straight' guys who say they're 'straight' and then suck dick are still 'straight' when it all comes down to it."

My heart sinks at the thought Rainn could possibly be like that, but I shrug it off and choose not to entertain the thought. Rainn might still be working things out, but he can do that in his own time. I'm not going to make him choose a label when he's not ready, and it's way too soon.

"He's allowed to identify however he identifies," I say.

"I agree, but at the expense of someone else's feelings? That's when the lines get blurred for me."

"Not everyone likes labels," I argue.

"Mm-hmm. He's probably totally cool with a straight label, though."

"He already came out to his cousin. He just kissed my cheek in public."

"In a queer-friendly space."

I want to argue he kissed me in the car outside my family's home yesterday morning too, but he'd probably argue, "Where people weren't likely to see you."

Ian's eyes soften in sympathy. "Just … watch for the warning signs."

"What warning signs?"

Ian holds up a finger. "Not defining what you're actually doing," he says. *Guilty.*

Another finger goes up. "Calling it an experiment."

I want to say, *Ha! He doesn't call it that,* but Ian keeps going.

Third finger. "He'll let you suck his dick and won't try to reciprocate."

Boom. Rainn has already reciprocated.

"Won't take you out in public or show affection in front of your friends."

He held my hand in front of my family, so I think I'm good there.

One out of four warning signs is not … horrible. Right?

"When he 'came out' to his cousin, did he actually say he's *bisexual*?" Ian asks.

I don't know. "Yes."

"Are you sure?"

I throw my arms up. "What's the difference?"

"There's a big difference between admitting you belong to this community and saying you're dipping your toes in just to get your rocks off."

I grit my teeth. "Rainn's not like that."

"Like what?" Rainn's voice makes me jump.

He stands in front of us, and I wonder how much he heard.

"Nothing," Ian and I say at the same time.

Rainn frowns.

Umm … how do I word this? "Ian here is reading way too much into the kiss on the cheek you gave me."

"Ah." Rainn stares at my face as if trying to read me.

I'm not sure what he sees, but it must not be good. I don't want him to think I was complaining about what we have.

"Okay, then." Rainn rounds the bar, and Ian and I turn on our stools to greet him. He walks right up to me, plants his hands on my thighs, and spreads my legs so he can stand between them.

"What are you doing?" I manage to ask even though my heart is in my throat.

"Well, if a little peck on the cheek confused him, I figure I should make myself clearer." Rainn doesn't let me reply before he's touching his lips to mine in an aggressive kiss that makes my toes curl.

It's claiming and possessive, and I didn't know it until this minute, but I like that trait in a guy. That's good to know.

I kiss him back and groan, but that's the precise moment he steps away and glares at Ian.

"Get it now?"

Ian's mouth hangs open.

"Rainn, stop kissing the customers and get back to work," Tanner calls out.

When Rainn's and Tanner's eyes meet, they share a smile.

"Better get back to it," Rainn says, and then he steps away and begins clearing tables of empty glasses.

I glance at Ian with a smug expression. *See?*

Ian relents. "You might have a good one there, but my warning still stands. Be careful. Your first straight-guy heartbreak is the worst."

"Thanks for your warning, but I'll be fine."

It's not like I'm expecting to marry Rainn or anything. You don't marry the first guy who touches your dick. Even old-fashioned me knows that, but even knowing it probably won't make it hurt any less when this does end, though.

I'm already in deep with Rainn, and I think I was before he kissed me.

Now …

Stop it. I'm overthinking everything again and getting ahead of myself because it's so easy to do when it comes to Rainn. I need to learn how to live in the now and enjoy this for what it is. *Whatever* it is.

Rainn catches my eye and stares at me with an expression that warms my gut and makes me believe everything will be okay.

That's all I need.

RAINN

Tanner eyes me all shift after my little public display of affection. Admittedly, it might have been a tad bit caveman-y, but I pretend Tanner's not eye-stalking me and avoid looking in his direction.

And, as I expect, as soon as there's a lull in customers, he's by my side.

"When I said not to do the asshole straight-guy thing, I meant let him down gently. That might've been *too* gentle."

I laugh. "The good news is he's taking it really well?"

Tanner looks like he wants to say something but won't because it's not his place.

"I … I like him," I say quietly. "I'm still figuring out what that means, but I have to say, it's been fun trying to work it out."

"Fair enough." Tanner points at me. "But no fucking in my bar."

"Wouldn't dream of it." Though, it's a nice fantasy. I could totally bend Whit over this bar and fuck him until he couldn't walk.

Shit, okay, not going to think about that. My dick likes the idea too much.

Whit continues to talk to Ian for a little while, but Ian eventually goes back to his friends, leaving Whit on his own.

Guilt eats at me. Not about kissing him in front of Ian but making Whit sit there while I work.

I approach him. "You can go and talk to people, you know. You don't have to sit here for me."

"I like it here. I like watching people. And I like it when you get a quick second to come check on me."

I give him a new drink. "If you're sure?"

Whit nods.

"You gonna come back to my place tonight?"

"I can, but I can't stay overnight. I need to get home for morning chores, and the drive the other morning almost killed me. Not to mention how much shit my family gave me for the walk of shame."

"We'll have to work out some sort of schedule. Maybe you can stay over on nights I have off. I'll make sure you get plenty of sleep." I smirk and hold up three fingers. "Scout's honor."

"I don't believe you."

"Fine. I'll make sure you get plenty of *rest* ..." I lower my voice and mutter, "In between rounds."

Whit smiles. "I'll take it." The heat in his gaze makes my cock respond in the same way it did imagining fucking him right here in the bar.

My shift needs to hurry up and be over.

The minute it is, it's a rush to get back to my apartment. Whit could be hit with a speeding ticket with how fast he pulls his truck onto my street.

It's his turn to park crooked, and like the other night, I don't care.

Neither does he.

We're all intertwined limbs, crashing mouths, probing tongues, and wandering hands as we enter the apartment and strip each other down.

In the blink of an eye, we're naked, and Whit's pinning me beneath him on the couch.

He's right about it being lumpy and uncomfortable, but with

Whit on top of me, it's the furthest thing from my mind. He grinds against me. Miles of skin on those lean muscles. Until Whit, I never realized how sexy a masculine body could be. There's still so much to explore of him, and I'm getting started right now.

I taste faint sweat and aftershave as I kiss Whit's neck. He moves on top of me, and the old futon creaks.

I worry for three seconds that we're going to break the frame, but then he shudders on top of me, and I don't care to stop him. I'm not *that* worried. Other than not being able to afford to replace it.

Eh. Don't care. My couch can be the futon without the frame.

I've never been so turned on by grinding against someone. I trail a hand down his back and grip his ass. His cock leaves a wet trail on my burning skin.

I run hot but shiver with want.

My hand inches closer to Whit's ass crack, and I don't really know what I'm doing until my middle finger is pressing against his hole.

He stills on top of me and lifts up to look into my eyes. "What … I mean … Is this—"

"I'm still firm on holding off, but I know you want more. I was thinking …" I tease his rim.

"Yes. I am so ready for that."

"Have you ever, you know …"

"Yeah. My ass is well acquainted with my fingers."

"Good to know." And hot to think about. Holy fuck, the thought of Whit fingering himself is probably even more arousing than the idea of me doing it to him.

Whit's eager for it, working against my fingertip, but then he pauses. "Wait." He sits up and takes my arm, bringing my fingers to his mouth.

He opens those fuckable lips and sucks two of my fingers right down so they're covered in spit.

I want to tell him I bought lube after the last time we hooked up, but I don't. He looks too hot with my fingers in his mouth while he's straddling my lap and slowly moving against me. The other reason I don't want to point out the lube situation is I don't want to give Whit false hope that I'm ready for more just yet.

I want to explore. I want more fun. I'm loving what we're doing, and I don't want that to change or to add pressure to what's already a heightened situation.

Whit's eyes close, and he looks desperate for it. I remove my fingers from his mouth and reach around him, cupping his head with one hand and pulling him back down on top of me with the other.

Our bodies move as one, our mouths collide, our breathing syncs, and our moans respond to each other as if this is our only form of communication now.

With Whit on top of me, I tease his hole but don't push inside right away. I let his hips get me there and leave him in complete control. He moves his hips, maneuvering to take my finger inside him to the first knuckle.

Whit's mouth breaks from mine, and a shuddery breath leaves his lips. "More."

He sits up again, and I add a second finger. His strong hands land on my chest as he rides my fingers.

This is the part I love. I love watching him lose his composure. I love seeing him let go.

With my other hand, I reach between us and stroke our cocks together.

"Oh, fuck." His grip on my chest tightens.

He moves with abandon now, as if he has no control over his body.

He rides me hard, and I grip us tight. His cock glides in and out of my fist, dragging along my own dick. It feels so good, but the sight of Whit, his eyes shut, a cute concentration line above his brow, that's the thing that gets me teetering on the edge.

I jerk us faster until my muscles ache and my body can't take anymore.

My cock erupts between us, cum spurting out in streams and covering my abs and groin.

"Rainn." Whit's voice is strained, and he follows me over the edge, coming on a hoarse cry.

He collapses on top of me.

I run my hand down his back. "We definitely need to work out a schedule so we can do this again. And again and again and again."

He nods against me. "When my season's over, I can come to the bar and stay on Saturday nights. On Sundays we can go do stuff. Like all the festivals and shit coming up."

"Festivals?"

Whit lifts his head. "Yeah, you know all the small-town events all over Vermont, like Cheese Wheel Race Day. It's treated like an Olympic sport."

"Oh. Uh, yeah, well, umm …"

"Not your thing, I'm guessing?"

"Not really. You know what my idea of a perfect Sunday morning is?"

"What?"

I lean up and kiss his cheek. "Waking up next to you. Getting coffee. Hanging out. I'm a pretty easy guy to please."

Whit doesn't seem to like that answer. "What about on your nights off? If I drive into town, will you at least take me to dinner?" His voice takes on an edgier tone I've never heard from him.

"Definitely dinner. As long as there's no singing, dancing, or … cheese wheel races, I'm all for it."

Whit stares at me as if I gave him the wrong answer again.

"What's wrong?" I ask. "Did you want me to say no? Is it too late to change my answer?"

"It's not that. For a second … I thought, maybe …" Whit climbs off me, and we shift around so we're both sitting up.

"Thought what?" Are we about to have a serious conversation completely naked and covered in cum?

"Just … something Ian said back at the bar, but never mind."

"You can tell me."

"He said a straight-guy warning sign is that you'd refuse to go out in public with me, so—"

"So when I said no to the cheese wheel thing, you assumed it was because I don't want to be seen with you or look like your date." I reach for his hand. "It's not that at all, I promise. How about this. On Tuesday, you come to my place after classes, and I'll take you to dinner. I'll hold your hand and everything. I'll walk down the street telling random strangers, 'This is my date.'"

Whit laughs. "You don't have to go that far, but are you sure you're comfortable with that?"

"I was fine with it at your game. And in front of your parents. I literally just kissed you in a bar in front of everyone I work with."

"Mm. True. Ignore me." He lowers his head.

"It's okay to have insecurities because this is new, and we're still feeling our way, but you can ask me about anything and call me out if you think I need it, okay?"

"Okay."

I'm not entirely sure I believe him, but he makes me want to do better.

I want to make him happy.

Sundays quickly become my new favorite days. Since I've started working at the bar full-time, I've gotten more of a set work schedule, so I only fill in at the bookstore if someone's sick or is on vacation.

As soon as Whit's hockey season ends, and he doesn't have weekday practices anymore, we easily fall into a routine where he stays over on a Tuesday or Wednesday. He usually leaves in the morning before I'm lucid, and I'll sleep through him sneaking out before the sun has even begun to think of rising.

But on Sundays, I get to wake up to Whit's mouth on my skin or his lower half moving against mine. Or both. Like right now.

Whit kisses along my collarbone while his hard-on drags along the outside of my thigh.

I'm mostly still asleep, in that semiconscious state where I don't know if I want to wake up all the way or not.

"What time is it?" I complain. "Your farm-boy body clock is dumb and—"

His hand dips into my boxer briefs and wraps around my dick.

"Awesome. Your body clock is awesome."

Whit chuckles against my neck and then maneuvers himself on top of me. His hard cock drags along mine.

"Good morning," he rumbles.

"Mm, I'll say."

We're all lazy kisses and slow, languid movements until we can't take it anymore and scramble to pull our underwear down enough for us to grind against one another in a rush to get off.

When we're a heap of exhausted muscles and both covered in cum, I rasp, "Sunday mornings with you are the best. They're my own version of going to church."

"You do call out God's name a lot, so there's that."

"But ..." I roll us over so I'm on top. "The Maple Festival is on this weekend, and I was thinking we could drive up to St. Albans. They have a pancake breakfast and sugarhouse tours. There's even a parade."

Whit stares at me as if he's waiting for a punchline. "That sounds exactly like the type of small-town shit you said you wouldn't like."

"But I know you'd like it. And there's no cheese wheel races."

He lets out a deep laugh.

"We can drive up there and be back before my shift tonight."

The sides of Whit's breathtaking eyes crinkle as he breaks out into a dimply smile. "You'd endure that for me?"

"*Only* for you."

I've been looking online to see what kind of events area towns are hosting with it getting closer to summer, and this was the first one that didn't make me want to fake my own death to get out of.

I'm willing to compromise and do things Whit wants to do, but I do have some limits.

Like anything cheese related.

Whit kisses me, and okay, I'd probably even do the cheese thing if he asked me to. I'd do *anything* for him. I just won't let him in on that secret yet.

We shower, but it probably would've been quicker if we did it separately.

We're all exploring hands and needy cocks, only proving to me that I will probably never get enough of exploring his body.

When we do finally get out, it's because the water starts to run cold, not because we're done with each other.

We manage to dress quickly and get on the road once we're not touching and groping.

Since Whit started staying over more, we've gone to dinner a couple of times at the same restaurant we had our first ... friend date.

While eating there, we haven't shied away from affection like I promised. I haven't felt the need to. It's not a hardship showing Whit affection. Not when it makes him smile at me the way he does when he's truly happy about something.

Arriving at the Maple Festival, though, it's different because it's somewhere new and this definitely feels like a couply thing to do.

For all intents and purposes, we are a couple. I may not have figured out where my sexuality lies among all this, but it's pretty clear I have strong feelings for Whit.

I like making him happy.

I really like making him come.

I want Whit to be my boyfriend.

I pull him around to everything the festival has to offer, holding his hand, and it's both somehow intoxicating and scary. Because what if I mess this up? It hasn't happened yet, but I've been waiting for the freak-out or the air to become stifling between us.

After we stuff our faces with pancakes and waffles, we walk the festival grounds. There's a tent and a mainstage with music, and there's a carnival that's mainly for kids, but unsurprisingly, Whit wants to play.

He is basically a big child, so …

He wins me a small stuffed toy on a shooting game, and I promise to cherish it forever before promptly giving it to a child who's crying because they didn't win.

Whit doesn't care. In fact, I think it makes him like me more. As we walk to the next thing to do, he leans in. "You do have a heart."

"Of course I have a heart. I'm a regular optimistic charity giver who's not selfish at all."

Whit grins. "That's truer than you want people to believe."

No, I still know I'm a selfish bastard. "Kids are my kryptonite."

"Oh, good. I shall use my nephew as leverage to get what I want from you."

I pause and turn to him. "Nephew?"

Whit's face falls. "Oh, shit. I wasn't supposed to tell anyone yet. Not until the wedding."

Finally—*finally*—he mentions the wedding. I've been waiting for it.

"Wedding?" I play dumb.

"Uh, yeah. Campbell's wedding is in a week, and Christie's pregnant, but, like, no one knows except me and our parents, and … Can you not tell anyone? Like your cousin or—"

"I won't tell Sommer on one condition."

"Anything."

"Are you going to ask me to your brother's wedding?"

He stalls. "You want to go to my brother's wedding? I figured

… I dunno. It's a family event, and you'd be my date, and that's a big step. It's huge. That's like—"

"Like what? Like we're boyfriends?" I step closer to him. "I don't know if you've noticed, but do you really think I'd come to a place like this with someone who wasn't my boyfriend?"

"I … uh … I … umm no?"

"Exactly. By the way, my cousin told me about the wedding weeks ago." I mockingly tsk him. "Playing hard to get is not a good look on you."

"But it worked, didn't it?" he calls after me as I walk off.

I guess it did.

Whit catches up and cuts me off. "You really want to come to the wedding as my date? I figured meeting every single person important in my life might be a bit much too soon. We haven't even had sex yet."

"Uh, we've had plenty of sex."

"Not, like, you know …" Whit gestures as if to say *fill in the blank.*

"I have a question for you. Say we stop seeing each other."

Whit's mouth drops open, but I hold up my hand.

"Hypothetically, we end. Then someday in the future, I happen to meet another guy I like. I don't see it happening, but then again, I never saw you coming, either. That's not my point. Do you really think, after everything we've done in bed together, I could say to him, 'Nope. I've never had sex with another man'?"

Whit thinks about that longer than I thought he'd need. "I guess not."

"I like what we've been doing, and I want to keep going. And I want to go to your brother's wedding."

"You'll get a lot of invasive and personal questions. You're my first boyfriend."

"What a coincidence. You're my first boyfriend too." I nudge him. "Besides, I've already met your parents and your brother. Who else would there be?"

"Farmhands who have worked for Dad for years and are practically uncles, their wives, their kids who are like honorary cousins. We may not have a lot of extended family, but our farm and everyone who works on it is our found family."

Okay, that's a little more daunting, but nothing I can't handle. I don't think.

"I'm not in the wedding party, but I'm helping out a lot, so it's not like I could be by your side the whole time."

"My cousin is going, so I won't be alone. Wait …" This is actually taking some *convincing*. My eyes narrow. "If you don't want me there as your date, you're allowed to say that."

Big hands grip my biceps. "No, no. I do. I …" Whit blows out a loud breath. "I'm worried it will scare you off, and the reason I haven't asked is because I didn't want you to feel like this is turning into more than we've discussed—"

"You're right. We should have had this conversation already, but like you, I'm … hesitant."

"About us?" Whit's voice is so small. It makes me want to hold him and reassure him.

"About saying we're more than what we are or defining it wrong or labeling us and then figuring out it's too soon. I don't want things to change, but this feels important to say."

The words *I'm falling for you* try to come out of my mouth but get stuck.

"I want you to be my date to my brother's wedding," Whit says.

"Then I will be there. Lucky I asked Tanner for the night off two weeks ago, huh?"

Whit shoves me. "Were you going to ever tell me?"

"Nope. I was waiting for you to bring it up." I step around him and head for the maple cotton-candy stand.

Whit's stare burns into me as I order two and give him one.

He leans in and kisses me, soft and sweet. "Thank you."

"It's just cotton candy."

He shakes his head. "Not for that."

"Definitely no need to thank me for doing something I should have had the guts to do after the second night we hooked up. I think I knew it back then, but it's taken this long for me to really get comfortable with saying it aloud, so thank you for being patient with me."

Whit takes my hand in his while we walk and eat. "A wise man once told me that everything happens on our own time. If you put too much pressure on yourself, you might end up a blubbering idiot in a bar full of people."

"Okay, I don't remember the blubbering idiot part."

"Oh, I added that in."

"Of course you did."

We continue walking around the festival while I hold my breath for something to go wrong. As if waiting for the universe to smite me for even thinking I could possibly have a relationship with someone and have a sort of plan in place for a future. I don't know what that future holds or what it looks like, but I can't imagine it without Whit.

Maybe if I don't make solid plans with him, it won't fall to shit.

He makes me happier than I've been in a really long time, and I don't want that to change.

"So, now that we're officially together and stuff, can you please finally fuck me?" Whit's words are so casual, I can't help laughing.

I'm thankful he brought it up because it's something I've been thinking more and more about too. I'm still nervous about making it good for him and making his first time memorable, but there's only one loud resounding answer to that question.

"The next time you're able to stay over and not leave me before the sun is up, it'll happen."

I want to hold him after our first time. I want to wake up to him the next day. I want to take *care* of him.

Whit leans in and kisses my cheek with his sticky, sugary lips. "I'm going to hold you to that."

"Good." Because I'm ready.

WHIT

"Nothing is ready," Campbell says. "The hay bales aren't in place, and the aisle isn't set up." He paces in front of me in the great room of our farmhouse, his shirt messily untucked from his penguin suit.

"Gordo's fixing it." I place my hands on my brother's shoulders. "It will be okay. You're getting married today."

I wish I could say my sole focus is on my brother, but it's not.

Tonight's the night.

Rainn said the next time we can spend the night together and not have to get up stupid-early the next morning is when we'll have sex.

I'm nervous as fuck but so ready for it. So, so, so ready.

"You finish getting dressed," I say to my stressed-out brother. "I'll go find Gordo and help him."

Campbell nods. "Okay."

We're behind schedule. The plan was to set up the barn yesterday, but a drop in temperature and threatening snow had us working past nightfall on the farm yesterday to prepare for the snowstorm that never came. Our past selves decided this morning would be the best time to set up all the wedding shit. Our past selves are assholes.

I find Gordo and Dad in a nightmare world of tulle and fairy lights, and I have no idea where to start or how to help them.

"Shouldn't you be good at this stuff?" Gordo asks.

"*Queer Eye* will not be choosing me to help make over anything or anyone anytime soon," I quip back. I turn to Dad. "We need Mom."

Speak of the devil. "You sure do." Mom enters and promptly gets into action. "Okay. Gordo, you climb up and wrap the lights around the rafters. Leighton, you organize the hay bales in something that resembles rows. You"—she turns to Dad—" you're on aisle duty. I'll cover this place in so many flowers it will look like it vomited petals here."

"See. We just needed someone to herd us," I say.

Mom scoffs. "Honestly, it's like herding cats."

With a system in place, we get it done, and as we're finishing up, two figures appear in the entryway.

Damn, Rainn in a suit. Holy fuck, he's the hottest person I've ever seen. His dark hair is slicked back, his bright blue eyes are shining, and he shaved. I don't think I've ever seen his skin as smooth as it is right now.

Beside him is a woman with a pretty face and black hair styled in an updo.

"Is that your boyfriend?" Gordo taunts. "Did he bring a date?"

I shove him. "It's his cousin."

"Sommer is your boyfriend's cousin?" he asks.

I guess with Sommer knowing Christie, they all must have hung out at some point.

We agreed for Rainn and Sommer to come a little earlier than the rest of the guests so I could meet the only family he has in Vermont. I'm probably more nervous about that than what I have planned for later tonight.

"Do you know if she's single?" Gordo asks.

I point at him as I walk away. "Hands off."

Rainn's cousin lets out a little squeak when I approach and lean in to kiss his cheek. I don't know what that's about.

"Whit, this is Sommer."

"I can't believe you're real," Sommer says.

"I, uh … I think I'm real."

Her arms come around me. "Yep. Real." She turns to Rainn. "And muscly. Good job."

"I can't take you anywhere." He pulls her to his side.

I step past them. "Come to the house. We're finished here."

"Are we too early?" Rainn asks.

"No, we're behind schedule. The weather is screwing up their big wedding plans."

"It looks amazing, though," Sommer says.

"I'll take your word for it." I lead them to the house where my brother looks more respectable than before but is still struggling with his bow tie. He's practically worn a path in the floorboards from all his pacing back and forth.

"Ooh, someone's nervous," Sommer sings.

Campbell relaxes into a totally fake smile. "Hi, Sommer." He holds his arms open to hug her, and as he pulls her close, he says, "You're not allowed to tell Christie I'm freaking out."

She purses her lips. "Well, that depends. Why are you freaking out?"

"I want today to be perfect for her."

"Aww."

"Making sure you're at the other end of the aisle when she turns up will make it perfect," Rainn says.

I pull back. "That … that might be the most romantic thing you've ever said."

"I'm setting a low bar of expectations, and I'm okay with that," Rainn says.

"I have to go shower and get ready." I point at Rainn and Sommer. "You two, it's your job to keep Campbell calm."

Rainn mock salutes me.

I get to the stairs when I hear Sommer say, "Your boyfriend is adorable."

"Say it louder. I don't think he heard you," Rainn mutters.

"Oh, I heard it!" I call out.

I shower fast, put on one of my post-game suits, and run back downstairs. My parents have joined them, and Gordo's actively hitting on Sommer, but my eye catches on Rainn and Campbell in the corner, smiling and laughing.

I guess Rainn's taking his duty seriously, then.

He looks relaxed around my family, and even though a small part of me is still expecting him to change his mind or run away, there's a bigger part of me that can't help picturing him in my life on a more permanent basis.

Rainn glances up at me, and I do a spin even though he's seen me in a suit countless times.

"It's not a penguin suit, but it'll do."

"Still want to be a penguin, huh?"

"Penguins are cool." I take my phone and check the time. "We'll be back in time for the ceremony, but I need to steal Rainn for a second." I grab Rainn's hand and lead him outside before my brother can protest me disappearing this close to the vows.

"Where are we going?"

"It's a surprise."

"I'm not like you. I don't like surprises."

I lead him to my truck. "Well, technically, this isn't really a surprise for you. It's just something I'm proud of."

"It's your dick, isn't it?"

"How'd you know? But it's not only my dick. Normally, I'd take the ATVs, but mud is not our friend today, and Campbell will kill me if we come back dirty."

"Now you're talking about cum, right?"

I snort. "I wish."

We drive down the road to the other entrance of the property and past the empty meadows that are soon going to be crops, and I explain to Rainn the plans for the expansion, but I'm not sure how much of it he's retaining.

"We need more than dairy to survive in the long run," I explain. "But this isn't what I wanted to show you. Eventually, we're going to add another entrance from the road that leads back here, but for now this is the only access." I pull up alongside the foundation and half-constructed walls of my soon-to-be house.

"What is this?" Rainn asks as we get out of the car.

"This …" I hold out my arms. "Is my future home."

The house faces the pond, and I wish I could've brought Rainn here at sunset for him to see the colors painted across the sky.

Rainn is quietly contemplative.

"Campbell and Christie's place is up a bit farther, but after Mom and Dad are gone, they'll probably take over the farmhouse."

"Because he's older?"

"Nah, because they'll fill it with a billion children. I'll probably be the weird uncle who lives in a cabin all alone." Or with someone special, but I don't want to push that idea onto Rainn even though imagining it makes me want it.

I grab his hand and take him to where my porch will be. "I'm going to drink my morning coffee here." *After I wake you up after I finish morning chores.* "Drink my beer and watch the sunset." *With you on the seat next to me.*

There I go getting ahead of myself and fantasizing about things that I really shouldn't.

"Sounds perfect," Rainn says.

"The plans are for two bedrooms, though I don't know what I'll do with the second one yet. Home gym maybe."

"You don't want kids?" Rainn asks.

"I dunno. I always thought that would be left up to my brother. I love the idea of being able to give them back when they're whiny or upset."

"That is a very good point. I don't get to see my nephews much, but when I do, I love it when I can be all 'Someone has a dirty diaper, and that's not my job.'"

"*Exactly.*"

"This is an amazing place, Whit."

"I like it." I step up behind him and wrap my arms around his waist. "And when it's done, you can spend your nights off here. You can sleep in while I go to work. I can come home for a nooner."

Rainn laughs. "Now who's the romantic one?"

"I can see us here," I whisper and hold my breath to wait for the protest or for him to stiffen.

He doesn't, though. Surprising me, he turns in my arms and kisses me. It could be in agreement or a distraction, but I really don't care.

This is me, putting myself out there, but not with anything too crazy. I'm talking about doing what we do now, just at my place instead of his.

I don't need to ask questions that don't need immediate answers, but I want him to know I am *thinking* about a future.

"We should get back," he says. "Before Campbell kills me for making his brother miss his wedding."

"That would be bad. I kinda like you, and it would suck if you died before you could fuck me."

Rainn scowls. "And you'd miss me."

"Oh, yeah, that too."

He hip-checks me as we walk back to the truck. When we climb in, he reaches over and squeezes my leg but doesn't say anything.

With one last look out at the place, it really hits me. "My brother and I have been talking about doing this since we were kids—building houses on the property and expanding the farm. It's surreal that it's finally happening." I lock eyes with him, and his expression holds some sort of awe. "What's that look for?"

Rainn averts his gaze and stares out the windshield. He looks like he wants to say something but either can't or doesn't know if he should. "I'm ... jealous."

"Of the house?"

He huffs. "No. Of your passion. I like my job, I like my life, but I don't have that passion anymore."

I want to tell him he still has it, he's just mad at it, but he needs to get there on his own. "You'll find it. You've been discovering a lot of new things about yourself lately."

"True."

By the time we get back to the farmhouse, we have to take a parking spot on the road because the other guests have poured in.

"Will you sit with me for the ceremony?"

"Of course. We'll have to find Sommer, though. I told her I wouldn't leave her side today. Oops."

"Are you ready to meet my extended family?"

"Nope, but I'll do it for you."

That makes me all warm and fuzzy inside. "I promise they won't interrogate you. Much."

"Oh, fun. I might use Sommer as a shield."

"I can't wait to see *that*."

We make our way toward the barn where my mother gives us a stern look.

I point at Rainn. "His fault."

Rainn's mouth falls open, but my mom doesn't believe me anyway and rolls her eyes.

Then she squeezes Rainn's arm and says, "Good to see you again, Rainn."

"You too," he murmurs.

She hurries off to take care of some last-minute detail, and I swear Rainn blushes, but that can't be right. "Are you blushing?"

"Shut up. I want your mom to like me."

"Aww, that's so cute."

"I will hurt you," he growls.

It only makes me laugh.

He pushes me toward Sommer, who's sitting near the back, and we bring her with us to take the spots saved for us in the front row.

My brother glares at me, probably for disappearing on him, but he shakes it off when Gordo slaps his back and mutters something to him.

When we stand for Christie's entrance, Rainn slips his hand in mine. I'm not even sure the move was intentional, but I hold on tight because I will take any excuse to touch him.

Christie looks beautiful in a gown that hides her tiny baby bump. Their reasons for moving up the date weren't sex-before-marriage concerns, but that she wanted to fit into the dress she'd already bought.

As we sit again and watch them exchange vows, it's hard not to think about my future. Not just with Rainn, but in general. Though, Rainn definitely plays a starring role in my thoughts. And I realize I've only known the guy a few months and that we've been dating even less than that, but nothing makes you think about relationship stuff more than attending a wedding.

I have no idea if I ever want to get married, but I do know I want what my brother has with Christie. They have that perfect kind of love people only dream of.

After the ceremony, I'm obligated to take part in family photos. Luckily, we get through them quickly, and, after making my escape, I find Rainn and Sommer by the open bar. They're talking to some of Campbell's high school friends, Nathan and Anton.

I approach and wrap my arm around Rainn's waist and pull him to my side. "Hey."

Rainn stiffens and turns to me with widened eyes, killing the conversation in the process.

I've done something wrong, but I don't know what. I take a hesitant step away from him, but he scrambles to wrap his arm around me and pull me close.

"Hey." He kisses me on the lips, but it's super quick.

"What did I miss?" I ask.

"What did *you* miss?" Nathan says. "What did we miss?" He eyes Rainn.

I'm confused. "You guys know each other?"

"College," Rainn says, and then it clicks.

Rainn is the same age as my brother, but Campbell never went to college, so it never occurred to me that they might have mutual friends. I carefully step away again, because being affectionate in front of my family is one thing. His friends are completely different.

Surprising me, Rainn turns to them. "Guys, this is my boyfriend, Whi—"

"I already know these losers," I say.

"We didn't know you had a boyfriend, little Leigh-Leigh," Anton teases. "Or that Rainn was gay. Especially because in college—"

"I swing both ways," Rainn says.

My knees almost give out. I was not expecting him to say that. Not here. Or anytime soon.

"Something I've only recently discovered." He pulls me to his side once again, and I let him. But he's stiffer than usual and not really present for the rest of the conversation.

Later, when I ask him to dance, he says no. He did tell me he doesn't dance, so maybe that's his reason. Sommer takes me out onto the makeshift dance floor instead. Eventually, Gordo cuts in, sweeping Sommer away with a grin. I glare at him, but apparently Sommer's more than okay with it.

I make my way back to Rainn and shrug. "Apparently, women like to dance with straight guys over gay ones. That doesn't seem right."

Rainn gives me a small smile.

"Are you okay?" I ask.

He leans forward and places his drink on the table. "I'm just thinking of when we're allowed to get out of here. I have promises to follow through on."

I promptly stand so I can get the toasts out of the way.

We don't need to stay for cake.

RAINN

Somehow, despite today being a good day, it's brought a million insecurities forward, and it's hard to comprehend.

If I was ever going to have doubts, I thought it would be about the elephant in the room I haven't really addressed yet. The big *queer* word. I didn't think I'd be freaking out over our future.

When he showed me his house and his future plans, he was his animated and lively self, and that's when the panic began. Because creating a future with him sounded … perfect.

I know how perfect plans end.

I desperately want this to go somewhere, but I don't feel good enough to deserve it. Not with Whit.

The drive home is quiet.

I don't think it has anything to do with what Whit and I are about to do but everything to do with what comes next.

What happens tomorrow and the next day and the next?

Can I really see myself driving out to Whitaker Farms every week to spend nights in Whit's cute little house he made for himself?

Then I'd come home, go to work at V and V, and return to my crappy, small apartment, and do it all again the following week.

It's not … me.

Then again, I don't even know who the fuck that is anymore anyway.

Whit's hand lands on my thigh. "You okay?"

I try to smile, but I'm not sure if I pull it off. "Little nervous."

Maybe I am just nervous about sex. It feels like *I'm* about to lose my virginity, and that ship sailed almost a decade ago.

"I make you nervous?"

"Making this good for you makes me nervous."

"You don't need to worry. I trust you."

I groan. "God, that makes it even worse."

Whit laughs. "No, it's a good thing. I'm comfortable with you. I won't hesitate to tell you if I don't like something."

I nod.

"Are you sure you're okay? You've been weird today. I thought maybe you were second-guessing."

"I'm not second-guessing you." *Just myself.*

Whit reaches for my hand. "Good, because I've been waiting for this forever."

"I think your expectations need to be taken down a bit. I'm terrible in bed, just so you know. I kinda stick it in and wiggle it around a little bit."

Whit bursts into laughter. "Sounds hot. And it still counts."

I huff. "My dick is a weird shape."

More laughter. "I've seen your dick countless times. I've had it in my mouth. It's a beautiful dick."

"Okay, now you're making things weird."

"I'm not making it weird. You're making it weird by trying to talk me out of it."

"All those months of not going through with it because you couldn't find the right guy and I called you picky … I told you to wait for the right person. I … I …" Shit, why can't I tell him I don't think I'm the right choice?

"You are the right person," he says as if he can read my mind. "You're my first actual boyfriend."

"But—"

"I wasn't being picky, Rainn." Whit pulls his truck into a space by my apartment.

I didn't even realize we were this close to home. I've been too spaced out.

Whit turns to me. "I could've taken any of those guys home. The reason I didn't is because the person I wanted was *you*."

"Me …"

"And by some miracle, the universe let me have you." He unclicks his seat belt and leans across the console to kiss me.

The touch of his lips on mine, that familiar feeling I get when he's near me, it's all-consuming and makes all those niggly little doubts melt away.

When he pulls back, I can't help smirking.

"Are you saying the universe has control over my dick?"

"If Cupid is real, he must be gay."

"Must be." I lean in and lower my voice. "Let's go inside."

"That's what you'll be saying later."

I shove him. "You're making it weird again."

When we enter the apartment, we hover by the entryway, both of us seemingly too nervous to get this started.

"Drinks," I say. "We should start with drinks."

I go to the kitchen and find the bottle of whiskey.

"I'm having déjà vu," he says as soon as I pour him a glass.

He tosses his back immediately, and I do the same.

As soon as he's swallowed it down, I wrap my arm around his back and pull him close. "Come here."

When he kisses me, he tastes like whiskey and smells like pine aftershave. It leaves a lingering scent even as he pulls away and leads me to my bedroom.

No more words are spoken.

His hands are soft and tender as they roam my chest and start undoing the buttons in my shirt. Mine do the same to his.

I don't take my eyes off him while we continue to undress each other.

I want to make him feel good. I want to be inside him and claim him.

When we shed the rest of our clothes, I push him toward the bed.

Whit lies on his back, his long, muscular body laid out bare for me. The look of hunger in his eyes doesn't cover the nervous way he bites his lip.

"We're going to take this slow," I say.

I have supplies stashed in my bedside table, but I get the feeling if I bring them out, Whit might rush this.

I know he wants it, but we've been holding out on doing this for so long, that I worry he's been building it up too much. It's why I'm going to take my time with him. He deserves that much respect.

I crawl between his legs and lay myself on top of his hard body. Our cocks line up, and Whit rolls his hips beneath me while reaching to cup my cheek.

This is more intimate than anything I've experienced before.

Everything with him is heightened.

My sense of touch.

The concept of need.

It's all so powerful it's hard to comprehend.

Like everything when I'm with Whit, in the moment, nothing else matters. I move against him, and the real world fades away. Labels, families, and future plans dissipate into an atmosphere of unimportance.

The way Whit writhes beneath me and throws his head back while I grip us and move my hand over the heads of our dicks … I could do this all night.

Then Whit moans, and I realize all night is an impossibility. I'm already too close to the edge.

"Rainn," Whit croaks, letting me know he might be too close too.

His chest heaves, and his skin flushes. It's almost a shame to drag this out when he's giving me everything that I crave from him. There's nothing more sensual or sexy than seeing Whit lose control.

Knowing Whit's refractory period, I could get him off now and again later, but I don't want to diminish his orgasm when I'm inside him. I want this to be the best experience he can possibly have for his first time.

With willpower I had no idea I possess, I release our cocks from my strong grip to help us both breathe easier.

I lean down and explore his wide chest with my lips and tongue.

Whit squirms, and his hips lift.

"Getting impatient?"

Whit's eyes meet mine. "I need you."

And it happens as easy as that. Three simple words. The clarification. The epiphany. It's a realization I never asked for, but it hits me with certainty.

I'm falling in love with Leighton Whitaker.

WHIT

The way this man touches me. The way he anticipates what I need.

Rainn moves down my body, and I'm so ready for more, but something makes him pause.

He lifts his head, locking eyes with me.

"Rainn?" I rasp.

Dark hair falls into his eyes. "Uh … umm. Supplies. I need supplies."

I don't know what has changed in the last thirty seconds, but after he reaches for the lube in his bedside drawer, he comes back like a man on a mission. A lubed finger pushes against my hole, and I shiver. He eases down until his head is between my legs, and his mouth is on my cock.

Sex is amazing.

I bear down on Rainn's fingers and relax enough to let them in. The suction of his mouth distracts me from the stretching sting of his fingers moving in and out of me.

I'm impatient, I want more, but as he works his way in farther and adds a third finger, the pain reminds me of why it's important to go slow.

Not until I'm a trembling mess of want and my ass is craving more do I let it out.

"Rainn," I whine.

He doesn't stop.

Every press of my prostate as he stretches me makes my feet tingle and my whole body flush. He's so careful and attentive, and I knew it wasn't a mistake waiting and doing this with him.

When he looks at me like I'm the only thing in this world that matters, an emotion I can't even describe takes over. It's something I've never experienced before. It's warm and all-encompassing.

"I'm ready," I say.

He pulls off my cock. "I want to be sure."

I pant. "I am sure. I … Fuck! I need it."

Rainn finally pulls his fingers free, and I gasp for breath. I want him to fill me up. This is the most intense experience of my life, and we're nowhere near done.

Rainn rolls a condom down his hard cock, and even though my hole is contracting, anticipating him being inside me, I just hope it doesn't hurt.

I said I was ready, but the sight of his swollen cockhead makes me worry if he's even going to be able to fit the tip in.

Deep breaths, Whit.

You had a billion fingers up there a moment ago.

"Look at me," Rainn says softly. "Look at my face."

My gaze flits upward.

"We're still going slow. I won't hurt you."

I trust him completely.

"Do you want to roll over? It will probably be easier—"

"No. I want to see you."

Rainn nods. "Tell me if you need a break."

"I will."

"Oh, and, Whit?" He smiles. "Breathe. Sex is supposed to be fun. Erotic asphyxiation is only sexy if it's intentional."

My laughter helps me relax. Then the head of his cock pushes past my tight ring, and it's not funny anymore. I do as Rainn says and breathe through it.

There's more stretching pain but not any worse than I was getting with his fingers, and he moves so slow, so cautiously. I fuse my eyes shut.

Rainn pauses. "So, a gay virgin walks into a bar and asks the straight bartender to be his wingman."

My eyes fly open. "Are you seriously making a joke about this right now?"

Rainn's chuckle settles him more deeply inside me. "Yup. Because you need a distraction."

"A distraction is good," I agree.

"I'm still working on the punchline, though. Our story is a great setup for a joke …"

"Dicks," I say. "The punchline has to have something about dicks."

Rainn chuckles. "Okay. Anything for you."

"I … umm … I think you can move again now."

This time, when he moves, it's not as hard to take.

I focus on his facial features, the way his eyes flutter shut as he goes deeper.

When he pushes against my prostate, a spark ignites.

"Do that again," I say.

Rainn's short and shallow thrusts send tingles shooting down to my feet and warmth to my gut. He hovers above me, staring into my eyes like he's trying to assess my reactions. I love seeing the restraint in his strained face, the fight between controlling himself and making sure I'm okay.

"Let go," I say. "I can take it."

Rainn lets out a ragged breath. "You feel too good. God, I …" Another thrust, another loud breath.

This is what I've been holding out for. It's what I've been anticipating since coming out, and without a doubt, I'm so glad I waited for Rainn.

His big cock moves in and out of my body languidly while he whispers my name like I'm some goddamn superhero.

We're both sweaty, we're both breathing heavy, and we're a heaving pile of intertwined limbs and connected bodies.

I lift my head, glancing down at the small gap between us, and watch as he repeatedly drives into me over and over again.

My cock is leaking like crazy, the sticky precum leaving a wet trail on my stomach.

"Rainn, I need to …" I try to reach between us, but all his thrusting is getting in the way.

"Let me." He sounds so strained, like he can't hold out much longer.

I want to get there with him, but I need that contact and fric—

Rainn's hand closes over my aching cock.

My ass contracts, and my hips thrust upward.

Rainn strokes me hard and fast, while his pace increases, and he lets out a warning moan. I've heard it a lot these last few weeks while I've been sucking his dick.

He's close to the edge, and I want to push him over it.

As if reading my mind, he stills inside me. He grunts as he lets go of his release, but his hand doesn't stop pumping. With him inside me while he's jerking me off, I get closer and closer with every stroke.

"I need you to come," Rainn says. "Come, Whit."

My whole body tenses, and cum shoots from my dick. Streams of it hit my abs and lower body, the wave of pleasure crashing over me more than once.

It's an intense but quiet moment as I realize it's over. The only sound left between us is heavy breathing. Once my dick stops erupting, Rainn slowly releases me and pulls out.

The sensation is *weird*—weirder than that first uncomfortable breach when he entered me. This is a sensation of loss and relief at the same time. My ass is thankful to be getting a break, but I also want to feel full again.

"Are you okay?" Rainn rumbles.

Am I okay? Fuck, I've never been better.

Large hands try to shake me awake, but I don't want to comply. I bury my head into the hard chest I'm pressed against.

"We need to go if we're going to make your family brunch."

"Post-wedding brunch. Who *does* that? I need more sleep," I complain.

"It's past nine. I think this is the latest you've ever slept." Rainn's hand absently strokes my hair.

"I guess a good dicking is what I needed to reset that body clock of mine you hate so much."

Rainn snorts. "Guess so. I'll keep that in my back pocket and whip it out whenever I want to sleep in."

"You get to sleep in when I'm not in your bed."

"True, but I never do. I often find myself reaching for you and wake when I don't find you."

My eyes finally fly open, and I look up at him. "Really?"

"Really."

I have to kiss him, and when I close the small gap and touch my mouth to his, his cock hardens against my thigh.

But in the next second, he pushes me off him.

"Wha?" I'm dazed and still not fully awake.

Rainn gets out of bed and starts dressing. "We're going to be late, and I don't think you want to explain to your family why."

"Can we skip it?"

"Shouldn't I be the one asking that? They're *your* family. I'm still waiting for the interrogation I know is coming. I'm thankful weddings are busy and they didn't get their chance last night."

I wave him off. "Nah, my family isn't like yours."

"Like mine?"

"Yeah, Sommer cornered me at one point and did the whole, 'Don't hurt Rainn. He's already lost enough in his life' thing."

"She didn't."

"Oh, she did. It was cute."

"I'm going to kill her."

"Don't. I saw her leaving with Gordo. That's punishment enough."

He pauses with his pants halfway up his thighs. "Gordo … the best man? Is he a decent guy?"

I laugh. "It's adorable how you two are protective of each other."

"She's practically my sister. I see her more than my actual sister."

"You should make time to go see your family in Rhode Island."

"It's hard with work and everything, but I should."

That means he won't. I've been around him long enough to know his dismissive tone. He used the same one when both Coach and I told him he should contact the hockey camp guy.

I slowly climb out of bed and reach above my head, stretching out all of my tired and aching muscles.

Rainn watches me, his eyes taking all of me in, but then he shakes his head. "Nope, nope, nope. We're going to be late." He turns and walks out of his bedroom but not before glancing at me over his shoulder. "Keep moving, Rainn," he mutters to himself.

I love the way he's obvious in the way he wants me now.

He's been hard to read from the start, but the more we're together, the more he's letting down his guard.

Whatever weirdness he had last night at the wedding is gone this morning, and I'm chalking it up to nerves about sex. It was subtle, but I know he was in his head about something.

He had nothing to worry about. Even though my ass is a little tender this morning, I wouldn't have changed the way it happened.

I know I'm lucky and not many people get to say the man of their dreams came through for them, but mine did. This is not how the straight guy and the gay friend story usually goes.

"I've already got my shoes on," Rainn sings from the other room.

I get my ass in gear and dress quickly so we can get on the road. Luckily, we thought to shower last night before falling asleep, or we'd be even later.

As Rainn predicted, we're the last ones to brunch, and Mom, Dad, Campbell, and Christie are already at the dining table when we walk into the farmhouse.

"Sorry, we're late," I say as I take a seat. "Rainn slept in."

"Lies," Rainn says.

"Fine. I slept in. For maybe the first time ever in my *entire life*." My dramatic tone is not lost on my mother.

She rolls her eyes. "Guilt trips don't work in this house. You know that."

"You work me so hard!" I exclaim, and my brother and father give me the same look they always do when I complain about how much work I do around here. It's the "you have it so easy" look.

"How was your first night in the new house?" I ask Campbell and Christie. I'm not using it as a diversion tactic. Nope, not at all.

Their house has been ready for a few weeks now, but they wanted to wait until their wedding day to move in.

"It's amazing," Christie says. "You'll find out soon enough when yours is finished."

Mom has her usual spread on the table that she cooks up for the farmhands, but they would've eaten an hour ago.

This brunch is just for us.

With the wedding craziness over, Mom and Dad have a better chance to ask Rainn some questions, and as Rainn and I pile our plates full of bacon, eggs, toast, and hash browns, they don't hold back. It's not an interrogation, but I realize they hit him right where it hurts first.

Mom smiles at him. "What do you do for work?"

Ouch. Sore spot right out of the gate.

"I currently work at Vino and Veritas in Burlington." Rainn plays it off breezily.

"Are you in graduate school?" Mom asks.

"Uh, no …"

"Oh, sorry. Just how you said currently, I thought you had plans."

I wince.

"I, uh, had a pretty bad hockey injury my senior year of college."

"Oh, you play hockey too?" Mom asks.

"Played," Rainn says.

Mom doesn't pick up on the hurt in his voice. "No wonder you get along with Leighton. What did you get your degree in?"

Oh, geez. I really should've spoken to my parents about safe topics to bring up around Rainn. Like books, or … Well, shit, that might be the *only* safe topic.

"Recovery was kind of long, so I didn't finish out the last semester. I did plan to go back eventually, but I haven't managed to get there yet."

I have to hand it to Rainn, he's being open about it at least. And he's not grunting or scowling. That's better than when I met him and brought up all the same questions.

"There should be no rush to go back, either," my dad says. "I tell my boys to be young while they can."

"And then he works us seven days a week," Campbell quips.

"You love it," I say to Campbell because he does. We both do.

"It's why we keep telling Leighton to take that Healy guy up on his Pittsburgh offer," Dad continues.

I freeze, and I sense Rainn doing the same thing next to me. I try to give my dad the clear message to stop talking by glaring at him, but he doesn't take the hint.

"It's not every day agentless hockey players who didn't enter the draft have teams interested in them."

I make a slashing motion at my throat, but Rainn sees it.

"Whit?" Rainn's tone is confused and, if I'm not mistaken, hurt.

"It's nothing."

"It's not nothing," Mom says. "We keep telling him the farm will always be here, and he can come back anytime. He should go and explore the world while he's still young."

The world. Sure. Because the AHL is known for being *international*. Canada doesn't count. I can get in the car and be in Canada in two hours. I don't need to be a pro hockey player to accomplish that.

"Like I told you guys already, I'm not interested." I shovel food in my mouth, hoping they'll drop it.

"Pittsburgh wants you?" Rainn asks.

"Wilkes-Barre/Scranton does, but I'm not going."

"AHL?" The excitement in Rainn's tone is hard to miss.

"At least go meet with the man," Dad says.

"I don't need to."

Rainn's hand lands on my arm. "You should. Do you understand how big an opportunity this is? If you get on a development team, that's a straight shot to the NHL."

"Thank you, Rainn," Mom says. "That's what we've been trying to tell him."

"It's not though. It's an ATO one-way contract. They wouldn't be able to call me up to the NHL."

"But you'd have their eyes on you. You could still get an NHL contract out of it."

"I also know how many other people would kill for the opportunity to even be considered, but I'm not one of them. I love hockey, you all know I do, but it's not my everything. It's not even in my world anymore, and I'm okay with that because my future has been mapped out from when Campbell and I were kids, and I want *that* future."

"But ..." Rainn's brow furrows. "Futures change. I'm the prime example of that."

"Yeah, but you had no choice."

"Which makes this even worse. You do have the choice, and you're giving it up willingly?"

I turn to him. "We'll talk about this later. This brunch is supposed to be about my brother and his wife."

"Aww, that's the first time anyone's called you my wife." Campbell turns to Christie, and they give each other a sickeningly sweet smile.

Rainn grits his teeth but relents. He stares at his food while his fork moves around the scrambled eggs on his plate.

He won't understand this. It's why I never brought it up with him. It's why the night Healy approached me, I played it off in front of Rainn.

To him, an offer like this would give him everything back that he lost. I don't feel like hockey was mine to begin with.

I keep stealing glances at him throughout the meal, but he keeps his head down and he has that scowl that is so inherently *Rainn* on his face.

We have a serious talk coming, but the thing that gets me the most is that he didn't even blink at telling me to leave.

It makes me wonder what would happen if he had an offer just like mine. Would he even hesitate to take it? Would I be a factor at all? Sure, Rainn is part of the reason I'm not interested in whatever Healy wants to offer me, but he's not the only factor.

When Rainn lifts his head, his eyes are cold and distant, and I have my answer.

If he had some kind of offer on the table, he'd leave me in a heartbeat. I don't know how to take that. I thought we meant more to each other, especially after last night, but maybe I'm wrong.

And if I'm wrong about that, what else am I wrong about when it comes to Rainn?

RAINN

How do I smack some sense into Whit? I knew from watching him play—in practice and in a game—that he has natural, raw talent that would be an asset to any professional hockey team.

Yet, it's like he doesn't believe it or … something's holding him back.

It can't be the farm. Like his mom said, the farm will always be there. Pro hockey careers aren't known to be long unless you're one of the greats. Five years average. Whit could go do his thing and still be back on the farm at twenty-eight.

What's stopping him if it's not—

Oh, shit, am *I* the thing holding him back? Surely, I wouldn't even be a consideration at this point. I'm the dude he lost his virginity to, but that kind of thing doesn't mean shit nowadays.

I care about him. I could possibly be falling for him. Last night I was sure of it. But right now, I can't think of anything other than him needing to take this opportunity without considering me.

I know what it's like to live with regrets. If I hadn't taken that hit. If I had rehabbed my leg properly the first time without going back on the ice too early. There have been too many what-ifs in my life, and I don't want that for Whit.

But I also don't know how to talk to him about it without the conversation blowing up.

The drive back to my place is quiet because of that. I don't have the right words. I don't even know how to broach the subject.

"I didn't tell you about it because I knew you wouldn't understand," he says after about fifteen minutes of silence.

"You're right. I don't understand."

"And you don't need to because it's my decision to make."

There's an edge to Whit's voice I've never heard before. He's not a serious guy. I didn't think it was even possible for him to be mad.

"So I don't get a say? At all?" I ask.

"Nope." His mouth makes a popping sound on the *p*.

"Why not?"

"Because it's my future. I don't get a say in yours."

"You might not get a final say, but I appreciate your opinion."

Whit scoffs. "No you don't."

I frown. "Where's this attitude coming from?"

"Oh, I don't know. Maybe my boyfriend telling me I should move five hours away without another thought."

"Wait, you think I want you to move to get away from me?"

"No, but did you even consider us before telling me to go?"

"Of course I did. I don't want to hold you back. I don't want you to have regrets like I do."

Whit shifts in his seat. "Okay, then let's hear those regrets. What are they? Not finishing college? Not doing anything with your life? Why don't we talk about that?"

"That's cold, Whit."

"No, it's not. You want an open discussion on my life, and this relationship thing is supposed to go both ways. I haven't pushed you into doing anything. I haven't told you to call that hockey-camp guy. I haven't told you to enroll for classes next semester. I've done none of that even though I've wanted to because it's your decision to make when you're ready. Just like this is my decision to make."

"I think you're making the wrong decision, though."

"So are you."

I huff. "A college degree will always be there. I can go back whenever I want. This is an opportunity for you that won't come by again. I'm not saying you have to take it, but at least find out more."

"There's no point."

"You're being so stubborn."

"I'm stubborn?" Whit exclaims. "Me? You're the most stubborn person I know. Stop being so headstrong and face your fears. It's been long enough."

"What fears? I'm not scared of anything." Although, that's not entirely true. I'm scared of failing. Of never being happy again. But most of all, in this moment, I fear losing the one person who's understood why I am the way I am. The one person who hasn't pushed me to deal with my shit until now.

"You're so fucking scared of trying to be happy because you know what it's like to lose something you care so much about. You threw your whole self into hockey, and when it didn't go the way you thought it would, your world crumbled and it destroyed your future. And I get it. I really do. But at the same time, you haven't even tried to get any of that happiness back. You work in a job you like but have no passion for. You avoid everything to do with hockey—"

"I didn't avoid you. In fact, I'd say I did the complete opposite."

"Still doesn't negate the fact you're avoiding even planning a future because you're—" His mouth slams shut, and it's as if I can see a lightbulb appear above his head. "That's why you started acting weird yesterday."

"Say what now?" I pretend I have no idea what he's talking about.

"I thought it was nerves about having sex with a guy, but I

was looking at it all wrong. You started getting weird after I showed you my house. I have a *plan*, and that freaks you out. I'm like that terrible blind date you had. She was ambitious, she had a plan, and you shut her down for it."

Hearing him lay out my issues like that feels like he's slamming me into the boards over and over and over again.

"Think what you like," I snap. "You're trying to turn this whole issue around on me when you're the one who we should be focusing on."

"This has nothing to do with me. Not really. You're pushing me away. That's what this is."

"Just because I'm telling you to take an amazing opportunity, that doesn't mean I'm pushing you away."

How much longer is this drive? I need air. I need to get out of this truck. I really need to buy a new fucking car.

"If you say so," Whit mutters.

Suddenly, Whit's not so interested in talking anymore, and that's fine with me. Because he's wrong. I'm not pushing him away.

When he pulls up outside my apartment and doesn't throw the truck in Park, I know he's not coming in.

"That's how it's going to be, is it?"

Whit's hands tighten on the steering wheel. "Yeah."

I unclick my seat belt and open the door, but I don't get out. I'm trying to find the right words when he stops me altogether.

"I'm not going to Scranton. End of story."

"Why are you so determined to fuck up your future?"

Whit laughs. "Me? You can turn that one around on yourself."

"I'm happy at Vino and Veritas. It's a great place to work."

"You might be happy, but you're not fulfilled. I'll get both of those things from staying on my family's farm. It's you who has a problem with this, not me."

"You say your decision has nothing to do with me, but if that's the case, why did you keep it from me?"

"Because I knew you'd react *this* way. Hockey might have been your calling, your life, but it's not mine."

"Can you seriously sit there and tell me that the reason why you're not even contemplating it has nothing to do with me?"

Whit's jaw hardens.

"Take me out of the equation," I say. "Is your answer still the same?"

"That's the problem, Rainn!" He turns to me, his eyes colder than they've ever been. "I shouldn't be taking you out of the equation. You're my *boyfriend,* and unlike you, I can't dismiss that label as easily as you apparently did with your past girlfriends. You are a factor in my life because you're important. Don't you get that?"

Last night, I would have loved to have heard that. Last night, I would've kissed him stupid.

Today, it's too much.

It's too … permanent.

I can't handle it. It's too much pressure and too much like making a future plan.

I can't put myself in the same situation to be hurt again when it all goes away.

"I'm not your forever, Whit. I know that's hard to hear, but it's a reality. It has always been the reality. Because I'm no one's forever. Nothing is permanent, and everyone is temporary. At least in my world. So don't hold back because of me. Don't stay in Vermont because of *me.*"

Whit's hardened jaw doesn't move. He averts his gaze and stares out the windshield, giving me a curt nod. "Got it."

"Whit—"

"I should go. I'm double-parked."

Meaning, *get the fuck out of my truck.*

I don't want to. I really don't.

But I know I should.

My feet have barely hit the ground, and the door isn't even completely shut when he drives away.

I'm confident Whit just needs time to cool off, but it's taking longer for that to happen than I thought it would.

Because I took the weekend off, I'm filling in on my usual nights off, and I'm certain he'll show up at the bar, park his ass on his stool, and smile at me like Sunday didn't happen.

I'm back to where I was months ago, lifting my head every time someone enters and getting disappointed when it's not him.

I've had days to go over the fight in my head, and I've thought about it countless times. I can see why he thinks that was me pushing him away, and maybe I was, but I didn't mean to. I don't want to lose him, but I can't be the reason he doesn't pursue hockey.

If it were a person who had kept me from playing in the NHL, I would hate them with all my being. I don't want to be that person for Whit.

He says he's not interested and that he's happy here, but his flat-out refusal to even go meet with the guy is stubborn as hell.

Then there's the other side of his argument—the part where he thought I'm projecting my issues on to him—but I'm not ready to explore that.

One, because I'm scared he's right. But more importantly, I shoved all that shit down years ago, and I'm not about to open that can of worms now.

I have to hope he'll come around.

"Geez, and people say I'm absent." Molly's voice breaks me out of my stupor, and I realize I'm standing at the bar, customer in front of me and my coworker Molly serving them around me, while I stare into nothingness.

I snap out of it. "Shit, sorry."

Molly waves me off. "Please. Gives me a break from being the screw-up for once."

"You're not a screw-up." *Intentionally*. I don't say that part out loud, though.

"Want to talk about what's on your mind?" she asks sweetly.

"Thanks, but I'm good. I'll get over it."

"Leighton might not," a voice comes from behind me.

For a second, I'm excited by the deep-toned voice, because it's familiar, but then it clicks that Whit would never call himself *Leighton*. And he doesn't talk about himself in the third person, anyway.

I turn to find Campbell sitting where his brother usually does. His stature is similar to Whit's, his hair a few shades darker, but the resemblance makes my chest twinge.

I glance around the room at the customers here tonight—the typical diverse variety of people and pairings—and wonder if Campbell knows this is a queer-friendly space.

"What can I get you?" I ask him.

"IPA, thanks."

I'm trying to work out his tone. It's definitely not as friendly as it has been the last few times we've seen each other.

I slide him his drink with a smile, but he doesn't return it.

My shoulders slump. "We had a fight."

Campbell scoffs. "Yeah, worked that much out. He's been moping around and treating everyone like shit, really."

I'm genuinely concerned. "That doesn't sound like Whit at all."

"It's not." Campbell leans forward on the bar. "What will it take for you to contact him?"

"Uh, umm … I thought giving him his space would be best. I figured if I stayed away, maybe he'd see meeting with the guy from Scranton is a good idea."

"So, you want him to leave." It's not a question.

"No, I don't, but I happen to agree with your parents. He should go out and experience as much as he can. He's lucky that his plans for the farm will always be there for him."

Campbell takes a sip of his drink and purses his lips.

"What?" I ask at his hesitance.

"What's your deal? I know you said at brunch that you were injured, but why are you working here?" He looks around the space with an analytical eye. "Doesn't seem like your kind of place."

"I like it here," I argue. "It's easy, the tips are good—"

"Hmm."

I start getting frustrated. "Can you say what you came here to say so I can get back to work?"

"I'm thinking you don't really have a leg to stand on, and I can see why my brother is pissed."

"What?"

"You can't exactly tell him what he should do about his future, when you can't even work out your own."

A big *fuck you* is on the tip of my tongue, but it doesn't come out. Because deep down, I know he's right. Both he and Whit are right.

Campbell finishes off his drink and stands. He reaches for his wallet, but I put up my hand to stop him.

"It's on me."

He puts the cash in the tip jar instead. "For what it's worth? Leighton doesn't see going to Scranton as the big opportunity you do. He knows the farm will always be there, and we can manage without him for a few years. Gordo could step up into his place easily. But to my brother, that would be exactly like you putting your life on hold to work in a bar when you know your destiny is hockey, whatever form that might take. Mom and Dad can't see that, just like you can't."

Campbell walks away before I can stop him.

His words hit me square in the chest.

I want to call Whit and apologize and to drop the whole argument, but I can't. Because I can't go back to him without proving to him that I understand where he's coming from.

Campbell ripped off the lid to that can of worms I didn't want to open, and now I have to clean that shit up.

As soon as I get off work, I send Whit a text. It's not much, but it's all I can think to do.

I'm sorry.

WHIT

When people hear I'm a dairy farmer, they automatically think I milk cows all day. Yeah, no. Machines do that. Most of my time is spent fixing fences because cows are dumb fucks and will damage that shit every chance they get.

One of our working girls lets out a loud moo beside me as if she hears my thoughts. She's one of our best milkers, but her age means we'll likely retire her soon.

"Don't take that tone with me. I'm out here because of you."

She makes a whiny, grunting noise that reminds me of Rainn, and I get mad all over again.

"You're the one who did this!" I point to the fence.

She huffs.

"Please tell me the cow isn't answering back." My brother comes up on my other side.

"Ha, ha. So funny."

"Take enough anger out on the post yet?" Campbell asks.

I look to find I've hammered it into the ground more than I really needed to. "Maybe."

Campbell shoos me out of the way, taking my tools with him. "I have an idea, and you're not going to like it."

"Oh, then please, tell me what it is. I'm so excited."

Campbell looks out at the field. "I think you should go to Scranton."

"Not you too."

"Well, Mom and Dad think you're being too quick to dismiss the opportunity, right? Rainn thinks you're a downright dumbass."

"Thanks. Thank you so much for bringing him up."

"The only way to make the right and best decision is to have all the information. So go there with an open mind, and hey, who knows, maybe you'll get there, love it, and want to stay. Or maybe you were right all along, and it's not for you. At least then you can tell all three of them you gave it a real shot and were right all along. Even throw in an 'I told you so' taunt to Mom and Dad."

Campbell makes a really good point. Damn him.

"What if …" I bite my tongue.

"What if what?"

What if I do like it there? I don't let the question past my lips, but the thought alone makes me realize that while I'm ninety-nine percent sure staying here and following my passion is the right choice, it might be a good plan to check out what Healy has to offer. If I don't, I might always think about what could have been.

Still, when I think about the reality of hockey, the grueling schedule, the weight training, the strain it puts on my body, I know a pro career isn't for me. If I'm going to take over this farm, I need my body to be in working order. One injury on the ice could jeopardize that.

But if I take Healy up on the offer to at least meet and have a talk with him, it will get Mom, Dad, and Rainn off my back. So I should do it.

Then, if Rainn and I ever get over our egos, he won't question me staying in Vermont.

"I'll give Healy a call."

"Good." Campbell claps my back. "Then you can call that boyfriend of yours. He looks as miserable as you do, by the way."

I frown. "When did you see Rainn?"

"Last night. Drove into town and went to his bar."

I try to hold back a smile. "You know that's a queer bar, right?"

"All-inclusive, isn't it? Doesn't that *include* straight people?"

"Please tell me some dude hit on you."

"I wasn't in there long enough for that. I told Rainn to stop being a dickhead to you and then left."

I burst out laughing. "Thanks for defending my honor, but clearly, he didn't get the message."

"He hasn't called you?"

"Nope. He texted a half-assed apology saying he's sorry, but I don't even know what he's sorry for."

Campbell whistles. "Damn."

"Is this what a relationship is? All anger and resentment?"

"It was a fight. All couples have them."

"When does it constitute a breakup? We haven't spoken in days. In gay terms, that's like a month."

"Lucky for you, from what I understand, Rainn isn't gay," says Campbell, the smart-ass.

I'm not in the mood for it, though, and ignore his attempt at getting me to lighten up. "I think I'm more invested in our relationship than he is, and that's never a good thing, is it?"

"I … honestly don't know."

"Of course you don't. You've been with Christie forever."

"We're not perfect. We've had fights. She broke up with me when we were eighteen."

"Really?"

He shrugs. "Because we've been together since we were kids, she didn't know what else was out there, you know? She had to figure out what she wanted, even if that meant taking a break from the one thing she thought was a definite."

"Wow. Really subtle with the comparisons there, brother."

"You know I'll support you in anything you do, and I understand why you're making the choice you are. We've been talking about expanding the farm forever. So go check out what your alternate life would look like and come back home certain."

"I already am certain." Why can't anybody understand that?

"I know, but relationships are also about compromising. If you make the effort, he will too."

For the first time since I drove away from Rainn, I'm able to let go of the annoyance and anger at him for pushing me away.

"You're very wisdomous today," I say.

"Bullshit. I'm always this wisdomous. You just never listen to me."

"That's possibly true."

My brother pushes me toward my ATV. "Go call Healy. I'll fix … your definition of fixing this fence."

I point at the cow. "She did it."

"Mmhmm."

As soon as I get home, I take out my phone and find Healy's card.

His voice comes on the line almost immediately. "Frank Healy."

"Hi, this is—"

"Leighton Whitaker."

"How did you know?"

"You're the only person I can think of who'd be calling from an 802 area code."

"Oh. Sorry to bother you—"

"Not a bother at all. I've been hoping you'd call."

And just like that, I agree to give this thing a shot. It's only a meeting.

We set something up for this coming Friday, and he says he'll get the team's assistant to send me the travel details.

It's so tempting to go to Rainn and be all, "Look, I'm being the bigger person, you stupid jackass!" But I know it'll be better if I don't have pressure from him about this trip weighing me down.

As soon as I get back, though, there'll be no stopping me.

I'm going to get my man.

RAINN

My stomach is in knots as I walk around the familiar campus. I used to act like I owned this place, but now it's intimidating as fuck.

And come September, I'll be back here. Not because I want to prove something to Whit, but because it's time.

Am I scared? Terrified. But if I want to let go of my fear of making plans because I don't want to be disappointed, I have to do this. I have to push through and just hope someone will be there if it all goes to shit.

I wonder if I had someone like Whit by my side when I was injured if it would've taken so long to get back here.

Whit helped me take these steps. He opened my eyes to a lot of things, the obvious being that I'm not straight, but it's more than that.

He's more than that.

He's the light to my pessimism. He sees the good in me when I can't.

I'm still a selfish ass, but when it comes to Whit, I don't feel so self-absorbed. I'd do anything for him, and I'll do anything to win him over.

I keep an eye out for him on campus, but this place is huge, so I doubt I'd be that lucky.

After it's all official and I've submitted the paperwork to the registrar, I take a deep breath and head for Coach Keller's office.

The hockey facilities are empty with the season being over, and I slow my walk and take in the emptiness. These halls are used to chaos, and the stillness of the off-season is a stark reminder that hockey is not the be-all and end-all.

I've let this sport hold me back from so much, and for what?

I want to get to a place where I can have my passion back without it overtaking my entire life. With my new outlook in place, I don't hesitate to knock on Coach's doorjamb.

He glances up from his computer and smiles at me. "Twice in one year? Careful, you might give the impression you want back in the game."

"I do."

"Finally!"

"I'm coming back to school to finish out my senior year."

Coach doesn't look pleased. "I thought you might be here to get the number of the guy I was telling you about again. Because there's no doubt you threw that number away seeing as he says he never heard from you."

"I don't know what the future holds for me, but coaching is definitely an option. The thing is, one of your players has taught me a valuable lesson."

"Whit?"

"I should have a backup plan for my backup plan so I don't get completely crushed when plan A doesn't work out."

Coach nods. "That's smart."

"I was hoping … Well, I remember one year I was here, they had a volunteer assistant coach for the team? I'd love to do that if there isn't already someone in that position. It would give me coaching experience, and—"

"Done," Coach Keller says immediately.

"Thanks."

Coach stands and shakes my hand. "Welcome back."

I do an internal victory dance as I make my way back out to the parking lot where my new car awaits. It's nothing fancy or anywhere close to brand-new, but it should be reliable. And I get to test it out properly on my drive to Whitaker Farms.

I must have PTSD because the whole way to Whit's farm, I'm not thinking about groveling to Whit or fearing he might still be mad. No, what I'm worried about is breaking down in the middle of nowhere, Vermont, with no cell service.

Perhaps the guy who sold me the car was telling the truth, because I make it there with no problems whatsoever.

But as I pull into the long drive up to Whit's family's farmhouse, those nerves about Whit finally hit me, and my hands shake.

I've never really had to do this before. The whole *I'm sorry* thing. There's a reason I don't have many friends left from college, and that's because I never apologized for being a jackass during my recovery.

I pushed people away.

Whit thought I was pushing him away too, but that was different. I was thinking about what was best for him and not me. The one time in my life I try to be selfless and look how I aced that shit.

My boyfriend is mad at me and hasn't spoken to me in what feels like forever.

The text I sent him has gone unanswered, and I don't blame him. Saying sorry isn't enough, which is why I needed to make a plan and follow through on it before going back to him.

I need to prove that I heard him. That I'm *trying*. Not so I can tell him how he should live his life, but so that he can see I'm living mine.

With a deep breath, I get out of the car and bound up the porch steps to the front door. I go to knock, but Whit's mom beats me to it.

Her eyes are wary, but her voice is warm. "Rainn, so good to see you."

"You too, Mrs. Whitaker. Can I talk to W—Leighton?"

"Oh. He didn't tell you. He's not here."

Damn. Missed him.

"I looked for him on campus earlier but couldn't find him."

"He's … He's in Scranton. Flew out this morning."

My heart sinks.

Even though I wanted this for him, and I am definitely happy for him … He left without saying goodbye?

"He's due to come home tomorrow morning. He only went for a meeting."

I force a smile I don't feel, because the team is gonna love him. And if he actually made the trip out there, that means he's interested.

I can't hold him back from this opportunity. I *can't*.

"If it makes you feel any better, he was rather reluctant," Mrs. Whitaker says.

No, that doesn't. Not at all. Because if he's on the fence about staying or leaving, I can't be the deciding factor.

"Could you … Uh, is it all right if you don't tell him I stopped by when he gets home?"

"Are you sure?"

I am. Even if I hate it. "He needs to make this decision on his own."

Her expression holds so much sympathy it hurts. "That's noble of you, but if you want him to stay, you should tell him."

"I don't want him to miss out on opportunities because of me."

She smiles. "I don't think he'd be losing out if he chose you."

I'm grateful for her words, but that's the thing. I don't want him to have to choose. Not between me and something else.

"Thanks, Mrs. Whitaker."

I turn on my heel and march back to my car.

The drive home is totally different than my drive to the farm.

The car is the last thing on my mind. All I'm thinking about is Whit.

If I lose my first love to an injury and lose Whit to hockey, it will be full circle.

I hate that this is what I wanted for him, and now I'm pissed he has it. I don't want to be upset, but I am. Which is so stupid.

When I get home, my melancholy has set in full force. I trudge through my apartment building and throw open my door. Then I remember the other thing I did to show Whit I'm taking him—taking *us*—seriously.

My mom is sitting on my futon.

Yep. I called my mom, told her I was sorry for cutting her off for no real reason other than I was being sulky over losing hockey, and invited her to come for a visit to meet my *boyfriend*.

She was taken aback at first, obviously. A lot has changed in my life since my injury, and I didn't let her in on any of it. The long two-minute silence she gave me after I came out was from shock, not disapproval, and once she got over it, she started talking animatedly and rearranged her work schedule to have a few days off to come up here and see me.

The distance I put between us after my career died is all on me, but she's here now.

"Where's the boyf—" Her mouth hangs open when she realizes I'm alone.

I shake my head. "He's, uh, got an opportunity to meet with an AHL team, so he's in Scranton."

Mom's face falls as she stands. "Oh, honey, are you okay? That must be hard seeing him get your dream."

I huff because I realize something. That's not why I'm upset at all. I'm upset because I'll be losing him. Not that he gets to live the life I wanted.

"I'm in love with him," I blurt. "And I'm scared I've pushed him away. He didn't even want to go, and I made him do it."

My heart is breaking, but this was my own making.

Mom hugs me, while I quietly hold back tears.

I can't lose him.

But I can't hold him back.

Long distance? It won't work.

"Rainn?" Mom pulls back. "Did you hear what I asked?"

"Wha?" She said something?

"Dinner?"

"Oh. Right. Yeah, looks like we're on our own."

Like I will be once she leaves. Again.

Not that long ago, I was resigned to thinking that was my life. I was okay with it.

After being with Whit, I can't imagine going back to being by myself.

And I don't want to.

WHIT

Okay, I can't even deny that walking into a professional arena is intoxicating.

I thought I'd be meeting with Healy and maybe the coaches or something. The season is done, so I expect the arena to be empty, but they're pulling out all the stops.

Three guys from the team who didn't leave for their off-season vacations or summer jobs are here in full gear, waiting for me to suit up in team pads and skates to meet them on the ice so Coach can see what I've got.

Two on two won't demonstrate the full range of my skills, but I still give everything I have.

I'm playing with a dude named Zeke Montgomery, who goes by Monte. We instantly bond over having nicknames derived from our last names.

We're skating against Lawton and Finnce, and holy fuck, they're fast. All three of them are. I keep up, but it's a workout.

The locker rooms, the facilities, hell, even the way these guys skate … It's a big step up from playing in Vermont, and it's intimidating, but I'd be lying if I said it hasn't piqued my interest. I told Campbell I'd come into this with an open mind, and I am.

I push hard, but it doesn't feel like it's hard enough. It's like playing against a team who keeps scoring and it's impossible to find the net. I manage to get around Finnce a few times, but it's easy to score when there's no goalie.

This isn't about winning or losing, though. This is about showing what I can bring to their team.

We're not on the ice long when the coach calls it, and I don't know if that's a good thing or a bad thing.

So after I shower in the best locker room experience I've ever had, I meet Healy and the coach in the offices.

Coach leans back in his seat. "Tell me a little about yourself."

"Umm." I shrug. "I'm just a gay dairy farmer from Vermont who likes playing hockey."

Coach doesn't even flinch. "Interesting …"

"How so?"

I expect him to say something about being so open about my sexuality and about maybe not letting it get in my way.

He proves me wrong. "Most kids who come in here answer that question with 'I'm the next best thing in hockey.'"

"I assure you, I'm not that. I love hockey, but it's not all that I am. And I'm not delusional; I know I'm not the next Mario Lemieux."

He smiles. "Healy told me he saw something in you during your game against Colchester. He's really backing you here."

That makes me uncomfortable, and I shift in my seat. Why is my hockey career more fascinating to everyone else but me? "I'm not saying I don't have talent or what it takes to make it in pro hockey, but I am saying it's not in me to be one of the greats."

"I like humility in a player," Coach says. "Especially at this level. We get players in here all the time claiming they're ready for the Big Show only to refuse to develop into better players."

"Believing you can't grow anymore, that's when you've peaked."

"We want to invite you to come to preseason training," Healy says. "We'll see how you gel with the rest of the team, but a contract offer could be on the table. You'll need to get an agent, and we can go from there."

I suck in a sharp breath. Today was fun, there's no doubt, but … I still don't see this as my big break or an amazing opportunity. Chasing three of these guys around the ice was enough to know my heart isn't in it.

Rainn doesn't have the physical ability to be a hockey player. I don't have the love for it.

Healy and the coach sit there blinking at me.

"You need to think it over?" Coach asks.

"It's not that I'm not grateful for this opportunity, but it's a big move."

Not to mention rookie AHL players earn peanuts.

If I could really, truly see myself trying to develop my skills to make it to the NHL, then yeah, this would be the opportunity of a lifetime. But I don't want that life.

I could waste the next few years skating and fart-assing around in the AHL, or I could do exactly what I've wanted to do since I was a kid.

We stand and shake hands again before I make my way outside. The three players are there, standing around talking.

Monte turns to me. "Hey, rook, coming out for a drink?"

I go with it. "May as well. That's better than hanging around my hotel room."

But if I'm honest, I'd rather head straight to the airport and try to get an earlier flight so I can go home to Rainn, to the farm, and to my real future.

This. The butterflies in my gut, the overwhelming feeling of excitement mixed with nausea, this is how I should have felt walking into that arena in Scranton.

Instead, I'm outside Vino and Veritas where it all began, wondering how I can go in there and demand that Rainn let go of all of his issues so we can be together and live some happily ever after like a fucked-up fairy tale.

I know I wasn't supposed to fall head over heels in love with the guy I lost my virginity to, but I did, and I don't want to let him go.

I don't want to scour hookup apps for lonely guys across New England to share a few sweaty hours with me.

I want Rainn Richardson.

I just have to hope he wants me too, despite my lacking NHL ambitions.

If he tells me I'm giving up an opportunity for him, I may lose my shit again. I need him to understand.

I still don't know how I'm going to play this when I walk through the doors, but then I see him, and I know exactly what to do.

He's busy behind the bar, but my usual seat is free. It's only one of two that are available.

As calmly as I can, I make my way over to it without flat-out running so no one else can take it. I slide onto the stool and wait for him to notice me.

It's busy, and I'm hoping the fact he hasn't acknowledged me means he hasn't seen me and not that he's ignoring me.

His coworker approaches, and I want to tell her I'm waiting for Rainn, but instead, I order my usual.

As soon as "I'll have a Shipley Cider" falls from my mouth, Rainn freezes a few feet away. I like that he knows my voice, but I like even more when his eyes meet mine and he says, "I've got this."

He gets me my drink, and when he slides it over, I look up at him and lick my lips.

"I need help with something," I say.

His expression softens. "Anything. I'll even help you move all your shit to Scranton, if you ask me to."

"It's not that. I need advice. Like, dating advice. And because you're my wingman, you're all I've got."

Rainn grins. "A gay guy walks into a bar and asks the straight bartender to be his wingman. I think I've heard this one before."

"We never got to the punchline, though."

Silence falls between us in the bustling, crowded bar.

"Whit ... I—"

The loud crashing sound from the back room startles Rainn.

"Oops," comes the other bartender's voice.

Rainn swears under his breath. "I'll be right back, okay? I'll help Molly clean up whatever mess she's made this time, and then I'll go on my break."

He retreats to the back, and I wait, tension coiling inside me. He's still talking about me moving to Scranton, and I worry this will end in another fight when I tell him it's not going to happen.

While Rainn takes his time, I sip my cider and try to come up with a way to tell Rainn exactly what I want without freaking him out. What I have to say will definitely scare him.

I have the dreaded Big Future planned out, and it includes a lot of him.

He appears in front of me, wearing a smile I don't entirely believe. "Let's go."

"Are you sure you can take your break now? It's kind of busy."

"I'm overdue for one. It's been a busy night all round."

I finish off my cider and follow him out to the street. My hands go to my pockets so I don't reach for him. It's not like we spent every single day together, but I've missed him like crazy, and all I want to do is hold him.

But I'm not sure where we stand, and I don't want to push things. At the same time, I'm about to tell the man that I'm in love with him. So, yeah, there's that.

If I'm not comfortable touching him, should I really be confessing my undying love here?

"Are you hungry?" Rainn asks.

I shake my head. My stomach is too tied up for food.

"I want to show you something."

The quip almost falls out of my mouth: *Is it your dick?* But I rein it in.

Hey, look at that. I've finally learned how to control my mouth, and all it took was a seed of uncertainty.

"What is it?" I ask.

Instead of answering, Rainn leads me to the nearby parking garage and stops in front of a random car.

"It's mine," he says.

"Y-you bought a car?" It's an old Honda and not much, but it's a step he hasn't been willing to take, and that's something.

"That's not all I did."

"What else did you do?"

He sucks in a sharp breath. "I … I'm going back to school and finishing my degree."

My eyebrows shoot up. "You are?"

"Yep. I've only got one semester left, but I'm going to split it over two. I should get my BA in sports management next May. That's if I can handle the classes while still working at Vino and Veritas."

"You will. I can help you study or whatever."

Rainn averts his gaze. "You can? So you're not … You—"

"I know you really wanted me to go for this opportunity with Scranton, but while I was there, all I could think about was being back here."

"Did you give it a real chance?"

"More than a real chance. I skated with three of the guys on the team and then went out with them afterward. They're great guys, and the arena they play in is insane. I mean, it's no TD Garden but still amazing. The offer to skate with them at their next training camp is without a doubt a great opportunity, but not when my heart isn't in it. My heart belongs somewhere else."

Rainn shakes his head. "What if I move to Scranton with you?"

My eyes widen. "What?"

"I mean, I'll need to finish my degree, but it's only one year. I could move there next summer, and—"

"You'd do that for me?"

"Whit, I'd do anything for you. Anything."

My heart feels full. "I don't think you know how much I needed to hear that, but Scranton's still not for me. It's not just you I'd be leaving behind, but the farm, my family—my entire life."

"I'm not going to pretend I understand turning it down, but I am going to be thankful you won't be leaving Vermont."

I take a small step toward him. And then another. "Why's that?"

His lips quirk. "I think you know why."

"Not really."

"Not seeing you, not being able to text you, not having the courage to tell you I'm sorry until I did something about my life … It's been hell, okay? I didn't want to be the reason you didn't do something, and you're right, I did push you away. But not because I don't want to be with you. I pushed you away because I'm scared."

His confession surprises me. Actually, this whole conversation is not going the way I thought it would.

"What are you scared of?" I ask, my voice low.

"I'm scared of putting myself out there again. Of plans not working out. My heart getting broken. I'm scared if I tell you I love you, you won't feel the same way, and then I—"

"I do."

His gaze flicks to mine. "Really?"

"It's why I haven't so much as let myself touch you tonight. I've been preparing myself for rejection because big plans scare you, and love? Deciding to spend your life with someone? That's the biggest plan of all plans."

"It is. But something you said before you drove off and left me on the side of the road—"

"Calm down. I left you outside your apartment, not in the middle of nowhere."

Rainn smiles. "That's not how everyone else will hear about it."

I laugh. "Of course it's not."

"Something you said then made me think. About the bar. My life. How long I'm going to continue to be bitter. I realized if I truly want something with you, which I do—I really, really do—I can't delay my future any longer. I want to be happy. And I want it all to happen with you."

I can't take it anymore. "Can I please touch you now?"

Rainn takes me off guard by practically slamming into me. His arms go around my waist, and his mouth lands on mine.

I stumble backward but hold on tight to his broad shoulders and wide back.

He licks into my mouth and moans.

My back slams against the door of his car, and then Rainn's there, boxing me in. He doesn't stop kissing me even when he pulls away to murmur how much he's missed me.

This can't be real life.

I can't be this lucky.

"Rainn," I breathe.

He puts his hand in his pocket and pulls out his car keys, unlocking the doors with the fob. "Get in the back seat." His voice has a serious growl to it, and I'm quick to comply.

I lie across the wide back seat, but my feet have nowhere to go and end up in the footwell. "It's small."

"Hey, at least it's not a Fiat."

I laugh. "True that."

Rainn climbs in and closes the door behind him.

Back seat, two large hockey players, it doesn't make for a comfortable hookup, but right now, I don't care.

My cock is hard and aching for him even after the shortest of kisses.

I look up into his eyes as he settles above me. "I love you."

"I love you too."

This time when he leans in to kiss me, his lips are soft, and it occurs to me I'm in love with the first person I've ever been with. While that fills me with some sort of hesitance, it has nothing to do with Rainn or us or how I feel about him.

Your first love is supposed to be your first heartbreak. That's the way life works. He's not supposed to be the perfect guy—the one who was made to be yours.

What Rainn and I have is deeper than I thought I could ever find in a lifetime.

Rainn moves on top of me, his hard cock rubbing against mine through our pants. "Fuck, Whit."

I burst out laughing. "What did you call me?"

The moment is broken, and Rainn buries his head in my shoulder and laughs with me. "Your name is really unfortunate."

"You could call me Leighton."

He lifts his head, those bright blue eyes on mine. "Really?"

I cup his face, my thumb running along his permanent five-o'clock shadow. "The most important people in my life do."

"Leighton ..."

I lift my head and kiss him softly, turning what was supposed to be a quick hookup into a declaration of something so much more.

That doesn't last long, though. Especially when his hips move again, rocking into me, and he says, "I need you," in my ear.

I try to get my hand between us so I can undo his jeans, but he's too pressed against me.

He lifts up but hits his head on the roof. "Ow." He laughs and rubs the back of his head.

"You couldn't have got a bigger car?"

"My top priority was something that won't break down."

I roll onto my side to try to climb on top of him but accidentally push Rainn into the footwell.

"Fuck," he hisses. He tries to get back up on the seat but fails. "I think we're both too uncoordinated for this."

"No. We're hockey players. We're super coordinated. We just have to …" I shift. Nope, that won't work. "Hang on." I sit up so my back is against the door, and I spread my legs. "There. Climb up here."

"We don't have to do this now. As soon as I finish work, we can go back to my place."

"We have to do it now. Make-up sex is supposed to be the best, and I'm going to be pissed off if it turns out society is lying about that too."

"What else has society lied about?" Rainn manages to get back up on the seat, where his head is right above my crotch.

"That straight guys only cause gay guys heartache." I run my hand through his hair. "That queer bars are flamboyant and over-the-top."

Rainn's eyes flutter shut. "Mmm. It's a shame Tanner didn't make me wear boy shorts and no shirt during my shift. Imagine the tips. I could've got a bigger car."

"No one gets to see that but me."

He lifts his head. "You want me to wear boy shorts?"

That image is actually hot. "Definitely."

Rainn's hand sneaks up my shirt and over my abs. "We may not be able to manage make-up sex in here, but I'm in the perfect spot for a make-up blowjob."

"Is that a thing?"

"I'm making it a thing."

Rainn lifts my shirt and runs his tongue from my belly button to the waistband of my jeans while he undoes the button and zipper.

I shift to help him lower my jeans and underwear enough for my cock to be free, but he continues to kiss and lick all over me, purposefully avoiding my dick, and I squirm in frustration.

"I don't think you have time for teasing."

"Mm, true." He kisses my hip. "I need to get back to work, eventually."

Yet, he doesn't move any faster. He doesn't go near my cock.

"Rainn," I whine.

He chuckles. "I'm trying to show your body how much I've missed it."

"Mind showing my dick?"

Rainn full-on laughs now. "I guess I can be nice."

His gaze flicks up to mine as he finally lowers his head and gives me exactly what I want. He closes his mouth over the head of my cock, sending a shock wave of tingles through my body, all the while not taking his eyes off mine.

I suck in a sharp breath and forget to release it. With the way he's staring at me, I'm locked in place.

Rainn makes jokes about being able to give the worst blowjobs, and I wouldn't know because I have no comparison material, but I don't need experience to know no one else would compare.

Nothing compares to Rainn, and I'm certain nothing ever will.

It's not about the blowjob or the way he swirls his tongue over the head of my cock. It's not about the orgasm building. It's the way he takes care of me, the way he concentrates on my pleasure and what I want. It's the selfless act of giving because he wants me to fall apart for him.

He wants me to let go.

Rainn breaks eye contact and focuses on taking me deeper.

My hand flies to the front seat and holds tight. "Fuck. That's so good."

He responds by sucking harder. He's so eager and enthusiastic, it's hard to believe I'm the only guy he's done this with. He sucks me all the way down until my breaths come out in wispy pants, and I'm shuddering all over. His loud slurps and grunts drive me closer and closer to the edge until I'm making lewd noises of my own, and I can't hold back anymore.

My free hand weaves into Rainn's dark hair while I release

into his mouth and try to control my hips as they thrust freely, chasing to draw out my orgasm.

Rainn takes it, swallowing me down until my muscles uncoil and I sink into the uncomfortable back seat.

My head falls back against the window, and I take a moment to close my eyes and come down from that high.

Rainn shifts and moves my legs off the seat completely so he can sit opposite me. He palms his cock through his black jeans.

"Let me." I half-heartedly lift my hand. "In a second." I'm having trouble catching my breath.

He unzips his jeans and takes his cock out, stroking it teasingly with his large fingers. "It won't take much. Do you know how hot it is watching you come?"

"About as hot as watching my cock disappear between your lips."

Rainn continues to stroke. "Best make-up blowjob ever?" His voice is raspy, and precum leaks from his tip.

"Hmm, hard to tell." I've finally recovered enough to sit up and lean over so I can return the favor. "We have to see if I can beat it."

I use my tongue to lick over his slit and lick up that salty flavor left by the precum.

Rainn's eyes track me as I lower my head. I contemplate teasing him like he did to me, but we don't have much time.

We've been feeling our way through this whole sex thing, but I have to say, we're getting good at it. So good, my mouth has a Pavlovian response to the thought of sucking Rainn's cock and salivates. I'm getting decent at deep-throating too. Practice makes perfect.

I don't even warm up before diving right in, swallowing him to almost his base.

"Fuck, fuck, fuck."

It's really hard to smile with a cock in my mouth.

Rainn's right when he says he's close to coming already. His cock is hard and heavy in my mouth, and I taste more saltiness as

I swallow. He's thrusting hard, and I don't even think he knows he's doing it.

I wish he didn't have to go back to work because I could do this all night. Or at least until my jaw got sore.

"*Leighton*." Rainn comes on a harsh whisper, and I've never loved the sound of my name so much.

I swallow and keep sucking, waiting for his cock to stop erupting in my mouth.

When Rainn's finally as relaxed as I am, I pull off him with a wet pop and wipe my mouth. His eyes are hooded, his lips curving in a relaxed and sated way, and his cheeks are a slight shade of pink.

"I figured out the punchline," Rainn pants.

"I can't wait to hear this."

"A gay guy walks into a bar and asks the straight bartender to be his wingman. The bartender says, 'How about we fall in love instead?'"

I frown. "That's not very funny."

"It could be. Aren't most jokes funny because they're true?"

"Yeah, but it doesn't have any dicks in it. You promised me dicks."

Rainn laughs. "There's only one dick you're allowed, and it's right here." He cups his softening cock that's still hanging out of his pants.

"Wait, I'm not even allowed my own?"

Rainn thinks about it. "Nope. That's mine now."

"Don't tell me you're going to start getting all growly and possessive."

"Start? I swear every time another guy so much as talked to you, I was so close to losing my head."

"Aww, that's sweet. I think."

Rainn leans in and kisses my chest, right over my heart. "That belongs to me too."

The way he's being so open about it, he really is the guy I've been holding out for. Once I got over my own insecurities and allowed myself to be truly loved for the first time, I met Rainn.

No one else will ever compare.

That notion is scary, but if Rainn can face his fears of heartbreak, then so can I. I'll face every single fear of mine if it means I can hold Rainn like I am right now.

For forever if he'll have me.

29

RAINN

One Year Later

"I think you'll be a perfect fit here."

When I found out the camp director Coach tried to set me up with a year ago was looking for someone to coach this summer, I called him immediately.

TJ Beckett sounded mature and put together on the phone, so when I arrived for my interview, I was shocked to meet a guy around my age.

The camp he runs is a nonprofit, giving underprivileged kids who want to play hockey the chance to develop their skills and earn scholarships to colleges. It's an amazing opportunity for them. And for me, if I decide to take it.

Maybury is about an hour south of Burlington, but it's only twenty-seven minutes from Whit's farm. Not a bad commute. Though, I'd have to finally have the balls to ask Whit to move in together.

This past year I've been working and going to Moo U in Burlington, and he's been busy working on the farm expansion. It's been easier to spend nights together since his house was finished, and we have the place to ourselves. It felt too weird staying in the main farmhouse with his parents.

They're lovely people, but it's … awkward. Especially since I can't be in the same bed as Whit without touching him. It felt like I was in high school again, sneaking around and trying to find secret places to have sex.

"Do you have any questions for me?" Beck asks. He told me to call him that as soon as I met him and called him Mr. Beckett.

He'd screwed up his face and said, "Eww."

I think we'll get along fine. So long as he's cool with me being in a relationship with another man. I don't see why he wouldn't be, but you never know with people. That's something I've learned since being with Whit.

Most people are fine with it, don't care, whatever. But there was one person in one of my classes that decided to avoid me after finding out I'm bi. Or maybe they don't like me for other reasons and I'm reading into it.

When I started dating Whit, the bi label didn't feel right to me. There was no doubt I was attracted to Whit, but other guys weren't all that appealing to me.

And in the big scheme of things, being attracted to one guy means I fit under the bi umbrella, but I felt like an imposter. Maybe that's some internalized biphobia stemming from ignorance about bisexual people, but something happened at V and V that finally made it all click for me.

Ex-NHL player, Brent Weyland, came into the bar, and both Whit and I fanboyed over him. When he left, I unwittingly found myself checking him out. Apparently, I do have a type, and that's hockey players.

Weird considering I'd spent years in locker rooms and wasn't aware of it. Can a lack of hockey make a hockey player crave it so much they start finding the players attractive? They should do studies. I'd volunteer.

Whit wasn't so impressed with me drooling over another man. Especially when I said, "I looked at his ass," with maybe too much enthusiasm. But when I explained why it was a good thing —that it helped me identify with a label that fit me because thinking of Whit as some one-off fluke also didn't sit right with me—Whit forgave me.

Blowing him and promising he's the only one for me went a long way in helping with that.

Beck looks at me expectantly, and I have no idea how long he's been waiting for my answer.

Legally, I know I don't have to tell him shit about my personal life, but I don't want to have to keep it a secret, and I'd rather find out now if there's going to be a problem working here, or if it will make things awkward like with my classmate.

"I only have one concern. Or, not really a concern, but … something I want to know, I guess."

"What's that?"

"I have a boyfriend," I blurt like that's an actual sentence that makes sense in this context.

I wonder if there will ever be a time where I don't have to hold my breath when I say it. It's something I never realized was constantly hanging over queer people's heads. Coming out over and over to everyone you meet.

Beck leans back in his seat. Without saying anything to me, he picks up his phone and dials someone. "Hey, can you come to my office for a sec?"

Has he called an HR rep on me? Someone official to see his response? I don't know how I'm supposed to feel about that. But then a good-looking guy with dark hair enters. I saw him on the ice earlier when Beck showed me around.

"Rainn, I'd like you to meet my partner, Christopher Jacobs."

He reaches for my hand to shake. "You can call me Jacobs. Everyone does. Well, except him." He points to Beck. "But feel free to ignore him. I always do."

Beck laughs and sends Jacobs a look full of so much love it makes me miss Whit, and I saw him just this morning when I woke up to him coming home for his first coffee break.

"Oh. Partner as in … not your business partner, but partner-partner," I stammer.

Beck turns his smile on me. "Well, technically, he's both, but yes, partner-partner. Does that ease your concern?"

I nod. "It does, and I agree with you. I think this job is the perfect fit for me too."

———

As I turn into Whit's long driveway, the gravel crunching under my tires as I pull up to the white clapboard cottage, I get the sense —and not for the first time—that I'm coming home.

With the new job in Maybury, it would make sense for me to move out here with Whit, but the job is more an excuse to bring up moving in together. It wouldn't be *just* because of the job. It's because I want to be here.

Whit works insane hours on the farm, and I want to see him as much as possible.

I pull up outside the house and am greeted by my baby. And by baby, I mean a two-hundred-pound calf I named Sidney.

"Hello, my gorgeous boy," I coo when I get out of the car.

Whit appears on the porch. "You'd make a terrible farmer, you know that? I told you not to name him."

"I told you not to introduce me." When I found out what they do with the male calves, I might have guilted Whit into letting me keep Sidney. Apparently, when dairy cows give birth to boys, they ship them off and turn them into veal.

"Don't worry," I murmur to Sidney. "I won't let anyone eat you."

"You're banned from going anywhere near the pregnant cows forever," Whit says. "We can't afford to fill our yard with bulls."

"I'm okay with that. If I pretend the whole slaughtering thing doesn't exist, I can save Sidney and still enjoy a nice steak when we go out."

Whit shakes his head. "You are seriously fucked-up."

I bound up the steps to the porch and grin at him. "It's why you love me."

"You do know Sidney is going to grow up to be a thousand pounds, right? At least."

"So, I should stop letting him come inside the house?"

Whit's face falls. "You didn't …"

"Just once. It was so cute."

"Rainn," Whit whines.

"I don't know why you're complaining. I named him after a Penguin. *For you.*"

He gives me a pointed look.

I change the subject. "Why are you home? Shouldn't you be out there killing baby cows?"

"I've been waiting for you to get here. How'd the interview go?"

I smile so hard I can't contain it. "I got it."

Whit throws his arms around me. "I knew you would. Congratulations!"

"It's going to be crazy over the summer, because that's when they have the most kids there. Since a lot of their coaching staff are college students, they're looking for someone full-time to help coach on weekends and breaks and before and after school during the semester. If I impress them this summer, the job's all mine."

"You're going to be great at it."

For the first time in a long time, I actually believe in myself, and I think I'll be great at it too. Spending a year helping Coach with the Moo U team made me realize Whit was right. I can still have hockey in my life.

When I made a difference on that team and could see my students growing and developing, none of the bitter jealousy I expected was there.

An accomplishment I'd never felt as a player settled over me because it wasn't only about me. It wasn't about scoring a goal or showing off. It was about helping someone else.

"You were right, you know," I say.

Dimples appear on my boyfriend's gorgeous face. "Was I? About what?"

"I was heartbroken."

Whit's big hand cups my face. "I know." He touches his lips to mine, but it's too soft and too chaste for my liking. "Come inside and tell me about the job."

He takes my hand and leads me inside to the amazing kitchen with marble counters and top-of-the-line cooktop and oven.

He turns the coffee machine on and gestures for me to sit at the table.

I watch him move about his space effortlessly. He settled in so fast here, and it feels like a home. My apartment is small and impersonal, which I never used to have a problem with. But now it feels empty when Whit's not there.

I'm not sure if I associate this place with being home because it's so nice, or because of Whit, but either way, I want to make it official.

"You know, Maybury isn't too far from here," I hedge.

"I know. It's why I'm excited. You can use the excuse to stay over more."

I lick my lips and swallow hard. "About that …"

Whit pours two cups and slides a coffee over to me while he takes his seat. "Oh, were you thinking of getting a place closer? An hour commute from Burlington would suck."

"I do want a place closer than my apartment."

He totally misses my hint. "I can help you look."

"I've already found the perfect place."

Adorable Whit is adorable. His confusion line deepens on his forehead.

"It's a house. Newly built."

"How much is it a month?"

I grunt. Now I'm getting the feeling he doesn't want me to move in here. Is it really that much of a stretch? I'm here whenever I can be.

"I'll have to ask the sexy landlord."

"Sexy—wait, you want to move in *here*?"

"Why do you sound so surprised? I thought we were heading in that direction, but maybe I'm wrong."

Whit grabs my hand on top of the table. "No, no, no. Not at all wrong. Shit, I've wanted you to move in since the house was completed, but I know how annoying it is to drive to Burlington every day for school, so I didn't want to ask. Well, that, and I figured moving in might be too much like *making plans* for you. I am surprised, but not because I don't want it. I do. I really, really do."

"Good. Because if you haven't noticed this past year, I like making plans with you. Big, future, permanent plans that might change depending on circumstance, and I'm completely okay with that. I'm prepared for it."

I've come a long way since meeting Whit.

"Oh, yeah? And what else is in these big, future plans of yours? Marriage? Kids?" Whit's tone is so dry, I know he's not expecting a serious answer.

If he was serious, I'd tell him I'll give him any kind of future he wants. He gave me happiness, and not just by loving me. He gave me back a life I'm excited to lead. He gave me back my passion.

I owe everything I look forward to every day to Whit.

"We already have a kid, and you told me I'm not allowed to have another one." I smirk.

He levels me with a look. "Cows are not children, and if you are going to live here, you're going to have to learn how to farm properly. Rule number one: don't name the livestock."

"But Sidney needs brothers!" I'm messing with him. Mostly.

"I decided I don't like it when you make plans. You should go back to being allergic."

"Never. You created this monster. I was happy living my life as a selfish, oblivious grump who didn't need hockey or a relationship."

Whit's eyes narrow. "Were you really happy, though? Truly?"

I don't even need to think about that. "Not at all. But it's still your fault I'm like this now."

Whit stands then pulls me into a hug. "Then I'll take that. Because it's worth seeing how happy you are."

I pull back and smile at him. "I'm happier than I've ever been."

"Good." Whit's mouth comes down on mine, hard and sure.

I press myself against him and hold him tight while I push my tongue past his lips. Whit moans and spins us to pin me against the table. He lays me down, sliding the coffee cups out of the way, and covers me with his body.

"How much time do you have?" I ask.

"Enough to get off and get out."

"Perfect amount."

Whit reaches for the button on my pants when a loud *moo* sounds behind us.

Whit turns, and I lean up on my elbows to find Sidney entering the kitchen door.

"See? It's like having real kids. I've heard they interrupt sex."

Then we hear clucking noises.

Whit's head whips back to me. "What the fuck is that?"

I might have befriended one of the chickens that Whit recently brought to a new henhouse he built in his yard. It thinks it's a human, and it's so cute. "That's a chicken. Wow, and you say *I'm* bad at farming."

"What's it doing in our house?"

"It's Sidney's chicken. He loves it."

Whit straightens up and adjusts himself. Then he points at me. "No animals in the house. Your responsibility."

Whit is usually laid-back and easygoing, but I've found when it comes to the farm, he's nothing but professional. It's admirable, and I have to admit, his bossy side is superhot.

"No more animals in the house," I say.

"No. No animals at all. You need to get Sidney out of here. And whatever stupid name you've called the chicken."

"It's Sidney's chicken, so I guess he's named her Moo."

Whit glares at me.

I tell him, "Chickens don't have names, silly. Only cows."

"Rainn, I swear to *cow*, if you don't get them out of here, you're not allowed to move in."

I hold my heart. "You're falling in love with them, I can tell."

"Get them outside." Whit puts his hat back on and walks out the front door.

"Love you," I call after him.

He grumbles something about "You too," but I swear he mentions damn cows in there too.

I turn to Sidney. "Come on, boo."

As I lead him outside, the chicken follows, and when I pick her up and take her up to the henhouse, I look back at Whit's home—the home that we'll soon officially be sharing—and I remember back to the day Whit showed me the bones of this place.

Whit has always known who he is and what he wants.

I might've stumbled and lost my way more than once, but with him, the future isn't daunting. I'm excited about our life together.

Some plans play out exactly how they're supposed to. Some blindside you, and you don't know what's happening until they've already fallen into place.

Being with Whit is definitely the latter.

He teaches me new things about myself every single day.

And I love him for it.

THE
END

ACKNOWLEDGMENTS

There's a long list of people I need to thank, but I want to start with Sarina Bowen and Heart Eyes Press for inviting authors to write in the True North universe. I'm honored to have been a part of it.

To my co-author of my CU Hockey universe, Saxon James, thank you for alpha reading Rainn and Whit and encouraging me to keep going when they were being stubborn, which was often. There's a reason I went with Headstrong on their title. It describes both of them *on* and *off* page.

I want to thank my assistant, CC Belle for keeping up with social media while I'm in my writing cave, my betas for loving Rainn and Whit as much as I do, and my readers who were supportive when I pushed back my release schedule so I could get this book written. Headstrong was an important project to me.

I should probably also thank my husband for encouraging me to take this opportunity when I already had a busy 2020 schedule. You regretting saying yes yet, honey? Sorry!

Finally, I want to thank my team of editors, Edie Danford for pointing out no sane couple would plan an outdoor wedding in April in Vermont (then again, who's to say Campbell and Christie are actually sane?), for Sandra from One Love Editing for those copy-edits and proofing, and Lori Parks for catching those ninja typos that always slip through. If they're still there after three rounds of editing, they've earned their place.

Lastly, lastly, thank you to every single person who's ever picked up one of my books. Without you, I wouldn't be living my dream.

Eden xx